THE SAPPHIRE LIBRARY

BOOK 3 IN THE LADY DIVINER SERIES

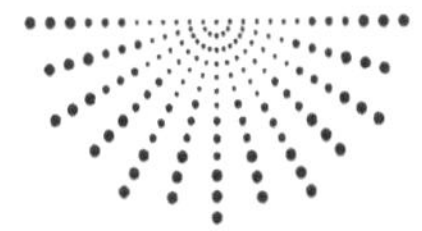

ROSALIE OAKS

Parkerville
PRESS

CONTENTS

IN WHICH MISS ZOOTH MEETS A WILD VAMPIRI

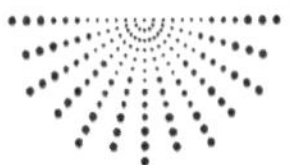

Dartmoor, Devon, 1804
Including some events previously recounted

Aldreda

Miss Aldreda Zooth flew over the bleak Dartmoor landscape, searching for the Moria Pearls. The moors were covered in mist, and it was in the darkest hour of the night, so it was hard to find the likely hiding spot of the pearls. Luckily, Aldreda had supernatural sonar as well as very good eyesight.

The wind crooned over her wings as she swept across the moors, which seemed too desolate and devoid of landmarks to hide anything. Aldreda didn't have Elinor's gift for divining jewels, so she had to rely upon her wits and her knowledge of her late companion, Henri. She was looking for something large or majestic, somewhere her beloved Henri would have chosen to hide his memory pearls.

That is why Aldreda did not notice the other bat until he was almost upon her.

The bat swooped down alongside Aldreda, then swerved underneath her. Aldreda pulled up short in mid-air, not believing her senses. Even as she hovered there, the bat spun in a circle around her and flicked his long wings up like a matador.

He was doing a vampiri bat mating dance.

Confounded, Aldreda flapped in mid-air. She took in the long musculature of his bat form – large even for a vampiri bat – and drew in a breath of astonishment. Here was another vampiri, out in the wilds of Dartmoor! She had yet to meet one in Devon, or even in England.

Aldreda squinted her sharp black eyes, shot into the air, and sped away.

The other bat followed.

Aldreda huffed to herself. He did another mating swerve underneath her. Aldreda plunged downward and flew close to the ground. *That* should give him the message that his attentions were entirely unappreciated.

To her annoyance (and slight astonishment), he attempted another curving dart, swinging underneath her, as low as she was. His body almost brushed against her own so as to avoid scraping the ground. He emerged on the other side, triumphant, and flung his wings up with a cocky flick.

This was insupportable. Gritting her teeth, Aldreda transformed into a woman.

The odd mixture of pain and pleasure shivered through her, but she focused on the tricky art of landing on her human feet as she fell. Black locks tumbled around her shoulders. Standing (somewhat shakily), she arranged her hair over her front to preserve some modicum of modesty. There was nothing she could do about the rest of her body, the stretch of pale white that was all too apparent.

As a vampiri, however, she was used to such contingencies, and she straightened her spine. The sooner she sent this pesky bat on his business, the better. She had left Elinor behind in the dark, near Totnes, and she did not have much time to explore the moors for likely hiding places.

The male bat pulled up overhead and hovered, eyeing her. Aldreda waited for him to transform. He simply flapped in a slow circle, staring down.

Aldreda gestured impatiently. "Human guise, please. It is only polite."

He hesitated. Finally, he shivered into human form and vaulted to his feet in front of her.

Before Aldreda stood a large vampiri – miniature compared to a human, but taller and broader than Aldreda, though equally naked. He wore a long bushy beard, and dark hair grew long and wild around his face. The rest of his body was hairy too, black hair covering his chest, only stopping to show a certain protuberance that somehow drew the eye. Clearly, mating was still on his mind.

"Desist in your seduction attempts," said Aldreda firmly. "I am on an urgent quest."

The vampiri opened his mouth and tried to speak. The words came out scratchy and slow, but there was nothing slow about the glint in his eye. "An urgent quest? So it is not that you are ... uninterested?"

Aldreda realised with a start that he was speaking French. She replied in the same tongue, narrowing her eyes. "I am uninterested. You may leave."

"Yet I have only just arrived. Perhaps I can help you."
He put his hands on his hips, muscled arms showing
between his long, matted hair.

"I doubt it."

"You are flying in my territory. Are you searching for
something?"

Aldreda avoided the question. "It appears as if you
have been out here for a while." It looked like he had not
seen civilisation for a decade. Or at least not a barber.

"I have indeed," he agreed. "Why do you not have a
gentleman to assist you on this urgent quest?"

"I do not need a gentleman," said Aldreda tartly. "It is
none of your concern. Good night, sir."

She drew a breath to transform. At the same time, he
threw up his hand. "Wait!"

Aldreda raised a brow. "Yes?"

He stilled and cocked his head, a frown darkening his
features. "I sense a Musor!" He sniffed the air and turned
an accusatory glare to Aldreda.

Elinor must be Discerning, Aldreda realised, which
was why this vampiri could sense her. "Yes, that is my
Musor. You are not permitted to dine upon her."

"Ha! I only dine upon horses."

"That explains a great deal."

He ignored her sniff, comprehending her other
words. "*Your* Musor? Are you mad?"

"It is customary for a vampiri to pair with a Musor,"
said Aldreda. "You seem to have forgotten the rules of
civilised behaviour."

Disbelief crept into his voice. "Did you learn nothing
from the Troubles?"

"What troubles?"

He narrowed his eyes. "Do not jest."

"I am not jesting," said Aldreda, keeping her voice calm. "I have been hibernating for the last eighty years."

"You slept through the Troubles?" A mixture of disbelief and envy passed across his face. "If only I had been so lucky."

"I assume you are referring to the French Revolution?" Aldreda knew the human version of it from Elinor: the common people of France had revolted against the nobility and chopped off many heads. "I cannot see what that has to do with the vampiri or Musors."

"You are uninformed, madame. Musors and vampiri were killed alongside the nobles, associated as they were."

Aldreda stared at him. "This is the first that I have heard of Musors being involved. Are you certain?" She did not quite trust the intense, bitter look on his face.

"I left before the end," he said, "but I know many died. Many of my friends. You are mad to liaise with a Musor."

"This is England," said Aldreda. "My companion told me the Troubles were twelve years ago in France." She glanced out into the dark moors, impatient to continue her search, knowing the selkies were also after her prize. "I have more important things to concern myself with presently. Goodbye. Thank you for your information."

Before he could distract her any further, she transformed. He shouted something as she lifted into the air, but Aldreda ignored him. She flew off in the direction she had been travelling before this unsettling little interlude.

Somehow, she expected him to follow her. When he did not, she peered over her shoulder. He was hovering mid-air with his head tilted, as if listening again. Then he wheeled slowly and began flying in the opposite direction.

If she had a human tongue, she would have cursed. He was going after Elinor.

Aldreda pulled up, almost spitting in frustration. She would have to cut him off.

Trusting that his instinct was weak, after years away from Musors, and knowing exactly where Elinor was, she flew back with all speed, high above the mist.

~

When she arrived, Elinor was divining. It was as loud as a bell to Aldreda's senses. Elinor's brother, Peregrine, sat hunched on a rock nearby.

Aldreda skidded to the ground and shuddered into a woman as quickly as she could. "Quick. My gown!"

Perry harrumphed and turned away. He was always a bit sensitive about the sight of her naked form, but Aldreda had no time for such niceties. Elinor came to herself and pulled Aldreda's gown out of her pocket. It was one of Aldreda's favourites: one Elinor had sewn with her own hands. Elinor herself was dressed in a riding habit with a dark cloak over the top, as befitted a midnight hunt for pearls. Aldreda had hoped that Elinor would be able to Discern the pearls if they were hidden in the moors, but so far neither of them had found success.

Aldreda dressed at a speed rapid even for her. Elinor straightened, pushing her blonde hair back from her face. "Did you find anything?"

"Not what you think. Another vampiri." Aldreda did the last tie with quick fingers. "I suggest we remove ourselves."

Elinor's eyes widened. "Truly? A vampiri? Do you think that is why my divination led us here?"

"A vampiri like you?" asked Perry, turning on his rock.

"No," said Aldreda shortly. "Not like me. I think we should leave."

"Oh, but does that mean a Musor is about?" asked Elinor eagerly.

"Not necessarily," said Aldreda. She could see it was not going to be easy to hurry them off. She put her hands on her hips. "Some vampiri go wild."

"Wild?" asked Elinor nervously.

Perry started, his hazel eyes widening like Elinor's. "Will it try to eat me?"

Aldreda shot him a withering look. "You do not look that delicious, Mr Avely. However, if you do see him, you may want to take off your cravat."

Perry clutched at the top of his coat. "Expose more flesh? Egad, no!"

"This vampiri is not going to bite you," said Aldreda. "He appears to have shunned human company for a long time."

"Why does he need my cravat then?" demanded Perry. "He does not sound like a very civilised sort of bat."

"Exactly," said Aldreda. "Do you want to see him unclothed?"

Elinor raised her brows. "Have *you* seen him unclothed, Aldreda?"

Aldreda ignored her. "Let us go. Before he arrives."

It was too late. The male bat swooped out of the night like a black arrow.

He made straight for Elinor, skidding in the air past her hair. She let out an involuntary shriek and stood up. The bat turned, in an impressive display of agility, and sped back towards her. She flapped her hands and shrieked again.

The bat shot towards Perry, who leapt back with an

oath. Aldreda, her hands still on her hips, shook her head crossly. "Keep still! You are confusing him!"

"He is confusing us!" shouted Perry.

Elinor had her hands near her ears as if her elbows could ward off the next attack. "What does he want?" she asked.

The vampiri transformed and landed on the rock Elinor had just vacated.

Elinor's eyes widened, taking in the sight before her. Aldreda was pleased to see that Elinor quickly raise her gaze to his face. The new vampiri stared back with his yellow eyes.

Perry let out a curse, whipped off his cravat, and hurried forward.

"Here you go, old fellow," he muttered. "Egad, I hope this doesn't mean I'm going to have a pet bat now as well. No offence, Miss Zooth."

The male vampiri let the white folds fall down around him, making no attempt to recover his modesty. Aldreda tutted and pulled her skirts a little closer to her person, hoping it would give him some indication of his barbaric conduct.

Elinor rose to the occasion. She was quite accustomed to nakedness, after all, thanks to her friendship with Aldreda. She was unfazed by a miniature, hairy man.

"Good evening," she said politely. "How do you do?"

'Mrgh.' The vampiri seemed to struggle to find his voice again. Aldreda tutted once more.

"I am very well, thank you," said Elinor, doing her best. "Do you have a name, kind sir?"

"Nothing kind about that display," muttered Perry.

'Mrghgh,' said the man. His eyes shifted to Aldreda, who put on an expression of supercilious disdain, though in fact she was quite curious to find out his name. She hadn't wanted to ask before. Human companions were useful sometimes.

The vampiri cleared his throat. "Urgh. Pags."

"Pags?" enquired Elinor. "Your name is Pags?"

The vampiri nodded slowly as if *she* were the half-witted one. Yet Aldreda knew that couldn't be his full name. So abominably rude.

"Lovely to meet you, Mr Pags," said Elinor, without even a hint of sarcasm. "What brings you to this corner of Devon tonight?"

The man just stared at her.

"He sensed your divination," explained Aldreda. "I doubt that he has felt a Musor for a long time."

"Oh." Elinor was embarrassed. "Does he want something – er – to eat?"

Aldreda spoke sharply. "Musors only bond with one vampiri at a time."

"Not me," said Perry hastily. "Don't look at me."

The male vampiri gave Perry a scornful glance. Then he cleared his throat and spoke in French to Aldreda. "I do not want any dinner." There was a glint in his eye again, as if it were something else he wanted.

"What did he say?" demanded Perry, whose French, it must be admitted, was not very good. "Did he say I looked tasty? Or not tasty?" He seemed uncertain which was more offensive.

Elinor frowned at her brother and directed a different question to Pags. "You speak French?"

"*Oui,*" said Pags.

"Well, thank goodness for that," Elinor spoke rapidly in that tongue. "I quite thought you were unused to civilised company." She cast a glance over him. "Would you like to clothe yourself, Mr Pags? You must be cold. My brother won't mind if you use his cravat."

Pags glanced down at the crumpled cravat, ignored it again, then stared at Elinor. His eyes gleamed in the moonlight, and he shifted a warning look to Aldreda.

Aldreda pursed her lips together.

Perry was pacing behind Elinor, perhaps feeling vulnerable without the protection of his cravat. "What did you say, Elinor?" he demanded. "I hope you are not offering me up as a snack."

Elinor turned impatiently to her brother. "Mr Pags doesn't want you for dinner. Nor does he want your cravat." She turned back to Aldreda. "Has this vampiri spoken to you, my dear?"

"Mrghgh." Pags cleared his throat again, and this time he spoke in accented English. "I have come to warn you."

There was silence.

"Warn us?" said Elinor.

"Warn you," repeated Pags.

"We heard," said Perry. "Why do you want to warn us?"

"Warn *you*," said Pags once more, fixing his gaze on Elinor. "You are a Musor, *vraie?*"

Elinor nodded cautiously.

"You are in danger."

Elinor looked around. "From what, my good sir?"

Pags didn't reply, but his eyebrows rose.

"Is there something out here in the moors?" she persisted. "Some danger to Musors?"

Pags shook his head. "Do not let *anyone* know you have the Gift. You should not even have confessed it to me."

"Anyone? Who? Someone in particular?" Elinor glanced at Aldreda. "Miss Zooth already knows of my abilities, and I trust her implicitly."

"Vampiri or humans," said Pags. "I have warned you."
Then, dismissing the topic, he turned to look at Aldreda.
His gaze travelled over her neat gown and rested on the
tips of her bare toes peeping from under the skirts. Aldreda
hastily flicked her gown over them. He gave her a feral grin.
"May I beg an introduction to your vampiri companion?"

Elinor glanced across in question. Aldreda tilted her
nose in the air and folded her arms in a stance that defied
an introduction. However, Elinor clearly could not bring
herself to refuse this suddenly polite request. "This is
Miss Aldreda Zooth. Who may I have the pleasure of
introducing?"

He bowed deeply, an odd sight, as his beard almost
touched the floor. "I am Pagrilliard Deponzel. Enchanted
to make your acquaintance, Miss Zooth."

Aldreda gave the barest of curtsies, her face shuttered.
Pagrilliard Deponzel? Wasn't that ... ? She couldn't
believe it. He must be from some other branch of the
family.

The vampiri winked at her and turned to the rest of
the company. "*Adieu.*"

Then he shrugged into his bat form. His arms folded
out into long wings, and his hair melded into the furry
body of a bat. He lifted into the air and hovered for a
moment as if showing off.

Then he vanished into the night.

A long silence settled over the remaining company.

"Thank goodness he is gone," said Perry finally.

"Mmm," said Aldreda. "I think he has dined on horses
for too long."

"I half expected him to neigh," agreed Perry.

"Or baa," said Elinor. "What a strange creature. Do
you think he was quite sane, Aldreda?"

"He might be a little unbalanced. I suspect he has been alone for a long time."

"What do you think he meant by a danger to me? Do you think he was simply raving?"

"I am not sure." Aldreda frowned. "Perhaps something to do with the French Revolution. He may be a little confused and not realise we are in England now."

"Well, I humbly suggest we remove ourselves," said Perry, "before he comes back. You never know, he might decide he is hungry after all." He hurried forward and snatched up his cravat. He gave it a doubtful look and then stuffed it in his pocket rather than put it on again. "That was a fine cravat. Don't see why he didn't like it. Complete barbarian."

"I quite agree," said Aldreda. "An utter savage. I apologise on behalf of my species."

2

IN WHICH BERESFORD BEARS BAD NEWS

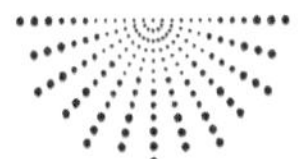

Elinor

Four days later, Elinor and Aldreda were ensconced in the civilised setting of Elinor's room. It was late for Elinor, but early for Aldreda, as was their usual practice. They had a lot to discuss, including the fascinating particulars of Elinor's forthcoming wedding.

Elinor snuggled into her armchair, waiting for the tea to brew and sighing with contentment. She was finally engaged to Lord Beresford, with no silly business about it this time. The last three days had been the happiest of her life thus far. It was so wonderful to be certain of his affection, to brush her hand against his, and to see the smile in his eyes when their gazes met. Elinor only hoped Aldreda did not feel neglected. Though, of course, the vampiri slept during the day when Beresford called and took Elinor walking, or invited her to his house, or took her on long, unnecessary tours of the manor grounds.

No date was set for the wedding yet. Beresford had told his mother, the Countess of Beresford (soon to be the dowager countess), and negotiations were in full swing.

Elinor poured tea for herself and Aldreda, placing the thimble and cup on the bedside table. "The countess wants a London wedding," she explained to Aldreda. "Even though both James and I wish to be married here in Devon." Elinor still experienced a small thrill in saying his Christian name.

Aldreda was curled up on the bed with Samuel stretched out purring beside her. The contrast of the vampiri's curling black hair against Samuel's creamy fur made a pretty picture. Aldreda frowned. "I hope Jaq will not be the best man."

"James says his friend Lord Worthing will travel to perform the office. If not, perhaps Jaq will do." Elinor sipped her tea with a sigh of relish.

"I can just imagine that selkie posing through the ceremony, tossing his dark locks." Aldreda sniffed. "Selkies do not have the same sense of decorum as vampiri do."

Elinor laughed. "You cannot say that about your Pags."

"He is not my Pags!"

"He did try to rescue you from that tea-chest in the selkies' cave," pointed out Elinor. "Have you seen him since? Perhaps we can invite him to the wedding so you will have company."

"Certainly not," said Aldreda. "One needs clothes to attend a wedding. I can assure you that I've seen quite enough of Pags, despite his abortive rescue attempt. The sight of him peering into my tea-chest gave me a fright." She paused and changed the subject. "How is Perry?"

"A bit moody." Elinor looked up curiously. "Did he

and Jaq have some altercation in that cave when we came to see you? Jaq apologised, I believe, and they went fishing together yesterday. But now Perry is avoiding Jaq again, and I cannot determine why. Do you know what the trouble is about?"

Aldreda cleared her throat. "I suspect that the two of them became ... rather intimate on the day you all came out to the cave to rescue me."

"What on earth do you mean?"

"I – er – apprehend that a kiss *almost* happened."

"Almost?" Elinor wondered how that looked. She knew Jaq had become a seal to swim Perry out to the selkie cave. Of course, before Jaq transformed, he would have stripped off his clothes. Perhaps Perry had been overcome by the sight. She giggled.

Aldreda sniffed. "Well, I heard Jaq teasing Perry about it in the cave, claiming that Perry had almost kissed him. Perry denied it, however."

Elinor bit her lip thoughtfully. That was the day that Perry and Jaq had consumed rather a lot of Beresford plums, in the form of a delicious, spiced plum pie. She cast a sideways glance at Aldreda. Now was a good opportunity to mention a certain salient fact.

"I haven't told you this, Aldreda, but there is a perhaps unfortunate side-effect to the Beresford plums. You know their healing properties? Well, on a perfectly healthy person, the effect is – er – libidinous."

Elinor felt herself blushing, but she was glad to see Aldreda took this revelation calmly. If anything, the vampiri looked slightly relieved. "Oh? That explains a lot."

"Does it?"

Aldreda shifted a little on the bed, an odd look crossing her face. "I thought I felt a bit ... strange after you fed me in the cave. Did you all eat copious amounts of plum pie before you rescued me? The plums must have affected Perry and Jaq that day too."

"Yes," admitted Elinor. "You think that was purely the reason for Perry's indiscretion?"

"Mm." Aldreda looked thoughtful. "Does Perry know about this side-effect?"

"No." Now that the secret was out, Elinor giggled again. "I am not so certain we can blame it entirely on the plums. I think they opened Perry's eyes to something that has been there all along." She thought for a moment, remembering Perry's rather close friendship with a schoolfellow, and seeing it in a new light. "I think he tends that way, after all, as well as towards pretty girls. And Jaq is so beautiful and charming that even Perry cannot deny it to himself anymore."

"Hm," said Aldreda. "Perry can tend whichever way he wants, as long as it isn't towards selkies. You know how Daziel betrayed Henri: Jaq might do the same to Perry. I don't trust him."

"You are prejudiced," said Elinor gently. "You indict a whole species on the basis of one terrible act. Jaq is not so bad; he helped rescue me." She sighed. "Yet goodness knows what happened on the fishing expedition, for Perry is once again giving him the cold shoulder. Really we owe Jaq our courtesy at least, as he has been so under-standing about the Moria Pearls."

Aldreda sniffed. "How is your transcription going?"

"Very well, so far. I have one of the pearls here with me." Elinor slid open the top drawer of her bedside table. A large pearl nestled in a handkerchief, purple and lustrous in the candlelight. Elinor was transcribing its contents into a journal, using her talent for Discernment to read the spells placed there. She would then pass that knowledge to the selkies, as this particular pearl contained the Musor teachings on Illusion.

A flash of worry crossed Aldreda's face. "Is it safe there?"

"Safe enough. The rest are still at the Manor. I like having the excuse to visit Beresford, but I have spent quite some time with this pearl." Elinor knew Aldreda disapproved of this pandering to the selkies, but the vampiri had grudgingly agreed Skerry could have access to the Illusion teachings, as long as she, herself, kept Henri's pearls.

Aldreda cocked her head as if listening to something. Elinor strained her ears also, but to no avail.

"Someone is riding to Casserly," explained Aldreda.

"At this time of night?" Elinor put down her cup of tea and stood to peer out the window. All was still, and in the distance she could see the ocean, calm under the dark sky.

Aldreda followed and tugged on Elinor's skirts peremptorily. "The hooves have stopped now, some way from the house."

Elinor lifted her to the windowsill, and they both watched for several minutes in silence. Finally, Elinor saw the familiar figure of Beresford striding up the path. She smiled and turned her head to whisper. "It is James. I wonder what he wants."

Aldreda raised a brow. "A late-night courtship?"

Elinor blushed. "He would not be so improper. He insists we observe at least some of the proprieties. And he has banned the plums." She grinned and leaned out the window. "James!"

Beresford came to a halt and stood frowning up at them. A riding cloak was flung over his admirable shoulders, and Elinor looked down at him in appreciation.

He spoke quietly, but his deep voice carried on the night air. "Good evening, Elinor, Miss Zooth. There is a meeting at the manor tonight. Both of you are required to attend."

Typically autocratic, thought Elinor fondly. She smiled down at him. "A meeting? Whatever for?" She felt a sudden fear it was something to do with his upcoming trip to France on behalf of the Crown to investigate Napoleon's flotilla. "Is this to do with your ... sailing trip?"

His gaze dropped to his boots. "No. You will find out soon enough. Quickly now. You can ride back with me. And please do not let your mother know."

When the three of them arrived at the Manor, they found Jaq already there, pacing in the library, his elegant form in some disarray, but his countenance still devastatingly handsome even with a dire frown upon it. The Countess of Beresford was there too, seated in regal splendour in the armchair near the fireplace. She nodded a greeting when Elinor came into the room. Then she gave a little shriek when she saw Aldreda sitting on Elinor's shoulder.

"Oh my goodness," the countess exclaimed. She cleared her throat, embarrassed. "Ah, you must be Miss Zooth. I do apologise, I was a little startled. Yet I have heard much about you."

Elinor, curtsying, felt Aldreda drop a curtsy too, no mean feat on a dipping shoulder. "Good evening, Lady Beresford," they chimed together.

"Goodness me, you are indeed a little lady," Lady Beresford marvelled, recovering her composure. "I scarce believed it when James told me of you, but he spoke only the truth. You must be smaller than my hand."

In fact, thought Elinor, Aldreda was about the same size as Lady Beresford's elegant hands, which now lay on her lap, holding a slip of white paper. However, it pleased Elinor that Aldreda was so readily accepted. The countess had known about the selkies along the Devon coast and had heard old tales of vampiri, so perhaps that was why she managed to overcome her surprise so quickly.

Jaq stalked around the library, his beautiful face sulky. Elinor put Aldreda down on a rosewood side-table, and they both examined his perambulations with interest. Elinor hoped Perry hadn't done something particularly rude in his attempts to avoid Jaq.

"What is all this about?" Elinor demanded.

Beresford stood next to the fire by his mother and clasped his hands behind his back. "We have been burgled."

Elinor turned quickly. "Burgled?"

"The pearls?" gasped Aldreda from her table. "Did someone take the pearls?"

Beresford nodded. "Out of my safe."

Elinor's mouth fell open. Those cursed pearls! Would they be no end of trouble?

Aldreda, however, had no hesitation in spinning towards Jaq. "You!" she exclaimed. "You took them!"

The selkie, thus accused, broke into an ungentlemanly snarl. "I did not take them!"

Aldreda glared. "Who else would know how to break into the safe?"

Beresford interposed. "Someone who watched me lock it, perhaps. Miss Zooth, do you know anyone called Pagrilliard Deponzel?"

Aldreda's face paled. "Pardon me?"

The countess held the white sheet aloft in her hands. "This letter is signed by him. Would you like to read it?"

Elinor strode forward and took the letter, carrying it over to Aldreda. It was on a human-sized sheet of foolscap, but the writing was tiny. Elinor squinted as she read it, shielding Aldreda from the view of the others.

To the Earl of Beresford,

My deepest apologies for intruding upon your inner sanctum and availing myself of the key to your safe. As you see, I have taken the Moria Pearls. I deem it best they are delivered to the King of England without delay. He may be in need of the knowledge contained within them. Furthermore, His Majesty will know best how they are to be disposed, and he is best suited to make the decision that weighs so heavily upon you all.

For these reasons, I have taken the pearls into my custody and departed for London forthwith.

I offer my abject apologies for this ungentlemanly and unilateral action.

Yours sincerely,

Pagrilliard Deponzel

The Fifth Dukel of Demontaine

P.S. Please pass on my sincere apologies and regards to Miss Zooth.

"That ... dastardly rat!" said Aldreda. From her initial pallor, she was now angrily flushed. "How dare he!"

Beside her, Elinor drew in a long breath. "The nerve of him! I'm so sorry, Aldreda. We should have been more wary."

"Who is this Pagrilliard Deponzel?" enquired Beresford. "I can see it says the Fifth Dukel of Demontaine, but I am unfamiliar with the title."

Aldreda did not answer. Her little hands were clenched by her side, and she appeared to be too busy seething to respond.

Elinor spoke hesitantly. "He is a vampiri. We met him out in Dartmoor."

"What interest does he have in the pearls?" inquired the countess.

"None!" sputtered Aldreda. "He has no right!"

"An interfering little bat," put in Jaq. "I expect nothing less from a vampiri."

Beresford's deep voice was calm. "Understandably, we are all very upset. Yet we must keep our heads."

Elinor smiled at him with approval, but she saw Aldreda hunch her shoulders impatiently. "When did you find the note, James?"

"About two hours ago," replied Beresford.

"Before sunset?" demanded Aldreda.

"Yes."

"So ..." Aldreda tapped a little foot rapidly. "Pags must have put the note there last night. He has a night's travel ahead of us." She stretched out her fingers by her side as if she wished to turn into a bat immediately and give chase. "I say we follow him."

"Ay," said Jaq, with a ferocious scowl.

"Wait," said Lady Beresford, listening avidly. "If this is to be a council of war, let us call for cream tea."

Elinor looked up thankfully as the countess rang the bell for Frobisher. Aldreda ducked behind a vase, muttering it was not the time for cream tea. Elinor affected not to have heard her. It was always time for cream tea, and it would give everyone a chance to cool their tempers and think about the matter calmly.

Frobisher arrived, showing no curiosity at the late-night gathering. The countess gave her orders for tea, chudleighs, cream, and the Beresford plum jam.

Beresford cleared his throat. "May I request strawberry jam for a change?" He cast a glance at Elinor, and she gave him a secret smile.

She objected, just to tease him. "Oh, but the Beresford plum jam is so divine!"

"Yet I have consumed too much of it in my lifetime."

"Surely impossible, my lord," she twinkled. "I'm sure you can survive a little more for our sakes."

Everyone else watched this exchange with some confusion, except for Aldreda, who now knew of the jam's side-effects. Beresford's lips twitched, but he shook his head firmly. "Elinor, I beg you to indulge me in this. Frobisher, strawberry jam."

Frobisher nodded and departed, though the countess frowned. Elinor raised her brows in mock reproof at her beloved.

Beresford grinned back. "I must insist, Elinor, or else I cannot answer for the consequences."

Aldreda stepped out from behind her vase to give directives. "Enough fussing about jam! We must give chase to Pags immediately. I can set forth now."

Beresford interrupted. "Excuse me, Miss Zooth, but may I ask a question?"

Aldreda halted to stare at him. "Yes? What is it?"

"Do we still have the pearl which Elinor took to Casserly Cottage?"

"I do," said Elinor. "It is in my bedside table."

Jaq leapt up from where he had been sitting and

clutched at his hair. "Good Gad, we must secure it at once!"

Beresford agreed. "That is the important pearl for the selkies, is it not?"

Jaq began to nod, then turned it into a shake of his head. "There is another – there are two pearls with Illusion teachings. We need both! We must go after this Pagrilliard. Just wait until I lay my hands on him!"

The countess gestured imperiously for the letter, and Elinor carried it over. Lady Beresford scanned the note thoughtfully. "Does the king have Musing powers too?" she asked. "It appears this Pagrilliard fellow believes that to be the case."

"Ah!" said Elinor, arrested. "Indeed, he must! Why else would Pags take the pearls to him?"

Jaq stalked across, read over Lady Beresford's shoulder, and then shook his head. "It merely says the king may be in need of the knowledge contained within. That does not necessarily mean he is a Musor."

Lady Beresford argued the point. "It does, however, say the king 'will know best how they should be disposed.' That at least implies a knowledge of magic and such things." She waved the sheet of paper. "It occurs to me that the king is the best person to have these Moria Pearls, after all. Can the selkies possibly make do with the pearl you already have? As I understand it, you now have an Illusor to help you as well, Jaq."

"No, we cannot!" shouted Jaq. "I knew I should not have trusted you all. This is what comes of consorting with humans and vampiri!"

Aldreda spoke coldly. "None of us have betrayed you. I am just as furious as you. I say we go after Pags at once, even if the king is a Musor."

Elinor held up a hand. "But isn't this what you

wanted, Aldreda? To have the pearls honoured and safe? Perhaps Lady Beresford is right, and they are better off in royal safekeeping."

The butler came in, bearing a tray. Aldreda had already vanished behind the vase. Elinor reflected it was lucky that vampiri hearing was so acute and reflexes so quick that the servants remained unsuspecting.

Everyone fell silent as Lady Beresford began to pour. Elinor was glad of the ritual, as it gave Aldreda time to consider. It was galling to have the pearls taken from them, but Elinor couldn't help feeling that it might be a good thing to give up responsibility for such a valuable necklace. However, it was irksome that an unkempt vampiri had been the one to relieve them of it.

When the butler left again, Elinor peered around the vase. "Aldreda, might it not be what Henri wanted?" she murmured quietly. "The pearls honoured in the royal collection?"

Aldreda's face emerged, mutinous, but it softened a little at that. "I suppose London is far from the selkies of Skerry."

Elinor nodded, though that was not quite what she had meant.

Aldreda stepped out from the shadow of the vase to address Jaq. "Do your seal-people have a treaty with the King of England?"

"Only brokered by Lord Beresford recently," snapped Jaq. "Up until then, it had been a case of politely ignoring one another. Selkies don't travel well in London."

Aldreda pursed her lips. "London is unfamiliar terri-tory to me too." This was partly because Aldreda had been asleep for the good part of a century, and partly because she had lived most of her life in France before that.

Elinor coughed. "London is a rather difficult place for me, as well." She was referring to the scandal which had blackened her name only six weeks ago in high society – the reason Elinor had fled to Devon in the first place.

The countess clapped her hands together. "We can all go to town! I will smooth over the gossip, and you and James can be married there. It is perfect!"

Elinor was filled with misgiving. She did not particularly want to face the gossips again, even with Beresford at her side. He would have to face the embarrassment of it all over again: to be reminded of how she had humiliated him at the Duke of Planx's garden party.

Beresford frowned at his mother. "If Elinor does not want to be married in London, she will not be married in London."

Aldreda interrupted before the family dispute could stir up. "Perhaps you are right, Lady Beresford, about the royal prerogative. Maybe it is better we stay here in Devon."

Elinor blinked in surprise. There was a long silence as the assembled company stared at Aldreda.

Jaq was the first to voice his thoughts. "That does not sound like you," he said suspiciously. "Are you in cahoots with this vampiri fellow?"

Aldreda drew herself up. "Certainly not! Pags is completely lacking in manners or decorum."

"He has gone wild," put in Elinor. "A far cry from our dear Miss Zooth here."

"What do you mean, wild?" asked Beresford.

Elinor grinned. "Pags eschews clothes, as far as I know. And drinks from horses."

Beresford and his mother both raised their eyebrows in identical expressions of concern.

"He is French." Aldreda seemed compelled to defend

Pags somehow. "And perhaps suffering from some loss. I know myself how it is to lose a human companion. It can derail one's mind."

Respectful silence met this reference to Aldreda's still-fresh grief for Henri.

Elinor tipped her head towards Aldreda. "Yet Pags did attempt to rescue you from the selkies when you were captive in that tea-chest. And he seems to have his wits about him enough to steal our pearls."

Aldreda spoke reluctantly. "I believe he thinks it is for the best. And I am content to agree – as long as I am assured the pearls were properly delivered to the king." She turned to Beresford. "My lord, could you make it your business to find out? I am certain you have connections who can make enquiries."

"Very well," said Beresford. "I will send an urgent message to London to determine if the pearls have been delivered. And if they are, we leave them in royal safe-keeping. Are we all agreed?"

Everyone nodded slowly, though Elinor wondered why Aldreda had capitulated so quickly. Was Aldreda keeping something from her? They had promised not to have secrets between them anymore.

Elinor glanced around. Jaq looked sulky, and Lady Beresford wore a rather mutinous expression. However, Elinor knew both were bound to obey Beresford's decree. And perhaps it was for the best that the pearls went to London without them.

"May I have more cream?" Elinor asked brightly.

After the tea, Beresford appeared at Elinor's elbow. "You

wretch," he murmured in her ear. "You know why I don't want any more plum jam."

She laughed softly. "No, why, my lord?"

"I am convinced that a lifetime consumption of the stuff has changed my constitution. Why else do I find it so exceedingly difficult to restrain my passions around you? It is unbearable."

"So unflattering, my lord. Could it not be my charms instead?"

Beresford sneaked a hand around her waist. "Of course, it is that, but I do not need the jam making my life more difficult than it is already."

She turned to smile up into his eyes. "I am grateful that you will determine if the pearls arrive safely."

"I only hope my people will know," Beresford replied. "Don't forget, I have to sail to France in two days."

Elinor put a hand on his arm, trying to enjoy his warm presence rather than worry about the future. "I have not forgotten."

3

IN WHICH MRS AVELY IS TOO DISCERNING

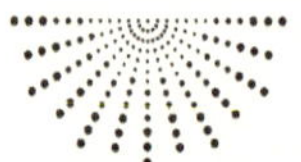

Aldreda

Aldreda suggested that she and Elinor leave soon after the tea. She had much to think about, and it was difficult to reflect with Jaq scowling suspiciously at her and Elinor flirting desperately with Beresford.

Yet it was consideration for Elinor which had made Aldreda renounce the pearls. Hiding behind the vase, she had recalled that Pags – the Dukel of Demontaine! – had told her that Musors were endangered.

It had occurred to Aldreda that London might be unsafe for Elinor.

There was a lot Aldreda did not know about the last eighty years, and a lot she didn't know about London. She had put Elinor through much already for the sake of the pearls. Perhaps it was time to let them go into royal safekeeping so that Elinor and Aldreda could stay safe in the relative isolation of Devon.

Besides, Aldreda didn't want to go chasing Pags all over the country. He no doubt expected her to do so. If Aldreda ignored him, dignified and unruffled, Pags would be served right.

No, she definitely did *not* want to chase Pags to London. Unless it was to wring his hairy neck.

Once in Beresford's carriage, Aldreda and Elinor sat silently for a while. Eventually, Elinor spoke.

"You know, we *can* go to London. I can brave out the scandal."

Aldreda sighed. "It is not scandal I am concerned about."

"What do you mean?" Elinor's hazel eyes were worried. "Is this something to do with what Pags said out on the moors? About danger to me? I suspect you are not telling me everything."

"Pags mentioned something when I was alone with him," admitted Aldreda. "I thought it was the ravings of a mad bat, but ..." she frowned. "I refuse to call him his gracel, Lord Deponzel – he introduced himself as Pags, and Pags he will stay."

Elinor smiled. "Indeed. But what did Pags tell you?"

"He said that Musors and vampiri were killed in the French Troubles. Not just the nobles. And he insisted on warning you of danger."

Elinor nodded. "Yet that was France! Twelve years ago!"

"We do not know the political situation in England. What if others are nursing a hatred towards Musors?"

"Who?"

"Mundanes, I suppose. Those who resent the power the Musing gives you."

Elinor leaned back thoughtfully. "The Musors must

have been more open about their power in France. No one is aware of its existence in England. I had no inkling." She frowned. "It would be good to know exactly what happened in the Revolution. Why were the Musors swept up into it?"

"We do not know enough, which is why we should stay away. The pearls will be safe for now."

Elinor raised a brow. "You trust this mad Pags with them?"

"If he says he is taking them to the king, I believe him," admitted Aldreda. She had not forgotten Pags's misguided attempt to rescue her from the selkies. While arrogant and mannerless, he had nonetheless appeared lucid – and honourable, at least according to his own code. "Furthermore, this way, you can be married in Devon."

Elinor gave her a grateful smile, and Aldreda changed the subject to the wedding gown, which was guaranteed to distract them both.

A mile from Casserly Cottage, Elinor called for the carriage to stop, so it would not disturb her mother and Perry. However, when the two of them tried to slip through the front door (with Aldreda tucked into Elinor's pocket), they had an unpleasant surprise.

Mrs Avely was awake.

Elinor's mother stood in the doorway to the sitting room, a walking cloak drawn around her, her grey-blonde hair piled on her head. Aldreda, peeping with one eye from the folds of Elinor's gown, saw that Mrs Avely was frowning, her eyes anxious.

"Where have you been?" she demanded of Elinor.

Elinor's heart was beating fast; Aldreda could hear it. "I went walking. I could not sleep."

"Walking! At this time of night!"

"I didn't go far. I am sorry to have worried you, Mother."

Mrs Avely brought a hand up to her eyes. "You cannot just wander off into the night, Elinor. It is unsafe and unseemly."

"Yes, Mother."

"Were you hunting for jewels?"

Elinor's voice took on a tone of wounded innocence. "Of course not, Mother."

Mrs Avely's hand dropped, and she stared at Elinor. "Were you meeting Lord Beresford?"

Elinor hesitated and turned it into a gasp of outrage. "Mother!"

"Were you?"

"Indeed not."

Aldreda silently concurred. They had met Lord Beresford, a selkie, and the countess. Quite different.

Mrs Avely, however, did not seem convinced. She gave Elinor a narrow look and told her to go into the sitting room and light some candles. Elinor did so and then sat, being careful not to squash Aldreda, who waited for Mrs Avely to look away so she could hop out of the rather cramped pocket.

However, Mrs Avely had her eyes fixed upon Elinor in a very examining sort of way.

"Elinor," she began, then paused. "I want to know the truth."

There was a silence.

"The truth, Mother?" said Elinor, with admirable calm.

"I know you have been lying to me. I know something is going on. I want to know what it is."

Elinor swallowed. Aldreda grimaced inside her pocket. Mrs Avely had never approved of Elinor's ability to divine jewels. She certainly wouldn't approve of a vampiri companion, selkies cavorting about the countryside, and a powerful pearl necklace.

Understandably, Elinor said nothing.

Her mother continued. "Last week, I found you in the cellar with Lord Beresford, and you were keeping something from me then, too – and not just your courtship. These secrets cannot continue."

Inside the pocket, Aldreda bit her lip. That was when Beresford had called upon herself. It had looked rather compromising when Mrs Avely had found Elinor apparently alone with Beresford in the cellar. Mrs Avely wasn't to know that Aldreda had been keeping a sharp eye on proprieties, albeit from behind a keg at that point in time. However, perhaps Mrs Avely had seen something?

"Well?" demanded Mrs Avely. Her voice took on a warning cadence. "Tell me." She paused and said with deliberation. "And I will know if you are not telling the truth."

"Er." Elinor gulped. Then she sat up straight and gasped. "You will know if I am not telling the truth?" Her voice sounded suspicious.

Aldreda cocked her head. It sounded as if Elinor was following a new line of thought. And suddenly, Aldreda became aware of the sense of Musing thrumming faintly through her veins. Elinor, certainly, would not be divining jewels right now: therefore, the Musing must be emanating from Mrs Avely. Aldreda caught her breath.

"Indeed. I am your Mother," pronounced Mrs Avely.

Aldreda poked Elinor in the leg as hard as she could, hoping to convey the truth.

There was a silence. "You are my Mother," agreed

Elinor slowly. "Could it be that I inherit my Discernment from you?"

There was a pause.

"I have no idea what you are talking about," said Mrs Avely.

Aldreda heard the faint note of bluster and slipped open the pocket to peer up.

Yes, Mrs Avely was definitely blushing.

"You do know what I am talking about!" exclaimed Elinor. "You can tell if I am lying! In the same way that I can sense the presence of jewels." Her mother remained silent. "It's true, isn't it? Come to think of it, you've always known when I was lying. I thought it was simply motherly instinct, but this is something more!"

Mrs Avely found her voice. "Nonsense. It is maternal intuition. I know you and Perry very well. It is only natural that I can tell when you are up to mischief."

"You can tell it in others, too." Elinor made it a statement. "I remember you in a rage at that dressmaker. And that time you were so cold to Lord Powlond, even before we knew he was misleading us about his title. Even that maid, who you dismissed for no apparent reason!"

Mrs Avely finally let out a sigh. "Very well. It is true." She wrinkled her nose. "I can see you have a bit of a knack for it also."

"I inherited my Gift from you," Elinor said, marvelling over the fact. "It passes through the family line!"

"I am afraid so."

"I have heard about your type," Elinor continued excitedly. "Discernors occasionally have the ability to sense truth and lies. You must have a natural talent for it as I do for jewels."

Her mother's eyes sharpened. "You have heard about my type? What do you mean?"

Elinor drew in a sharp breath, stopping herself before she could reveal any more.

Mother and daughter stared at each other: two pairs of hazel eyes locked with equally guarded expressions. Aldreda watched with interest to see who would back down first.

It was Elinor who relented with a sigh. "I suppose I cannot keep much from a mother who can Discern the truth. I have a new friend," she admitted. "She knows things about Musing – which is what she calls my divining."

"Who is she?" demanded Mrs Avely. "Don't tell me Lady Beresford is Gifted!"

'No," said Elinor carefully. "A Miss Zooth. She is a vampiri: a tiny woman with the ability to turn into a bat."

Her mother's eyes were fixed in amazement on Elinor's face, but Aldreda saw that Mrs Avely did not look incredulous. Perhaps that was the advantage of explaining the impossible to a Truth Discerner: Mrs Avely believed it immediately, for she knew Elinor was not lying.

Elinor continued, gaining in confidence. "Miss Zooth used to live in France a long time ago – eighty years ago, actually – when there were many people with such abilities. They called it Musing. Discernment is only one of eight possible talents. There were secret circles and teaching and protocols." Elinor clasped her hands together. "For all we know, there may still be such people; only, Miss Zooth has been asleep for eighty years. She has been trying to teach me what she knows, but it is not very much."

"Hmm," said Mrs Avely, her tone dripping with disapproval.

"She is very proper," said Elinor defensively. "That is

to say; when she *is* dressed, she is dressed very well. I've made her a few gowns myself."

"When she *is* dressed?"

Aldreda raised her brows. Perhaps Mrs Avely had some secret gift for interrogation as well, to make Elinor babble so much.

Elinor stuttered. "Er, Miss Zooth's transformation from bat does not allow for clothes." She cleared her throat. "Miss Zooth is a lady. She regards herself as a spinster and is determined to remain unmarried."

Her mother looked taken aback, but she obviously decided not to pursue the matter of vampiri matrimonial alliances. Aldreda was glad about that. "Where do you meet? At night, when you are out walking?"

There was a pause while Elinor obviously debated the merits of agreeing to this and thus explaining her behaviour, and then remembering that such lies were doomed to fail. "Er, sometimes."

Mrs Avely's eyes narrowed. "Sometimes?"

"We also meet in my room, where Miss Zooth attempts to impart her knowledge."

Aldreda nodded to herself at Elinor's cleverness. This partial truth avoided the larger fact that Aldreda currently lived in the attic and drank from Elinor's blood. It seemed to work, or at least her mother was distracted.

"Impart what knowledge exactly?"

"How to Discern – apparently it is easier with the element of water present, and there are some things called Talisman stones which also help, though I don't know where to find one." Elinor babbled on. "Miss Zooth says I have to balance wilfulness and openness, and I should be able to Discern anything I like. Imagine that,

Mother! A wide-ranging ability, not merely limited to jewels!"

Her mother did not look enthusiastic. "That way lies trouble. Look where your divining has led us already. Out to the wilds of Devon." She paused. "When can I meet this Miss Zooth?"

Elinor was quiet for a moment. "You wish to meet her?"

"Of course. It is only proper you introduce your acquaintances to me. I need not add that I will be able to detect if she is lying about anything."

Elinor coughed, embarrassed. "Miss Zooth would not lie about anything, Mother."

Aldreda decided that was her cue. She stuck her head out of Elinor's pocket and cleared her throat. "Perhaps if I may introduce myself now?"

Mrs Avely's eyes found her and widened. Aldreda smiled in a gentle way, trying not to reveal her tiny fangs.

Elinor helped Aldreda out and placed her on a side-table. "Mother, I present to you Miss Aldreda Zooth, my vampiri companion from France. Miss Zooth, my Mother, Mrs Judith Avely."

Aldreda curtsied very low. "A pleasure, Mrs Avely."

Mrs Avely collected her composure. After all, she was the one who raised Elinor, who was well trained in displaying imperturbableness. "How do you do, Miss Zooth. This is a long-overdue meeting, I gather."

Aldreda nodded. "I am relieved to finally make your acquaintance."

"Deception is exhausting," agreed Mrs Avely.

"Ha," said Elinor. "You would know! You have been hiding your Gift from me all this time!" Her voice became reproachful. "I have been looking for someone to teach me, and you have been here all along!"

Mrs Avely shook her head. "I cannot teach you. I do not know much. I have not sought to learn more about it."

Elinor leaned forward. "Are there others like us in London? Tell me, Mother! I must know."

A piqued expression crossed Mrs Avely's face. No doubt, she was realising that truth cut both ways. Aldreda watched with interest to see what she would say.

"There are a few. Not very many."

'Mother! Why didn't you tell me!"

"It is not talked of much. I didn't want you to be pulled into that world of secrecy. I wished for you to find happiness as an ordinary person."

It was Elinor's turn to be speechless.

Aldreda intervened. "Indeed, and Elinor has, with Lord Beresford."

"For which I am thankful." Mrs Avely sharpened her gaze. "You'd better not frighten him off, Miss Zooth."

Aldreda cleared her throat. "Lord Beresford has already made my acquaintance."

"Pardon me?"

Elinor nodded eagerly. "Miss Zooth was there that time you found us in the cellar. She was my chaperone."

This intelligence did not appear to soothe Mrs Avely. "Oh? Yet, forgive me, Miss Zooth, you are not a chaperone that could be publicly announced. Lady Beresford might look askance at such behaviour."

Elinor cast her eyes down guiltily.

Aldreda coughed. "Lady Beresford, too, is aware of my existence."

A look of incredulity and hurt crossed Mrs Avely's face. It was quickly hidden. "Am I the last person to meet you, then?"

Elinor looked up, remorse written on her face.

Samuel chose that inopportune moment to stalk into the room and leap up onto Aldreda's table, purring loudly. Mrs Avely's eyebrows rose further. "You have even made a conquest of the cat? Surely I rate before the cat."

"I thought you would disapprove," said Elinor, her voice faltering. "Even forbid our friendship. Please forgive me."

After a long moment, Mrs Avely nodded. "On the condition that there are no more secrets from now on. Is that understood?"

"Yes, Mother," said Elinor in a small voice.

Mrs Avely retired shortly after that. Elinor waited a few minutes and sneaked Aldreda and Samuel up into her room. She turned from locking the door with a very dejected expression.

"I ought to tell Mother that you sleep under her roof," said Elinor, wringing her hands together.

"One revelation at a time," counselled Aldreda, making herself comfortable against Samuel's soft fur on the bed. Aldreda had only bitten the cat three times, yet he was now her devout companion. She would feel more guilty about it, but it was pleasant to have some affection, especially as Elinor was so taken up with Beresford. "Let your mother grow accustomed to me first."

Elinor nodded despondently, then perked up. "I must say, it is a relief you are now in the open."

"Yes, it will make my attendance at your wedding much simpler." That was going to be a tricky affair, involving a heavily veiled basket, as the wedding could not take place in a cellar. They had been wondering how they were going to explain the presence of Elinor's 'sewing basket' at the church.

Elinor crossed the room and sat down beside Samuel. "Are you sure you don't want to give chase to the pearls? An adventure to London might be exciting."

"I have had enough adventure lately," said Aldreda, though reluctantly. "We can always visit London another time."

4

IN WHICH THE CELLAR IS GRACED

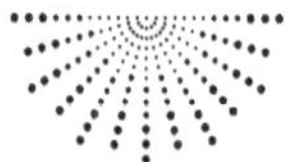

Aldreda

However, the very next day, Aldreda was woken from her deep slumbers early. She stretched and yawned, still tired. It had taken her a while to fall asleep, as her thoughts kept turning, unbidden, to where Pags might be with her pearls. She blinked wearily; it felt as if the sun was still up, and yet Elinor was rattling on her basket in a very businesslike fashion.

Aldreda stuck her head through the paisley shawl. "What is it?"

"I have some selkies to see you."

Aldreda twitched the shawl back. "I do not want to see them."

"It is important," said Elinor. "It is late afternoon, but I can carry you down to the cellar. They have something you need to hear."

Aldreda groaned. "Jaq and Seraphine?" The High

Prince and High Princess of Skerry tended to visit Elinor far too often, in Aldreda's opinion.

"Yes, I sought them out this afternoon."

"Why on earth would you do that?"

"If you weren't so prejudiced towards them, you might have thought of it yourself," said Elinor reprovingly. "I asked them what they know about the French Revolution."

Aldreda lifted her head with sudden interest. Of course, the selkies were from the seas between, and they lived long. They might very well know what had happened to the vampiri in France. And the Musors.

"Very well. Let me dress; then, you may carry me downstairs."

"Mother is out at the village, so hurry. Perhaps it is best to leave selkie royalty out of the picture for her, for now."

Soon Aldreda was appropriately attired. Elinor placed a thick blanket over the basket and swung it into the air.

Halfway down the stairs, Aldreda heard Perry's voice, muffled through the shawl and the blanket.

"Is something afoot, Elinor?" he asked. "Have you got Aldreda there?"

"We have royal visitors," said Elinor. "Would you like to join the tea party?"

There was a silence, but after a moment his footsteps followed them down. Aldreda wondered if Perry was going to pointedly ignore Jaq for the whole meeting. She hoped so. She still hadn't forgiven Jaq for claiming two of the Moria Pearls for the selkies.

Once in the cellar, with the door tightly closed, Elinor drew off the blankets. Aldreda stepped out of the basket, brushing her skirt down and looking around.

Ever since her last audience here, Elinor had made

some improvements in case it was required again as a receiving room. She had insisted the maid sweep and dust – giving reasons of rats – and had placed a couple of chairs about, with the excuse that they cluttered up the sitting room. She had even laid out a small carpet for the occasion today, and the result was quite cosy.

Aldreda was placed in the position of honour, on the top of a keg that was covered in another rug. She was pleased to see it was red, her favourite colour.

However, Seraphine, the High Princess of Skerry, did not look impressed. She was standing on one of the floor stones, holding her primrose skirts up and looking very unamused. Her gaze softened, however, when she saw Perry, whose slim, boyish form was neatly dressed in breeches and a morning coat.

"Ah, Mr Avely!" Seraphine cooed. "So lovely to see you again."

Perry bowed low, his dark blonde hair falling across his brow. "Your Highness, the pleasure is all mine." Yet, as he rose, his eyes slipped past her to Jaq.

Jaq was leaning against a rack of wine in a casual pose that somehow managed to show off his long legs. "Perry," he acknowledged. He didn't say anything more, just gave a smirk. Perry pressed his lips together and turned his gaze away, which Aldreda was glad to see. It was better for humans to stay away from selkies.

Elinor bustled about, pulling up a small table. "Now, shall I send for some tea?"

"What will your servants think?" asked Jaq. "Do they know about Miss Zooth?"

"No," admitted Elinor. "They will think we are highly eccentric. I have told them you are eager to inspect our wines."

Jaq raised a brow. "I do not need human wines. I have Skerry's."

Perry was curious, despite himself. "You have vineyards on Skerry?"

"The best," said Jaq. "We also import French wines and mermaid tears. You should try some one day."

Perry looked aghast at the prospect. Jaq dropped his eyes, and his lips quirked bitterly.

Elinor intervened. "Alcohol is not the subject for discussion," she said tartly. "Perhaps we will even skip the tea. No time to waste. I want you to tell Aldreda what you told me."

Aldreda's eyes widened. It must be an important matter if Elinor was willing to skip the tea.

Seraphine sat down with a huff in one of the chairs. "It is not enough that I demean myself with this ..." she looked around accusingly, "This dungeon! You will not even give me something to drink?"

"The matter is urgent," said Elinor. "Besides, you owe Aldreda a favour after arresting her and detaining her so unfairly."

"What else was I supposed to think?" said Seraphine petulantly. "I had good reason to arrest her."

Jaq pushed himself off the wine-rack. "Water over the reef."

Elinor nodded with approval. "Jaq, tell us about the French Musors."

"Well, Miss Zooth," Jaq paused. He searched for words and shuffled his feet on the stone. "I thought you were aware of this, and it is best that you know. The Musors suffered in the Revolution, alongside the aristocracy. Many died. So many, we fear there are hardly any left in France."

"Pardon me?" Aldreda stared at him. This matched

what Pags had intimated, but she still found it hard to believe. "When I left France eighty-five years ago, the Musor circles were thriving and growing. Though they kept their presence secret, of course."

"That was eighty-five years ago," said Seraphine. "Those Musors who escaped the guillotine fled, or they are in hiding. Much of the knowledge of Musing has been lost. That is why we need the Moria Pearls."

Aldreda looked from one to the other. "Why did you not tell us this before?" she demanded.

"I thought you knew," said Jaq. "I did not want to dwell upon it."

"You wanted the necklace!" Aldreda felt herself flushing with anger. "If what you say is true, the pearls are even more important than we knew!"

There was a silence. Jaq shuffled again on the stone. Seraphine gave an imperious sniff, but her eyes shifted away from Aldreda's.

"There is more," said Elinor. "Jaq? What about the vampiri?"

The handsome selkie twisted his hands together and stared at the floor. "The vampiri were killed as well, along with their masters. I have not seen a vampiri, apart from you, in ten years."

Aldreda felt her face pale.

"Companions," said Elinor abruptly. "Not masters. The point is, Aldreda, that for all we know, a similar situation is developing in England. We cannot be sure that the pearls will be safe in the metropolis. London could be a hotbed of seething dissidents who want to destroy all artefacts of Musing, just as was done in France."

Perry interrupted. "The pearls are in London?" The rest of the company turned to stare at him, and he flushed. "No one told me! How did they come to be in London?"

"Pags took them," said Aldreda. "I mean, his gracel, the Dukel of Demontaine." She wrinkled her nose. It still rankled that Pags was so nobly titled. He had even less right to parade around naked and attempt bat mating dances on unsuspecting females.

Perry was aghast. "That hairy vampiri?"

"Yes," said Elinor.

"Good Gad. After all that we did to find that necklace!"

"My thoughts exactly," said Aldreda. "I was prepared to leave the pearls with the king. Yet, if what the selkies say is true, London could be unsafe."

"Ah, yes," said Perry. "One of the king's advisors died only a week ago, in suspicious circumstances."

Everyone turned to stare at him again.

"What?" said Elinor inelegantly.

"It was in the newspaper." Perry looked around at the suddenly alert faces. "Lord Rapp, advisor to the king. Dead in his study."

"Show me at once!" demanded Elinor.

"No need to fly into a tizzle," said Perry, but he hurried from the cellar. The rest of them stared at each other silently until he came back, rustling a newspaper at them. "Here you go."

Perry opened the paper on the table and pointed. The selkies and Elinor crowded around him, with Aldreda perched on Elinor's shoulder. At length, Elinor looked up, frowning. "A shooting accident. So it is unlikely to be Pags who did it. Are vampiri strong enough to hold a gun, Aldreda?"

Aldreda considered. "We could lift one, but wielding it would be excessively awkward."

"Besides, the shooting happened a week ago," Jaq pointed out. "Before Pags left Devon."

Aldreda was glad that the nomenclature of Pags had been collectively adopted. His gracel, her footel.

Elinor thought aloud. "Could Pags have been in London before that?"

"Too far to fly," said Aldreda. "This must be someone else. Probably human, and possibly this Lord Rapp was a Musor." She squared her shoulders. "We must go to London after all, Elinor. Or rather, I should go alone."

"Nonsense," said Elinor. "If there are Musors in London, you cannot keep me away. And I want to give a piece of my mind to Pags."

Perry objected. "You want to chase Pags to London? One sight of him was enough!"

"I cannot agree more," said Aldreda, though, in fact, she had seen the sight twice (not that she was counting). "We shall not go near Pags. We will go directly to the king."

"More royalty," complained Perry, shooting a side glance at Jaq.

Jaq grinned. "Poor Perry. Nakedness and royalty: surely not a combination you enjoy."

Perry blushed bright red.

Seraphine ignored them. "Jaq, you must go too, of course."

Jaq shook his head. "I have to go with Beresford to France." He paused. "But after that, I imagine we will both head to the metropolis. I will recover the pearls, do not fear."

Aldreda wrinkled her nose. She didn't want Jaq underfoot, making claims to her pearls, but she could scarcely forbid him from going. At least he would be taken up with Beresford's mission first. By then, Aldreda should have the pearls well in hand.

Elinor was curious. "Won't you be too far from the sea in London?" she asked Jaq.

"It will cause me a slight strain only, nothing I cannot handle."

"A slight strain?" asked Perry.

"I shall feel a little dried out, as it were." Jaq grinned. "I'll just have to make sure I drink a lot. You'll have to show me the sights, Perry."

In no mean feat, Perry managed to look both pleased and suspicious at the same time.

5

IN WHICH ELINOR WARNS
HER FAMILY

Elinor

Elinor took the opportunity to pull Perry aside into her bedroom that evening.

"Perry, by the way – Mother knows about Aldreda now."

"What?!" Perry closed Elinor's door behind him and looked around furtively. "How?"

"I introduced them."

"Good Gad, why? Mother won't approve of Miss Zooth. No offence, Aldreda." Perry nodded at the bookshelf, where Aldreda sat primly atop a stack of books.

Elinor grimaced. "Well – you won't like this, brother, but we've discovered Mother is a Discernor also."

"What?!"

Aldreda looked as if she was repressing a grin. "Mrs Avely can Discern lies. So be warned, Perry."

Perry's mouth fell open.

Elinor nodded in fervent agreement, then rubbed her

own forehead. "Mother really put me on the spot last night. I felt like I was in the Inquisition, with all her questions and her gimlet stare."

"The deuces! That's terrible," said Perry, with feeling.

"I know." Elinor tutted. "She has frowned upon my Gift all this time when she has the same one!"

"Not that! She'll know when I'm fibbing!" Perry began to pace.

"Not necessarily *every* fib," pointed out Aldreda. "As Elinor knows, to Discern properly, one must concentrate upon the task. You can probably slip a few untruths past her."

Perry looked unconvinced. "I'd be too scared to try."

"She can't be Discerning all the time," agreed Elinor. "She'd be Bemused, all befuddled from Musing. However, like me, Mother seems to have a natural affinity for her subject. She probably will have an intuition if someone is lying nearby, just not know who exactly, or what about."

"Ha," said Perry. "So, I can only lie when surrounded by a multitude of possible other suspects?"

"You must not lie at all," said Elinor reprovingly, but allowed a twinkle to show in her eye. "As a good Christian gentleman should not."

With this new knowledge of her mother, Elinor disclosed all to Mrs Avely over several cups of tea the following day. With care, Elinor explained the history of the Moria Pearls, and how important it was to ensure their protection, and the necessity for removal to London – though she left out mention of Lord Rapp's death, as she did not want to cause an overabundance of worry or caution. As hoped, all the other information sufficed to distract Mrs Avely from any lies by omission.

"These pearls contain Memories of the Musor teachings?" asked Mrs Avely. "Then why don't you leave them with the king?"

Elinor regarded her mother narrowly over her cup, deciding that it was time to turn the questions around. "Mother, you mentioned that you knew a few Musors in London. Is King George one of them?"

Mrs Avely stiffened slightly. "I cannot speak for the king. I did not move in his circles, after all. But I will say this: Musors tend to be nobles; the power drifts upwards. Some of the highest families have secret abilities. Only a few, you understand, as the Gifts are rare, and they keep their talents hidden."

"Did you know any such families? Could you perhaps introduce me to them?" Elinor tried to justify her eager curiosity. "Then we can find out more about the political situation, and whether the pearls are safe with King George."

Mrs Avely sniffed. "I am no longer on speaking terms with the Musors in London. When you and Perry were born and your father died, I decided to end all such pursuits.

Elinor became arrested with new suspicion. "Was *father* a Musor?"

As far as Elinor knew, her father had died in military service ten years ago in the Battle of Turcoine. Her mother had always described Mr Avely as a brave and wise man, but perhaps she had left out other important qualities.

"No," said Mrs Avely sharply. "I do not wish to discuss it further, Elinor. Musing leads to danger, and I want us to lead safe, ordinary lives."

Elinor narrowed her eyes but did not press the matter. Her mother already had enough to cope with today. She sighed. "Oh, *vincit prudentia*, of course – you always want to take the cautious path."

Vincit prudentia was the Avely family motto, roughly translated as 'Prudence Conquers,' and oft-repeated by her mother.

Mrs Avely's eyes dropped. "Indeed. For that reason, I think we should avoid London for now, especially given the circumstances of our leaving it."

"But Mother, the Countess of Beresford wants to accompany us."

"Does she?" Mrs Avely was taken aback. "Lady Beresford is going to London too? She hasn't been there in years."

"Yes! Surely that will change our reception." Elinor twisted her hands together in her lap, realising that despite her bravado, she still felt nervous about the prospect of returning to London. "Lady Beresford says she will smooth over the scandal and try to gain us an audience with the king."

Mrs Avely thrummed her fingers on the table, an uncommon sign of perturbation. "Hm. Well, I suppose if the countess thinks you should go ..."

When Elinor showed Beresford the newspaper article, he frowned, nodded, and remarked that he wished Elinor would wait until he could accompany her too. Such a paltry attitude, however, was soon overruled by Elinor and his mother, not to mention Jaq and Aldreda. The selkie and the vampiri for once agreed about something, even if it was only to catch Pags and throttle him.

Beresford and Jaq left for France, after a tearful farewell. Elinor had to repress her worry for their safety, and Perry was also a little subdued after Jaq's departure.

The French coast was rife with danger for Englishmen and selkies as well. But they were both capable men, as Elinor told Perry, able to look after themselves. Furthermore, she was certain Jaq would swim to London if need be, even if only to go carousing with Perry. Beresford had promised to join them as soon as he could.

The countess was not worried; she was too busy packing what seemed a vast number of trunks. However, she told Elinor that she was travelling with a minimum, as she planned to order a whole new wardrobe in London, this time in colours. She was leaving her companion, Miss Trent, behind to keep the house in order, but she was quite determined to cast a veneer of respectability over Elinor.

"They won't dare snub *me*," announced Lady Beresford. "Besides, once society knows you are marrying James, it will put the whole *garden party* business in a different light. A mere lovers' tiff, so we will say, and any vulgar aspersions will soon be silenced."

Elinor was amused to learn that included within the countess's trunks were jars and jars of Beresford jam. They were an offering for the royal family in the hope it would smooth the way. A letter had been sent ahead, petitioning for a private interview, with cautious references to plum jam and pearls.

If that failed, Lady Beresford was determined to attend the court presentation of her protégé, Mademoiselle Laberche, a young French refugee who had been staying at the Beresford Manor. Mademoiselle Laberche was soon to make her debut in society, under the aegis of an old family friend in London. Lady Beresford planned to be there for the occasion and connive a word with the king.

6

IN WHICH ALDREDA
SEARCHES FOR MUSORS

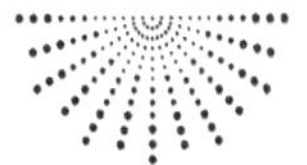

Aldreda

Aldreda was asleep in her basket, heavily curtained from the sun. She was woken on the embarkation of the carriage by the fact that Samuel was causing a fuss. He had been in the basket with her, curled up, all soft and warm. When Elinor tried to remove the cat, he objected strongly and clawed his way back in.

"I am going to London," Aldreda tried to explain to him from the shadow of her paisley shawl. The sun was too bright, though she was inside the carriage, and she felt faint. Samuel's green eyes stared at her uncomprehendingly. "I'll be back soon enough." Aldreda hoped it was true.

Samuel put a paw out and pinned her skirts with a sharp claw.

Mrs Avely smiled. She was overseeing the packing. "Perhaps Samuel understands more than you realise."

"You cannot go with Aldreda," said Elinor. "You belong here, Samuel."

He glared at her and wriggled himself further into the basket.

Aldreda sighed. "Let him travel with me for the first part. He will soon realise what is happening and return to Casserly."

"Cats have a homing instinct, don't they?" said Elinor. "Very well, Samuel, have a little adventure." She pulled the blanket over, casting them into darkness, and Aldreda sighed with relief.

So Aldreda had a comfortable pillow for the journey. When they pulled up at the first inn, she was sorry when Samuel leapt out to explore. No doubt, he would stalk back to Casserly. Aldreda felt a momentary pang, wishing she could go with him, where it was safe and familiar.

The first night on the road, while the Avelys and Lady Beresford dined together at the inn, Aldreda went exploring by herself. She had a whole night, after all, and she wasn't going to sit around twiddling her thumbs while everyone ate. She had already discreetly drunk from Elinor's wrist and was restless to act.

She swooped through the village. It was not much bigger than Deockley, though it was one of the major posts on the road to London. Her senses were cocked for the sound of Musing. Nothing struck her at this height, so she decided to work methodically through the houses. There was no saying where a Musor might be, though, of course, there was a stronger possibility in an aristocratic household.

She found only two. One was a kitchen maid, Heightening the food that she served at her master's table. She seemed untutored, Musing purely from instinct. Aldreda watched her a while, noting the girl only used her Gift occasionally (depending on which dish she was serving), which would keep her Bemusement in check. The maid might not even realise she was Gifted.

The other was a Diplomacor, a groomsman crooning at the horses. It was rare to find a Diplomacor with a talent for communing with animals. Aldreda watched him for a while and began to think she had been mistaken: he was just a groomsman. Then the stable cat came in, and the man gestured for it to sit on his shoulder. Aldreda felt the flash of Musing as the cat leapt up and rubbed against the man's cheek.

That was all. The rest of the household and village was dark of Musing. Of course, that could be simply because any others were sleeping or not engaged in practicing their Gift. If there were a Musor who could Travel, for example, Aldreda would be lucky to catch them in the act and most likely only sense the Musing as they vanished.

After some indecision, Aldreda stayed watching the groomsman. He was more likely to have found a vampiri companion. Yet no bat showed in the stables, though Aldreda kept a long vigil.

She returned to her basket just before dawn. To her surprise, Samuel was sitting next to it with a mournful look in his eye. He purred when he saw her, and they settled in for another day's journey.

The same thing happened in the following two nights. Aldreda found five more Musors, but all seemed as if they were working from instinct, erratic and alone. There was a Healor and an Illusor in Podimore, and a Memor in Amesbury. Two others had gifts Aldreda could not be sure of, only that she felt the presence of their Musing in fits and spurts. There were no bats, at least not of the vampiri kind. She found some other roosts of common bats, but they (rightfully) ignored her.

Aldreda reported these findings to Elinor each evening. Elinor was exhausted from the long days of travelling, and Aldreda was tired from her nightly forays, so their meetings were brief. On the third and final night, however, Elinor looked grave and stopped Aldreda from flying off immediately.

"Tomorrow night, we will be in London," Elinor observed. "What will you do then?"

"Same as I do now: look for Musors."

"London might be different. What if something happens to you?"

"I cannot imagine what." Unless Pags accosted Aldreda again. Pags must be *somewhere* in London. She would have to check the stables.

"Are you not concerned that you have seen no sign of any vampiri?"

"Not particularly. In France, we all flocked to the metropolis to be close to the Musors and their circles. No doubt, it is the same here."

Though she did not want to admit it, Aldreda was secretly concerned. Both Pags and the selkies had said vampiri were killed in the Troubles. She did not understand how that was possible. Vampiri were supernaturally quick and strong, difficult to catch and restrain, let alone kill. However, she did not want to worry Elinor unduly.

"Besides," Aldreda added. "We *have* seen a vampiri: Pags."

Elinor brightened. "Indeed, and I am sure he will seek you out. We can find out more from him."

"I hope to find out things for myself," said Aldreda, slightly cross. "Pags is clearly not to be trusted."

Elinor nodded. "We will be staying at the Beresford townhouse, which is near the centre of London. Don't go too far in your travels."

Aldreda agreed. "I hope I will have more interesting news to report after tomorrow night. If there are any secret circles of Musors, I am bound to find them."

"How exciting." Elinor's eyes sparkled.

Aldreda paused. "Do you have the last pearl safe?"

"Yes, in a locked box at the bottom of my trunk," said Elinor. "I will find a good hiding place for it tomorrow when we arrive at the Beresford residence."

When Aldreda woke the following night, she found her basket had been placed in her very own room. It was a vast improvement from the attic she had expected, which would have been musty and dusty. Here, her abode was made up in russet and yellow, with oak furniture polished and gleaming. The window curtains were drawn, the door shut, and her gowns laid out upon the bed.

She appreciated the courtesy. No doubt, the countess had given strict orders to her servants to leave the door locked. Vampiri had other ways of leaving a room.

Samuel was not with her. Perhaps he had returned home or been taken out earlier to be fed and petted downstairs. Aldreda wondered if he would scratch at the door later.

Too impatient to wait for Elinor, and leaving her clothes on the bed, Aldreda shivered into bat form and flew over to crawl under the curtain.

Someone had thoughtfully left the window open a crack. Aldreda slipped through, out into the night air.

It was later than she realised. She must have slept long after her recent exertions. The moon was high in the sky, and London was well into its evening's entertainments.

Smoke and the smell of excrement and horses assailed her nostrils, the familiar scents of a city. Aldreda darted higher up and looked around. The night was relatively clear, with a few clouds scudding across the sky.

Her window was on the upper floor in a grand house that looked onto a quiet street. The Beresfords were situated on a curving crescent of similar houses. Beyond that stretched the intriguing bustle of the city, with the shouts of servants and the rattle of carriages on cobblestone streets.

Aldreda set off, keeping close to the eaves of the houses. It would not do to fly too high, as she might not sense any Musing. But it was better to keep out of sight as much as possible, even though most would simply take her as an ordinary bat flitting in the night.

It was not long before she felt it: the strident call of Musing.

It was powerful, this time. It even seemed as if many were casting magic together. Finally – a circle of Musors. Aldreda was in civilisation at last. She let out a sigh of relief. She was sure to find vampiri here.

Aldreda shot towards the call. Her senses took her unerringly to a large building, grand in scale, with elegant columns lined ostentatiously across the front. She hovered in front, trying to determine how to enter. The door was well guarded, but at length, she saw an open upper window. She fluttered down and slipped inside the top corner.

The room was empty and grand. Wealth and power lay here, not just magic.

Aldreda kept high to the ceiling as she followed the

call of Musing. Humans did not look up very often, in her experience, and they would not notice a small bat flitting in the ceiling. Unfortunately, these were very ornate ceilings, designed to draw the eye upwards, and without many shadows. Aldreda began to feel nervous and kept to the edges, clinging to the cornices whenever she saw a servant.

Servants were all she saw and plenty of them. Finally, she found the room from which the Musing spilled. The sensation was like a heavy beat of drums, too loud. She began to have an inkling of what she would find within.

Aldreda hovered outside for a moment. Then, cautiously, keeping to the wall, she glided within and crept upwards to the ceiling.

Inside was a scene of dissipation.

Several men lay about in stupors, strewn about on the elegant, rich furnishings. There were empty glasses and trays of half-eaten food. Looking around, Aldreda saw the room was strangely round, with a large, arching dome overhead. The ceiling was blue, with the edges painted in looming grey clouds.

She found a hiding place quickly, clinging to a fold of some blue hanging curtains, and watched.

The men were quite obviously musedrunk. The throb of magic was so overpowering that there could be no other explanation. Aldreda tutted to herself. They were most likely Helicons, those Musors who deliberately sought the state of Bemusement, finding it an enjoyable way to spend the time. Helicons cast unnecessary, difficult magic, just for the sake of the mind-state that followed.

One was Musing now, a complex spell of Diplomacy. The room thickened with the smell of roses, and soft light somehow poured from the walls. Faint music played, sweet and lilting.

It was difficult to tell which gentleman was casting the spell. Some of the men nodded and smiled dreamily, lost in their own haze. One man in the corner giggled inanely to himself, amused at something only he could see.

"Brilliant, Your Highness," murmured another lazily. "You outdo yourself again."

The man so addressed was sprawled on a couch. He grinned with his eyes closed, and the music became a little more seductive. Aldreda swayed slightly with it, then pulled herself up sharply. A soft golden glow was arising in her belly, making her feel open and trusting. It was a powerful spell.

She tutted again and watched anxiously. His Highness? Could this be the king to which Pags referred? This man was not one to entrust with the Moria Pearls. If he was not careful, he might end up Bewildered: the lifelong state of Bemusement, the cost of pushing too far into magic.

No, he must be the Prince of Wales. Elinor had said the king was ill and elderly; this man was perhaps forty and still handsome. Though perhaps that was simply the effect of his Diplomacy that made him seem so attractive.

Aldreda examined the other men: all nobles, well dressed, and well drunk with magic. She settled in to watch from her perch, hoping to learn something else.

Unfortunately, not much sense was to be had. Eventually, the prince's spell faded, and he sunk further into his couch. He was still good-looking, observed Aldreda, with thick brown hair and warm toned skin. She felt a pang of hunger. She had not fed from Elinor that night yet, and the prince looked very ... warm-blooded.

Aldreda glanced around at the other men. Some were completely comatose; probably those who were not as Gifted as the prince, and more quickly overcome. There were six in all, in various states of disarray.

Her gaze sharpened. A bat was creeping over one of the couches. A vampiri! It had to be. Aldreda narrowed her gaze. The size and shape of it were somehow familiar. Or perhaps that was just her imagination.

As she watched, the bat began drinking from the wrist of one of the unconscious men. She drew in a horrified breath and almost flew down to chase him off. Such barbarism! To feed without permission! But she did not want to betray herself, so she stayed where she was, looking on, aghast. The human was so deeply asleep, he did not notice anything. Soon the bat withdrew and cast a somehow contemptuous glance around at the rest of the company.

No one had noticed him, except Aldreda. The bat flew to an alcove and took possession of a chair, hanging from a whorl of wood.

Aldreda glared down at him. That arrogant tilt of the wing was definitely familiar. The behaviour was certainly savage enough. Or perhaps the vampiri in London now operated under an entirely different code to France.

The only way to find out was to talk to him.

Aldreda stealthily made her way around the room and glided down to the alcove. When she swung onto the chair, the other vampiri fell off in a startled movement.

Seeing that long, muscled body, so big for a vampiri, Aldreda was more certain. Reluctantly, she transformed and landed on the seat, taking refuge behind a cushion to maintain her modesty.

"You thieving rat!" she accused, wasting no time.

The vampiri shook himself into human form. It was

indeed Pags, his beard still wild, his hair still in dire need of cutting. He struck a pose on the floor, putting his hands on his hips and looking up at her. He spoke in French. "Mademoiselle Zooth! What a delightful surprise! You are in London!"

"Of course I am in London, you hairy bandit," said Aldreda. "You stole my necklace!"

"I delivered it to safekeeping." Pags folded his arms in front of him.

"You had no right," snapped Aldreda. "It was already safe. You deserve the midday sun."

"It appeared to me that the pearls were the subject of some contention," countered Pags. "I was doing you a favour – taking them out of harm's way. You ought to be grateful."

"Grateful!" Aldreda glared at him. "You … cur!"

"Indeed, I was only trying to please you."

Aldreda frowned direfully, but Pags's expression was serious.

"I meant it for the best," he said. "The king will look after your pearls for you."

"Oh, so they *are* my pearls? And how can I know if the king is to be trusted?"

"His highness kept his country from following the same path as France," said Pags. "He is Gifted, as are some of his children. He will take care of the pearls and protect the knowledge they contain."

"So you say. Yet isn't *that* the king's first son?" Aldreda jerked her head towards the prince, who was now crooning softly to himself. "Look at him. He is a disgrace."

"The king is very different to his heir, who is young and rebellious."

"I can see that." Aldreda sniffed. "Where is the necklace now?"

"With His Majesty. Cursed heavy it was, too. I was glad to be rid of it."

She glowered. "I hope it gave you wing-crick. I will recover the necklace; you can be sure."

"What on earth for?" demanded Pags. "I have done you a service! The king has a dedicated Musor library, where your Henri's teachings will be honoured. It is all the more necessary after what happened in France."

Aldreda folded her arms. "What *did* happen in France? I want to know the particulars. You say that the vampiri died along with the Musors, but I cannot comprehend how. We are resilient creatures."

Pags's face became shuttered. At that moment, a shout broke into their conversation.

"Vampiri!" called one of the men. He stared at them, his eyes wide and accusing. "Over there!"

"Time to depart," said Pags. He flicked into bat form and rose into the air. Aldreda cast a glance around. Many eyes were now upon her, some wondering, some angry.

"Throw them out!" said the prince, his voice carrying authority though he still lay in a horizontal position, seemingly unable to stand. "No vampiri here. Such are the rules."

Aldreda decided she didn't want to enquire into the cause of their hostility. She changed into a bat and fled, following Pags out the door. Something hit the doorframe as she flew through. One of those sots had dared throw a pillow at her!

She winged her way through the palace – for it seemed it must be a palace – following Pags's quick, dark form. He took a different exit to the one she had found, through a back window near the stables. Of course. He headed for a tree and landed to hang upside-down from one of the branches.

Aldreda followed suit.

They waited as bats for a few minutes to see if any pursuit would eventuate. No one came. She could imagine the Helicons had returned to their musedrunken imaginings. When Pags transformed into a human and dropped to land on a thick branch, Aldreda did so too.

She tried to ignore the fact they were now both alone and naked in an oak tree, in a most improper fashion. And the fact she was now consorting with the enemy. But perhaps Pags really had meant his actions for the best.

"Why did they want us gone?" she asked.

He shrugged. "Because we might interfere with their pleasures. They know vampiri reduce Bemusement."

"It was not something more sinister?"

"Nothing like the Troubles," agreed Pags. He paused. "Many of us were captured then. The Mundanes used us to find the Musors, using our ability to sense magic."

Aldreda drew a breath. "Used us against our own companions? Surely that is impossible."

"They employed ropes made of Aubadesol," said Pags shortly.

He seemed to think Aldreda would know what he meant. She did not. Pags looked at her, seeing her blank expression.

"You do not know of the Aubadesol?"

She shook her head.

His voice went cold. "It is woven by the sun silk-worms, which were discovered on an island near the New World. These creatures spin silk with light embedded in the very fibres. The material weakens and binds vampiri. It can even kill us if we are kept tied in it too long. The hostile Mundanes used it to control us and make us do their bidding. That is how they caught so many Musors for the guillotine."

Aldreda was silent. She found it hard to imagine any vampiri turning against their Musor companion, even tied and weakened. Yet in times of great suffering, people did terrible things. Perhaps some vampiri had been willing to lead their captors to magic, even if it meant certain death to the Musor.

She cast a glance at Pags. He was staring into the night with a grim, closed expression. Had he been so caught and used? It would explain why he was so loath to ally with any human.

"That is terrible." She felt a little sick. "Yet you do not fear it might happen here in England?"

"King George III has kept a peaceful reign," replied Pags. "He is fighting the French, and he has passed laws against the use of the Aubadesol. That is why I fled to England."

"And what were you doing, feeding from a Musor uninvited?" Aldreda changed the subject. "How can you do such a barbaric thing?"

Pags looked momentarily embarrassed. "You saw that?" He lifted his bearded chin and stared haughtily. "I do not need permission. I refuse to form an alliance with a Musor now. Besides, it was for that man's own good. He verged too close to Bewilderment. This way, he will be kept from the edge."

"You merely wanted a good dinner."

"That is true." Pags grinned. "I must say I have grown tired of horses. Why can't I indulge, now I have found these foolish Helicons?"

"It is still wrong," said Aldreda, though her scorn was now tempered by the thought that Pags had possibly done the unconscious man a service. "You will be bonded slightly to him now."

"Only for a day. You know it takes a formal alliance to cement it."

"So you *do* remember some of the rules," said Aldreda. "Yet you choose to ignore all tenets of civilised behaviour. Scarcely appropriate for a dukel." She wondered briefly if Pags had been made a dukel in his lifetime, by becoming a companion to the noble house, or whether he had been born to it, succeeding in his mother's or father's duties. From his current state of barbarism and barber-lessness, it seemed he had been born to the lower orders. Then she remembered the signature at the foot of his cursed note: the *Fifth* Dukel of Demontaine.

He gave her a crooked smile. "A dukel may do as he pleases."

"Not exactly," she said coldly. "I must go now, Your Gracel." She put a world of irony in the honoured address. "Enjoy your evening."

"Wait. Where are you going?" He paused. "May I accompany you?"

"No, I thank you. I am going to find civilised vampiri society. So no doubt you will find it uncomfortable."

He grinned again. "Ah, but if you are there, it will be a delight. Besides, you are not dressed for it either."

It was true. Aldreda glanced down at her naked body. She had no evening clothes with her, a fact she had been trying to ignore, though of course, Pags had taken an opportunity to remind her. His eyes were alight with appreciation.

Aldreda ignored him. Usually, vampiri were escorted by their human companions to the social venues. Still, at this stage, she only wanted to watch from the shadows. Later she could obtain proper introductions.

She looked over at Pags. Perhaps he would be useful. He might know where the vampiri gathered. Besides, there were still questions she hadn't asked him.

"Do you know of a vampiri dance venue near here?"

"Certainly," he bowed. "May I lead you there tomorrow night?"

"Not to dance," she said hastily. "I simply want to observe."

Pags raised a brow. "We can remain as bats if you wish. I know of a discreet viewing point."

Aldreda nodded her assent. "Shall we meet back here tomorrow night?"

"I look forward to it, Miss Zooth," said Pags, and before she could think of a suitably crushing retort, he twisted off the branch into the night.

7

IN WHICH ELINOR RECEIVES
AN INTRIGUING CALL

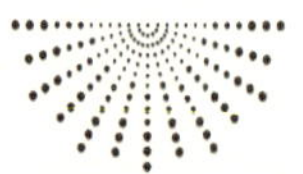

Elinor

$\mathcal{E}$linor went up after dinner to see how Aldreda fared and found her gone from her new room. Determined to wait, Elinor fell asleep on the yellow bed, tired from the day's travel and the excitement of arriving in London.

Elinor was woken by Aldreda, tugging on her little finger. Elinor sat, yawning, and saw the vampiri was dressed, and the night still dark outside.

"Well?" asked Elinor. "Any Musors in London?"

"The Prince of Wales, no less." Aldreda sat down, heaving a sigh. She did not appear pleased with her discovery.

"Oh?" asked Elinor. "Why aren't you happy about it?"

"Unfortunately, the prince is a Helicon – one who seeks Bemusement."

"Seeks it? Why would he do such a thing?" Elinor rubbed her eyes and curled her legs up under her. The room was cold; it must be very early in the morning. Vampiri didn't need warmth, but it would be nice to keep a fire going here regardless, if Elinor were to visit often.

Aldreda shrugged. "Some Musors crave the sensation, much as Mundanes like to be drunk."

"What did you call the prince? A Helicon?" Elinor propped her hand on her chin thoughtfully. It hadn't occurred to her that being Bemused was enjoyable for its own sake. She was usually too concerned with the Divining task at hand and found Bemusement a hindrance rather than a pleasure.

Aldreda explained. "Such profligates are named after Mount Helicon, where it is said the Muses drink from a sacred spring. I found the prince in a palace, revelling in musedrunkeness with several other men."

"Goodness me. How vulgar. Though, of course, I know Prince George is a bit of a wastrel."

"Extremely vulgar," nodded Aldreda. "Yet Pags – *his gracel* – tells me the prince's father is very different."

"You saw Pags?"

Aldreda nodded, her lips twisting. "I gave him a piece of my mind."

"Was he clothed this time?"

Aldreda shook her head.

Elinor repressed a smile. "I suppose you weren't dressed either," she remarked. "But never mind that – what did Pags say?"

"Both the king and the prince are Musors," said Aldreda, "but Pags assures me the king is more responsible than his son. I would like to determine that for myself."

"Perhaps I can find out today," said Elinor. "While you sleep, I can make my own enquiries." She yawned. "Now, however, I am too tired to think. Good night, my dear."

Elinor let herself out as Samuel slipped in, and she went down to her own bedroom. She fell asleep as she pondered what she knew of King George III: Farmer George, he was called, and a staid and cautious man by all accounts. He was always at odds with his heir, who was spendthrift and dissolute. Yet Elinor drowsily recalled that there were whispers that the king himself was subject to some kind of debilitating illness that kept him cloistered for weeks at a time. That might be a sign he too was unfit to guard the pearls.

That morning, before Elinor could decide what her first step should be to investigate the king, she received a noble caller: the Duchess of Planx.

Lady Beresford was out, calling on some dear friend of hers whom she hadn't seen in years. Mrs Avely was out shopping, and Perry was out walking – or brooding, rather. So it was that Elinor received the duchess alone in the drawing room.

The butler bowed her grace in, and the duchess's slender figure paused in the middle of the room, clad in a dashing yellow gown with black trimmings. Her gleaming brown hair was done up in fashionable ringlets, and she clasped a Norwich shawl around her shoulders.

Her face was attractive if somewhat marred by a cynical air of worldly sophistication. Dark eyes, a little piercing, fixed upon Elinor.

"Miss Avely!" The duchess had a well-modulated voice that Elinor remembered too well from the dreadful garden party. "How do you do! So pleased you could return to London."

Elinor curtsied. The fact that the duchess was calling upon the Avelys so soon was a welcome sign – if a little perplexing. Of course, it was probably the Beresfords her grace intended to call upon. James was still in France, but at least this visit would distract Elinor from her worry about him.

"Your Grace," said Elinor. "Thank you for calling." She gestured to a seat and gave the order for tea uncomfortably, aware of those dark eyes watching how Elinor dealt with the Beresford butler, soon to be her own.

The duchess threw off her shawl and sat down. "My dear girl, calling upon you is the least I could do after that *unfortunate* incident at my garden party. I am so sorry you felt you had to leave London. However, now it has all worked out for the best, has it not?"

Elinor blinked at this direct reference to the scandal that had blackened the Avely name after Elinor found a large amethyst pendant hidden in the Planxes' very own ducal garden. In trying to discover to whom it belonged, Elinor had been accused of its theft. At the time, the duchess had not done much to protect Elinor from the gossip, despite Elinor's attempt to blackmail her grace for an intervention.

"Indeed, Your Grace," replied Elinor cautiously. "Yet, your patronage will do much to smooth the way for me on my return."

The duchess waved a languid hand. "Oh, you don't need *my* patronage. I am here at the bequest of Queen Charlotte. She wants to make sure you are respectable again."

Elinor's eyes widened. "Pardon me? Did you say *Queen Charlotte*?"

"Apparently, you sent some missive to the king? Or the Countess of Beresford did so?" The sharp eyes were fixed again on Elinor's face in curiosity. "*Whatever* it is you said, the queen is convinced you need to be re-established in society. I, of course, do her bidding and am here to invite you to our little ball next week."

"I am deeply grateful," Elinor murmured, her mind busy. This was good news! Obviously, the Beresford letter, with its mention of pearls and plum jam, was an effective bid for royal attention.

At that moment, the butler entered with the tea tray, and conversation became general for a few minutes. However, as soon as they were alone once more, the duchess's tone became matter-of-fact.

"Miss Avely, we have a few things to discuss, do we not?"

Elinor took a careful sip. "We do?"

"Yes, which is why I took the unprecedented step of calling upon you without leaving my card first." She did not mention that as a duchess, she could probably do as she liked. Elinor took another sip and waited curiously for her grace to continue.

The duchess lowered her voice. "I received the most interesting communication from Lord Treffler."

Elinor almost choked on her tea. Lord Treffler! The last Elinor had seen of *him*, he was tied up in Beresford's boat, on the way to be dropped off to France with orders never to return. Lord Treffler knew rather a lot about Elinor – her jewel divining ability and her acquaintance with Aldreda. Elinor knew rather a lot about Lord Treffler, including his nefarious attempts to steal a stash of jewels, not to mention a ship. Until now, she had thought he would keep a safe distance under Beresford's orders.

"Oh?" Elinor enquired carefully. "A letter from France, perhaps?"

She watched her grace closely. Lord Treffler had been a secret lover of the Duchess of Planx. It was this piece of information with which Elinor had tried to blackmail the duchess. Had Lord Treffler been replaced by some other flirtatious nobleman, or was the duchess still in love with him? If, indeed, she ever *had* been in love with him.

Her grace put down her cup. "Lord Treffler had much to say about his unfortunate escapades in Devon." She coughed. "Including his – er – subsequent *escort* to France. I must beg of you, Miss Avely, to keep his misadventures a secret."

The dark eyes were fixed blandly upon Elinor's face. Elinor began to feel rather cross. "With respect, Your Grace, Lord Treffler tied me up and left me to die. I feel you ought to know that, if you know so much."

The bland look disappeared, to be replaced with a guarded expression. "I am certain he intended to return for you, Miss Avely. He had his eye on a larger prize at the time."

"I am surprised you defend his actions."

The duchess waved her hand again. "Ah, but it sounded as if you were *quite* in the way. And you were untied in the end, were you not? I perceive you safe and sound, after *all* your adventures. It sounds as if you made some new friends."

Their eyes met. Elinor sighed. "It appears we are equally in each other's confidence, Your Grace. I suppose we must rely equally upon each other's discretion."

"Exactly." The duchess nodded, pleased. "Yet I've always had your interests at heart, Miss Avely. Did you know I sent Lord Beresford to offer you marriage again, after that dratted garden party? I did my best to sort it all out for you. However, you seemed determined to be a martyr to the gossips."

Elinor's jaw almost fell open. "You sent Beresford ... ? Pardon me?"

The duchess took a complacent sip of tea. "Oh yes. I took James aside and told him to do the right thing. Sent him to your townhouse to propose properly, instead of trying to bully you into it in public as he did, the silly man. Much good it did. What on earth possessed you to refuse him again?"

Elinor pressed her lips firmly together. When Beresford had visited her townhouse, she had believed him to be acting purely out of his own conscience – not love – in repeating the offer made so disastrously at the garden party. That was bad enough! Now she was to understand he had only come at the order of the Duchess of Planx?

It stung, yet Elinor pasted on a smile. "I believe a marriage is best founded on something more than duty."

"Ah, you are a romantic." The duchess sighed. "If only we could all be so. I married my lord duke when I was young, and well I knew it was my duty."

Elinor repressed a fleeting sense of sympathy. The Duke of Planx was older and far larger than the stylish young duchess before her. He was also rich and powerful, bestowing both virtues on his wife by association. Furthermore, her grace had shown no compunction in pursuing her more 'romantic' pleasures elsewhere.

Elinor sipped her now cold tea, pretending enjoyment, but at a loss for words. Her heart sank with the thought that the duchess had a hand in Beresford's visit all those weeks ago, but why should it? Elinor was now happily engaged to be married to him, without any interference from anyone.

She decided to change the subject and begin her investigations. "Your Grace, may I enquire if London is safe at the moment? I heard Lord Rapp was foully murdered not long ago, in this very neighbourhood."

The duchess's cup tinkled in her saucer. "Foully murdered? Why, no such thing! It was an accident."

Elinor tilted her head. She had been wondering if she could learn Truth Discernment, for if her mother was quite skilled, surely Elinor could manage it? Perhaps this was a good opportunity to practice. Elinor opened her inner senses, letting out a breath and attempting to tune into the duchess's intent.

"Oh, an accident?" said Elinor. "I thought I heard rumours otherwise. How can you be certain that Lord Rapp's death was not something more … heinous?"

"Ah." A frown appeared between the sharp eyes. "It had nothing to do with my husband if that is what you are implying."

Hm. If Elinor were to gamble, she would bet that was a lie, but she could not really be certain. It could simply be Elinor's tendency to believe the worst of the duchess. How did her mother tell the difference? Elinor clutched at her cold cup of tea, remembering that liquid was meant to assist Discernment, and impatiently swirled the liquid around. She really had to find herself a Talisman Stone to help strengthen her abilities.

"The Duke of Planx?" she pressed. "I wouldn't dare suggest he had anything to do with it."

The duchess shrugged a petulant shoulder. "The scandal-mongers imply my lord duke was fleecing Lord Rapp at the gambling tables. Yet if Lord Rapp chose to play too deep, it is not my husband's fault."

Elinor raised her brows. That sounded like the truth. Yet it was evasive phrasing. "Are you suggesting Lord Rapp was so far in debt he took his own life?"

The duchess shrugged again. "I am not suggesting anything. I only fear the gossips imply it. And my husband does nothing to quench the scandal."

Elinor heard only the ring of authenticity in those

words, and she felt another stab of sympathy. She chose not to remark on the duchess's own scandalous activities – though in truth, her grace was very discreet. "So it is widely believed that Lord Rapp took his own life?"

"Very sad." The duchess cast down her eyes. "A terrible tragedy. The royal family is most distraught."

Again, there was a note of dissonance. Was that simply because the duchess was simply mouthing platitudes? Elinor blinked, feeling her mind cloud a little. Her attempts at Truth Discernment were taking their toll. It was better to stop before she became too Bemused and said something unfortunate. Yet her mind was suddenly empty of all conversation.

The duchess saved her. "Ah, I see you are reading *The Romance of the Forest*? Such a riveting book!"

On this topic, at least, the duchess was genuinely enthusiastic: Elinor could hear it in her voice. Elinor gladly let the Discernment go, and turned willingly to the topic of romantic literature, which she was well able to converse on until the end of the visit. And there was the added benefit that it allowed her to say silly things without appearing too odd.

Her grace left soon afterwards, having made her position clear. Elinor felt rather worn out though it was barely past midday. It was a difficult visit anyway, even without becoming Bemused. She wondered if all her social calls were going to be such a tricky dance, and she sighed despondently. Perhaps she wasn't cut out to be a countess, after all.

The rest of the day was spent unpacking and assisting Lady Beresford. Elinor realised she could scarcely set off to investigate the suspected murder. Instead, she would have to wait for the social cogs to turn and re-establish herself in London. Furthermore, she would have to be careful which questions she asked in polite company.

At least, Elinor reflected, in the meanwhile, Aldreda could go where a mere lady could not.

8

IN WHICH ALDREDA SPIES ON A VAMPIRI BALL

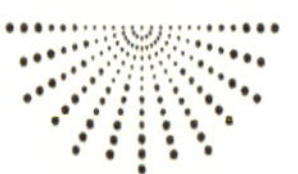

Aldreda

That evening, Aldreda set off to meet Pags at the oak tree by the prince's house. She carried no clothes, though she wondered if it was wise, with the uncivilised Pags as her escort. At least she would not put him out of countenance, for it seemed he had no wardrobe of which to speak.

She landed to hang upside-down from a twig, without any cumbersome gown to hamper her. Waiting, she listened to the night sounds of London: shouts, rattles, and faint music.

A rustle sounded in the branch above her. Aldreda peered through the leaves. A large bat swooped downwards. It was Pags, his strong, dark body more familiar to Aldreda now. He sliced past and darted out of the tree.

It was another impressive display of agility. Aldreda sniffed and followed.

Pags flew high, too high for Aldreda to sense any

other Musing as she tracked behind him. He winged his way to a large building in the quieter part of town. It was less ostentatious than the prince's haunt, but the house nonetheless clearly belonged to some wealthy aristocrat.

Pags flew to a high, small window, which presumably looked onto the attic room. He landed on the edge of the windowsill and tilted his head towards the aperture, indicating Aldreda to look within.

She landed on the other side and realised she was nervous. It was so long since she had seen other vampiri – apart from Pags. So long since she had danced in the vampiri revels in France and chatted with her own kind. She had always determined never to marry, being content with human companionship, but nonetheless, she missed the presence of other vampiri.

Momentarily, Aldreda closed her eyes and let out a breath. Then she sidled up to the edge of the window and peered in.

Immediately, she felt a pang of disappointment. What she saw was nothing like the Roost Revels she had attended in her heyday.

The room was set out elegantly enough. The attic floor was clean, and Vember furnishings (designed the size of a vampiri) lined the perimeters. Aldreda had not seen such chairs in a long time, with their velvet seats and high backs. She was pleased to see a table with expensive Vember glasses set out, miniature and exquisite, and a lovely Vember glass bowl filled with some kind of drink.

Yet, all this was to serve only fifteen or so vampiri. Two were playing a simple dance tune, and three couples were dancing. It was a minuet, one Aldreda knew from her own revel days. The other vampiri were standing around, talking quietly.

Aldreda sighed. She would have to risk human form if only to ask Pags more.

Backing away from the window, she became human and lay flat on the edge of the sill. She only hoped her pale limbs were not apparent from the street below. Pags followed suit, laying on the other side of the window.

Aldreda didn't waste time with pleasantries. "Why so few?"

"Good evening, Miss Zooth." Pags rested his chin on his hands. "To think you are the one who says *my* manners are bad."

Aldreda raised her brows. "I never said your manners were bad."

"Not in words, but your look said it with vehemence."

"And you are a consummate reader of my expressions, no doubt."

"I am learning."

Aldreda sniffed. "Good evening, Your Gracel. Can you please tell me why there are so few vampiri below?"

Pags shrugged. "There are not so many Musors or vampiri in England now."

"We had a hundred in Paris! You must remember the Roosts."

"I do." His face closed again.

"Surely some of those escaped, like you, and fled to England?"

"Or perhaps they went into hibernation," said Pags. "Like yourself."

"I did so long before those terrible times. You think that explains it? Everyone is sleeping?"

Pags's golden eyes dropped from her face. "I would like to believe so. Too many were caught. Very many died."

Aldreda swallowed. She crept a little closer to the

edge of the window, looking in once more. "Do you know these vampiri?"

"I have not introduced myself yet," said Pags.

"Why not?"

"I am not a sociable sort."

"Truly? You surprise me."

"My aim in life, mademoiselle." He smiled.

She turned away, annoyed at the blush that swept through her cheeks at his flirtatious response. Quickly she changed the subject. "It seems the darker-skinned lady standing over in the far corner has the most clout." Aldreda gestured towards the grandly-dressed and plump vampiri standing with a pleased smile on her face. "The others seem to defer to her."

"My thoughts also," Pags agreed. "Yet she is not the queen. King George's vampiri is young still, and the prince abjures vampiri. That lady you see rules over society in lieu of any royal companions."

Aldreda thought with a pang that her own queen from France would have also died in the Troubles if she had lived long enough. She examined the grandly-dressed vampiri again. "But she must be connected with the royal court or some high Musor?"

"I believe she is allied with the Duke of Planx, a Musor gifted in Healing. She came over from France in the exodus, ten years ago; she must have bonded with his grace then."

"And the Duke of Planx attends the Royal Court?"

"Yes," nodded Pags.

"What of this Lord Rapp?" asked Aldreda. "Was he a Musor?"

Pags's eyes narrowed. "What do you know of Lord Rapp?"

Aldreda frowned back. "Only what was reported in

the papers. He died two weeks ago, in his home. What do *you* know? You are beholden to tell me everything, after stealing my pearls."

Pags hunched his shoulders away from the window, lowering his voice. "Lord Rapp was a Musor."

Aldreda's skin prickled. "A Musor? Do you know what Gift?"

"No."

"How can you not know? You have been here at least a week."

"Musors are a secretive lot." Pags frowned. "And I keep to myself."

"Do you know who killed Lord Rapp?"

"They say it was suicide."

Aldreda stared, affronted by his dismissive tone. "Are you not worried that there is some trouble afoot?"

Pags shrugged again. "A little. Lord Rapp had a vampiri companion, Lordel Tildenhall. He has not been seen since his Musor died."

They flew back to the Beresfords' house soon after. Aldreda wanted to talk to Elinor, as she had not seen Elinor yet that evening. Pags insisted on accompanying Aldreda for her flight home. When they landed on her windowsill, he transformed. Aldreda sighed. It was only polite that she also do so.

Pags folded his arms across his hairy chest. "I am looking for Tildenhall. You don't need to worry about it."

"A Musor dead, and a vampiri missing! And this is the place where you take my pearls!"

"Tildenhall is probably grieving," said Pags. "Perhaps he has even gone into hibernation."

"Or he saw the murder and has been captured or killed," said Aldreda. "We must look with urgency to find him. He might be in hiding, with crucial information."

"*I* will look," said Pags.

"You do not even have *entre* into polite society. How will you make any enquiries?"

"I can easily gain entrance." Pags pulled his bare, muscled shoulders back. "I am a dukel, remember."

Aldreda rolled her eyes. "You look it. Well, I also can make enquiries."

At that moment, they both became aware of the door opening inside Aldreda's room. Their heads swung sharply to see Elinor walk in. She inspected Aldreda's empty basket then came over to the window.

"Aldreda! Good evening." Elinor opened the window wider, and her eyes fell upon Pags. "Oh! Pags! You rascal! How dare you steal our pearls!"

"Miss Zooth's pearls, as I understood it," replied Pags, looking for once a little uncomfortable.

"It matters not!" Elinor put her hands on her hips. "It was very bad of you."

"I meant it for the best," said Pags, and he coughed.

Aldreda repressed a smile, glad of her champion.

Elinor frowned. "Well, next time, you should confer with Aldreda as to what is best."

"Yes, Miss Avely," said Pags.

"And I see you still have no clothes – most impolite," continued Elinor, ignoring the fact that Aldreda was similarly situated. "Though I remark you have finally discovered the English tongue."

"Indeed, it was always in my repertoire, Miss Avely. And I do hope you are keeping your Gift discreet, as I advised. I have just been telling Miss Zooth how the Musors were guillotined in France."

Elinor narrowed her eyes. "There is no guillotine in England, my good sir. Don't try to distract me. I want to know if you are going to fetch the pearls back for us, you rapscallion."

Pags coughed again. "Unfortunately, they are now quite out of my power."

Aldreda cut across Elinor's interrogation. "Elinor, I am weary and must retire. Your Gracel, I bid you good evening." She stepped through the window and nodded stiffly. She did not want to curtsy while naked. It was the height of impropriety.

Pags had the temerity to wink at her. "I will look into the matter of Tildenhall," he repeated. "You need not concern yourself."

"As Miss Avely said, that is for me to decide," said Aldreda coldly. "You have done enough. Good evening."

"Good evening," echoed Elinor, supporting her vampiri. Then she ruined it all by smiling at Pags. "Have a lovely night, Your Gracel."

"I have already," he replied.

Then he shimmered into a bat and took flight.

9

IN WHICH ELINOR ENQUIRES ABOUT MAGIC

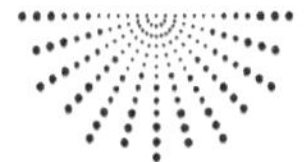

Elinor

"Well!" said Elinor once Pags had disappeared. "He is a bit of a rogue, isn't he?"

"Yes." Aldreda muttered something that Elinor couldn't quite hear. Then she spoke louder. "Thank goodness he is gone. I have much to tell you."

Elinor drew the curtains tightly and carried Aldreda across to the bed. "Indeed, who is Tildenhall, and why is Pags looking for him?"

Aldreda pulled her bombazine gown over her head. "Lordel Tildenhall was the vampiri companion to Lord Rapp."

"A vampiri companion! Does that mean ..." Elinor caught her breath. "Lord Rapp was a Musor?"

Aldreda's fingers were busy with her ties, but she looked up. "So Pags says."

"Ah!" Elinor leaned forward excitedly. "Do you think Lord Rapp was attacked *because* he was a Musor?"

"Possibly. We cannot ignore what happened in France." Aldreda hesitated, as if she might say more, then appeared to change the subject. "Also, Lordel Tildenhall, his vampiri companion, has been missing since the murder."

Elinor frowned. "Perhaps grieving, like you did when Henri died?"

"Or there is another possibility – that he is hiding because he is afraid." Aldreda smoothed her skirts down and sat on the edge of the bed, her black hair and gown stark against the yellow.

"You think this Tildenhall may have *seen* the murder?"

"Or know something about it. Tildenhall was prob-ably in Lord Rapp's confidence."

"Hm." Elinor became thoughtful. "We should find this vampiri soon if we can."

Aldreda nodded decisively. "Before Pags does." She went on to describe her viewing of a vampiri gathering.

Elinor was agog. "Truly? You saw a vampiri ball?"

"Far from a ball," sniffed Aldreda. "A little dance. I will try to find the patroness soon and make my own appearance."

Elinor clapped her hands together. "You are going to enter into vampiri society! Oh Aldreda, I shall have to sew you some more gowns." She began to think of what material she could spare and whether anyone would remark if she purchased only small scraps of black silk and lace. "Do you wish to stay in mourning clothes still?"

Aldreda smiled. "You are very kind, but I think I should visit a suitable modiste, one in my size. There is bound to be one somewhere in London, and it will save your fingers."

"Truly?" Elinor's eyes widened. "A miniature modiste? Can I come too, please?"

"Indeed, you shall have to accompany me. I cannot call on a dressmaker unclothed. It will not make the right impression."

Elinor giggled. "Oh yes, modistes are notoriously snooty. How exciting."

"Yet." Aldreda twisted her lips thoughtfully. "I wonder if it is wise for you to be seen with me, in the light of Pags's warning to be discreet."

"I wouldn't miss it for the world!" Elinor insisted. "The only question is how shall I waste the day away until then."

Elinor knew there was one person she could call upon as a friend: Lady Margaret Reeves. She and Elinor had become close a year ago, and Margaret was one of the few who had stood by Elinor when the garden party scandal broke. Margaret had also provided the Avelys with a refuge in one of her father's properties in Devon, but she herself had stayed in London.

In need of succour, Elinor decided to walk to Margaret's house that morning. All the carriages were spoken for, and Margaret lived only a few streets away in the same neighbourhood, for Margaret's father was the Baron of Reeves.

The day was overcast, but the sun lit up the clouds with white light. Elinor was glad of the chance to stretch her legs. She tried to ignore the jewels calling from behind the elegant facades of the houses. It was best not to follow the call with her mind, as she would end up a little Bemused. How strange that Prince George should seek Bemusement! He must be bored with his privileged life, that such things appealed. Or perhaps it was an escape, to flee from the pressure of his father's illness.

Margaret was home in bed, but she ordered Elinor to be sent up to her.

"For we must not stand on ceremony, my dear!" Margaret smiled, sitting wrapped in a silk dressing gown, sipping her breakfast chocolate. "Oh my, I had *such* a night at Vauxhall last night, which is why you find me so slothful. Please, you must have some chocolate too. Come, tell me what brings you to London! I was so happy to hear of your engagement!"

Elinor sat, glad to see Margaret's complexion was rosy, her auburn hair shining, and her grey-green eyes sparkling. "You look well, Margaret."

They chatted about Elinor's upcoming marriage and all their mutual acquaintances in London. Elinor, drinking chocolate, realised that even this was not the easy flow of conversation for which she had hoped. Elinor did not know if Margaret knew of the selkies in Deockley, and she wondered how much to tell of her own adventures there. The narrative might not make sense without the inclusion of Aldreda and Jaq in the tale.

"You seem preoccupied," said Margaret at last, putting her chocolate down on her tray. "Is there something wrong, my dear? I hope you are not worried about returning to London society."

Elinor sighed. "I confess I am a little apprehensive. I think it will be awkward for James as well as myself."

"Nothing Beresford can't handle," pronounced Margaret. "He is used to doing exactly as he pleases, without caring for anyone's opinion."

"Do you think so?" Elinor hesitated. "I found out

yesterday he proposed in London only after the Duchess of Planx told him to do so."

Margaret raised her brows. "Really? Why on earth would she do that?"

"I threatened to tell the world about her affair with Lord Treffler. I think the proposal was her attempt to help me." Elinor sighed. "Only I feel rather cross about it, that James came to me at her bidding."

Margaret examined her. "However, since then, Beresford has asked you to be his wife, with all the proper exhortations, has he not?" Elinor blushed and nodded. "Then why do you care?"

Elinor shook her head miserably.

Margaret continued. "I know what it is, Elinor – it is only your dignity that is threatened. When truly, you should be grateful the duchess acted on your behalf. Really, she is not so bad; she has been quite pleasant to me."

Elinor grimaced. "I know I am being irrational. And I am upset with James about it. I can't understand it."

"I can," said Margaret. "You are apprehensive about the marriage."

"You think so?" Elinor chewed her lip and sighed. "Yes, I suppose I am worried about becoming a countess, especially when all of London still sees me as a thief and a liar."

"They won't soon," said Margaret bracingly. "They will accept Beresford's choice of bride, you can be certain of that, especially if the countess is here to oversee it, and the Duchess of Planx is supporting you as well."

Elinor dipped her head in acquiescence, deciding not to mention that the duchess was effectively blackmailing her and only extending the hand of friendship because

Queen Charlotte requested it. Still, the queen was no mean ally.

"By the way, Margaret, can I ask you something rather strange?"

"Yes, indeed, how intriguing." Margaret moved her tray aside and tipped her head expectantly.

Elinor took a breath. "Have you ever heard of anyone being able to do magic?" Out of some instinct, she opened her senses, listening for the ring of truth in Margaret's response, though she felt a flash of guilt in using that ploy with her own dear friend.

Margaret's brows shot up. "You mean ... as in faerie tricks or enchantments? No, I cannot say I have. Why do you ask?"

Elinor flushed and let the Discernment go. Margaret's answer had rung with authenticity, as far as Elinor was able to tell. She must ask her mother about the knack of it, for she did not have the same clear sense as when jewels spoke to her.

"Oh, I heard a strange rumour that King George himself has magical abilities, as well as a few of his advisors. But of course that must be nonsense," Elinor finished hurriedly and bent her head to take another sip of chocolate.

"The superstitious beliefs of the lower classes, no doubt," said Margaret. "Or perhaps the king himself put that rumour around, to account for his bouts of madness: putting it at the door of a faerie bargain. Or perhaps Lord Olliot furthered the story. *He* is an advisor to the king, and that is just the sort of thing he might do to put on an air of mystery."

"Oh?" asked Elinor, wondering if this Lord Olliot was a Musor advisor like Lord Rapp.

But Margaret was not interested in Lord Olliot. "I have never heard such rumours, even from Lord Olliot. Indeed, I have only heard it is blasphemous to say such things. People would frown if they heard you."

"Truly? Not a breath of *anyone* possessing any magic?"

Margaret shook her head, decisively. "No. Is this like your fancy about the amethyst pendant being a Loyalty Stone? Elinor, you must not let your imagination carry you away again. It was disastrous enough last time."

Margaret did not know that it was Elinor's ability to divine that had led her to the amethyst in the first place – even if the amethyst had turned out to be an ordinary jewel and not a Loyalty Stone as Elinor had thought. Elinor dropped her eyes. "I suppose I like to imagine that the world has more to it than we can see. However, I shall endeavour to remain practical."

Margaret examined her narrowly. "Why do you mention the king's advisors? Have you heard of Lord Rapp's death? I assure you, it had nothing to do with magic."

"What do you know of it?" Elinor looked up, eager to hear what Margaret would say.

"Lord Rapp took his own life after an unfortunate contretemps with the Duke of Planx. It is the latest terrible scandal. One thing to be glad of is that it will eclipse any gossip about you."

"What happened with the Duke of Planx?" asked Elinor, leaning forward eagerly. Here was a chance to see if there was more to the story than the duchess let on.

"Lord Rapp was already deep in debt to the duke," explained Margaret. "Then, in one wild attempt, he tried to win it all back at a Planx card party a couple of weeks ago. He put his own house up in a ridiculous gamble.

Apparently, they bet on the matter of whether or not the duke had bats in his library. Lord Rapp claimed it was so, the duke denied it, they went along to inspect. They found the library empty, of course. As if there would be bats in the Planx library!"

Elinor stared at Margaret, fascinated. Could these be vampiri bats? Was that the subject of the bet, watered down through the gossip?

"How do you know all this?" Elinor asked.

Margaret shrugged. "There were several witnesses at the card party, and they all trooped along to inspect the duke's library. Apparently, Lord Rapp was very drunk, behaving oddly. He even claimed the duke was lying or hiding the bats, though there was no evidence to be seen of any such creatures. Rapp was lucky the duke did not call him out; his grace laughed it all off. Though, of course, he still took the vowels of promise."

"But that is ghastly!" said Elinor. "The duke cannot take Rapp's townhouse for such a silly bet!"

"More has been won and lost before over a gentleman's gaming table," said Margaret dryly. "It is a matter of honour that those debts are paid."

"What does the duke need with another house?" demanded Elinor. As far as she could remember, the Duke of Planx was rather large and jovial; his air of comfortable cheerfulness was probably born from his excessive power and privilege. However, Elinor had never suspected he was capable of such cruelty.

Margaret was cynical. "How do you think these great houses came by all their wealth? By such ruthless action. Though I do not know if the debt still stands, now that Lord Rapp has died. I suppose his poor heir will have to abide by it."

"Oh, it is too dreadful." Elinor shivered. "What a tangle. No wonder everyone believes Lord Rapp killed himself."

"Of course," stated Margaret. "What else could it be?"

10

IN WHICH A DRESSMAKER IS SURPRISING

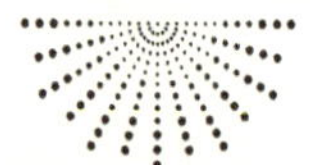

Elinor

*A*ll in all, Elinor was glad to be distracted that evening by Aldreda's quest for a modiste. Aldreda flew out at dusk and returned a half-hour later with a direction. Elinor could not travel alone either, so Perry was dragged along for the interview, as Mrs Avely and the countess were too tired from their first day in London.

Perry complained that he didn't want to go to a miniature tailor, but Elinor told him he should invest in a tiny jacket and breeches in case he should be confronted with Pags again.

"I don't want anything to do with Pags!" objected Perry.

Aldreda agreed with that sentiment from the top of the reticule but added: "Well, you want *me* to look civilised. You are the first to say I need clothes. Hence, I must acquire some."

Perry grimaced and acquiesced.

They took a carriage out, and Elinor told Aldreda and Perry what she had learned from Margaret and the duchess (though she did not mention the vexatious matter of Beresford's proposal at the duchess's bidding). "So you see," Elinor finished, "It appears Lord Rapp was trying to catch sight of vampiri in the Planx library."

"Ah, yes," said Aldreda. "The Duke of Planx is a Musor. He is a Healor."

Elinor started back. "Indeed? How do you know that? And why did you not mention it before?"

"I only found out the other night, from Pags: he said the vampiri who presided over the ball was the Duke of Planx's companion," explained Aldreda. "I forgot to tell you, amidst all the other news."

Elinor frowned thoughtfully. "I wonder if the duchess knows about her husband's Musor powers."

"Quite possibly not," said Perry. "Wives aren't always privy to their husband's secrets, and it strikes me that the Duke and Duchess of Planx are not particularly close."

"No," agreed Elinor. "Goodness, this puts a new complexion on the whole matter. If Rapp and Planx were both Musors, why were they arguing about vampiri? And did it have anything to do with Rapp's death?"

"One hopes the vampiri themselves can tell us more," said Aldreda.

Eventually, following Aldreda's directions, the carriage reached a rather grand townhouse in the west end of town. Aldreda assured Elinor the human owners would be quite accustomed to strange callers with nightly business hours. It had been so in France, where Musor companions provided lodgings as part of the terms of alliance with a vampiri companion.

Elinor looked at the townhouse: it seemed rather

familiar. Had she visited it during the last season or prior to her disgrace? She racked her mind, trying to remember.

Before she could recall, Aldreda directed the Avelys to drive around to the mews behind the residence. The carriage rumbled under the archway and pulled up at the first building on the left.

Elinor and Perry clambered out, examining the large carriage house in the moonlight and lamplight. From the third floor above, a black and white ribbon hung, visible only when Aldreda pointed it out. She informed them that the ribbon was a sign of a vampiri place of trade.

"Oh?" asked Perry. "You mean there are more such places scattered around town?"

Aldreda nodded, but Elinor was distracted. She had just spotted the crest high above the door of the carriage house, visible in the lamplight. It was the Planx ducal crest.

Elinor clutched at Perry's arm. "This is the mews to the Planx residence!"

Aldreda frowned. "Are you certain?"

Pointing at the crest, Elinor asked Perry to confirm it, which he did.

"Hm," said Perry. "So, this is where the dastardly bet took place?"

"Indeed," said Elinor. "I wonder if we can have a look at the library where it all happened."

"Don't be ridiculous," said Perry. "You can't just invite yourself into the Planx library. The duke will smell a rat."

"Aldreda, however, can do so without being noticed," pointed out Elinor.

Perry shook his head. "And provoke another scandalous incident? Heaven forbid the Duke of Planx stumbles upon Aldreda, unclothed in his library."

"Who, the duke unclothed, or Aldreda?" giggled Elinor.

Aldreda was still frowning. "Let us focus on the matter of the dressmaker. Perry, please pull on that ribbon." She ducked out of sight into the reticule.

Perry walked over and pulled the black and white ribbon, which curled all the way down to the ground. Elinor could not hear anything, but Aldreda said a bell tinkled. Shortly afterwards, a door opened in the side of the building, and a stableboy appeared.

The stableboy showed no surprise when Elinor asked to be taken to the modiste. However, she noticed the boy cast a wary glance down the mews avenue, and he shut the door quickly behind them.

Elinor and Perry were directed upstairs to the third floor, and they trod up the narrow staircase alone. Elinor wondered if the mews staff were under strict orders not to infringe upon vampiri quarters.

At the top of the stairs was a wooden door, locked. After hunting around, Perry found the key hidden under a flat stone and inserted it. Elinor supposed the vampiri must have different ways to leave the building if the door was locked from the outside.

The door swung open to show a hayloft. Exposed wooden beams arched above them, with hay heaped against the walls. Incongruously, an armchair sat in the corner, covered in rich brown velvet, and resting its feet between scraps of straw. Beside the chair was a small table adorned with a newspaper.

Elinor's eyes moved to the walls, and she saw something even more curious: deep wooden shelves along the far wall, occupied by tiny chairs and tables. It was almost like a dollhouse, but more serviceable than pretty. As her gaze travelled over in wonder, Elinor realised the shelves were at a height and size for vampiri to converse with humans.

Aldreda emerged from her reticule. Elinor lifted her up to the shelf to see what she would make of it.

"Ah, Vember furniture," said Aldreda with satisfaction. "This is more like it."

At that moment, a small door opened in the wall along the shelf. Elinor jumped, and Perry turned a gasp into a manly cough. Aldreda, it seemed, had expected it and already faced the tiny door.

The vampiri modiste emerged, clad in a severe cream-coloured gown that suited her brown toned skin. Her figure was plump, her thick hair piled high, and her features plain.

"Good evening," said this newcomer cheerfully to Aldreda. "I am the Duchessel of Planx. You may call me Lady Denier."

Elinor couldn't help but stare: this was the first vampiri to whom she had been introduced who was decently attired instead of stark naked. Lady Denier's gown, though simple, was very elegant. Elinor reflected that a modiste *would* attire herself well, even if she were sometimes a bat.

Lady Denier dropped a curtsy, her bright brown eyes openly examining her new client. Elinor, her social instincts on alert, watched as Aldreda curtsied deeply and decided to curtsy as well. It was not usual to do so to a dressmaker, yet this one called herself a duchessel and a lady, and she resided behind a ducal house, albeit in a hayloft. This must be the vampiri that Aldreda said presided over the vampiri ball.

The modiste's eyes travelled to rest on Elinor and Perry, and a frown creased her brow. "Musors too?" she asked. "Are you certain you wish to stay here? Perhaps it is better you go below."

Elinor spoke tentatively. "We will stay if you will allow us." Was the modiste concerned with proprieties for the sake of the stableboys?

The duchessel hesitated for a fraction, then nodded. She turned to Aldreda. "May I enquire as to your name?"

"I am Miss Zooth, and this is my companion Miss Elinor Avely. Are you the companion to the Duke of Planx, Lady Denier?"

The vampiri smiled. "Yes, I use one of the duke's other titles – he is also the Earl of Denier. Even then, I feel the title is a little lofty for one who is also a dressmaker."

Elinor was impressed. "You are a modiste *and* a duchessel?"

"If I want everyone decently fashioned, I have to do it myself," said Lady Denier, a little austerely. "Though I confess, before I became the Duke of Planx's companion, I occupied a much lower order, so I am long practiced at needlework."

"Goodness," said Aldreda. "We are honoured to be dressed by such nobility. What times are these!"

Elinor remembered what Aldreda had told her of vampiri hierarchy: the vampiri were given the same titles as their human companions, and they tended to stay with the same families over the generations. However, it was possible for a vampiri to bond outside their class and change their status, similar to how marriage worked in the human world. Perhaps in the upheaval of the Revolution, many vampiri had changed their positions, and a dressmaker duchessel was not so strange, even one with darker skin than was usual in the English aristocracy.

Elinor wondered if this indicated that there were

vampiri all over the world, and therefore Musors. It was a tantalizing thought, but she was not given much time to pursue it. Lady Denier invited Aldreda to sit on one of the little chairs and began a subtle interrogation.

"You are new to town?" asked Lady Denier. "I do not believe we have met, and your companions do not appear to know our customs so well." She cast another slightly appraising glance at Elinor and Perry.

"We have just arrived from Devon," said Aldreda, tucking her skirts around her. Elinor felt rather large and *de trop*, and she backed away so as not to loom over the consultation. Perry gingerly sat down in the armchair and took refuge behind the newspaper.

"Devon?" said Lady Denier. "Ah, that explains it; Devon is rather a backwater."

Aldreda nodded in agreement. "Before that, a long time ago, I was in Paris."

"I too!" announced the duchessel. "I thought I detected a Parisian accent. Delightful. When were you last in France?"

"1725. I have been in hibernation."

Elinor saw Lady Denier blink rapidly, then nod. "You are lucky," she said. "You missed the tragedies. At least you are safe now, in England. What can I do for you today?"

Things proceeded rapidly after that. Aldreda was measured, and reams of material were brought out for her inspection. Elinor hung back, not wanting to interrupt the delicate proceedings, but she was fascinated by the tiny reams of cloth and wished she could help with the selection. Perry ostensibly continued reading the newspaper in his armchair.

Aldreda eventually led the conversation back to the

'tragedies'. "Lady Denier – Your Gracel – I hope you don't mind me asking – I have been so out of touch with vampiri affairs. You said we are safe here in England. Is this true?"

"Indeed, there are different rules in England: we are kept more secret than in France."

"You do not fear a similar trajectory here, as occurred with the Troubles?"

Her gracel hesitated. "It is an entirely different society. We have none of the grandeur that was our lives in Paris. We are all brought low." She gestured down modestly, though in fact she must have risen, thought Elinor. "Though the truth is, I do enjoy needlework and do not mind dabbling in fashions."

Elinor thought the trade was quite possibly a form of wielding power too. The power of a dressmaker was immeasurable; she could make or break fortunes. Elinor determined to cultivate this woman's good opinion: she was obviously a political survivor as well as handy with a needle.

"I am certain you do a wonderful job of it," said Elinor. "Much better than my poor efforts."

Lady Denier cast a slightly disparaging look at Aldreda's current gown. "You cannot help it if your fingers are the size of pillows."

Elinor bit her lip, and Perry let out a snort from behind his newspaper. So he *was* listening.

Lady Denier looked at him curiously. "Is the gentleman also a Musor?"

Perry peered from behind the paper. "Me? Good Gad, no."

Elinor smiled sweetly. "Perry, didn't you have a request, while we are here?"

Perry lowered the paper as three bright pairs of eyes

rested upon him in expectation. He cleared his throat and glared at Elinor. "Not for me!"

"For someone else?" enquired Lady Denier.

Perry blushed and then hurried on under Elinor's gaze. "Er – yes, I suppose so. Could I commission some miniature – er – inexpressibles? And a coat. For a friend of mine. Just in case."

"In case of what?" asked Lady Denier.

Perry became slightly more pink. "For moments of – er – extremity."

Lady Denier took pity on him. She smiled. "Yes, often vampiri need spare sets of clothes, do we not! I can ask a gentleman's tailor to oblige you. Could your friend come in for a fitting?"

Perry shook his head emphatically, possibly after imagining escorting a naked Pags to the hayloft. "A standard size will be fine."

Lady Denier looked disapproving at this crass assumption.

Aldreda intervened by stating that perhaps a larger size was more appropriate. Elinor wondered if that meant Pags was bigger than most male vampiri. Pags certainly was larger than Aldreda.

Elinor asked a tentative question. "Your Gracel, could you estimate how many vampiri are in London?"

Lady Denier pursed her lips. "Perhaps forty, maybe fifty."

Aldreda's eyes dropped. "Not very many."

"Do many live in the Planx residence?" asked Elinor. "Other than yourself?"

Lady Denier looked up sharply from her notepaper. "Only me. I suppose you have heard those unfortunate rumours? I *did* have a little salon in the duke's library a few weeks ago. Nothing untoward, you understand; it was very discreet." She lifted her nose in the air. "Of course, with our supernatural hearing and speed, my vampiri guests were all able to disperse before any humans trooped in. No indiscretion took place, and no breach of the rules."

"Of course," murmured Aldreda. "You would not want any Mundanes to see you."

The duchessel sniffed and turned away. "No. Certainly not." She appeared quite ruffled and certainly did not want to discuss the matter further.

Elinor leapt into the breach. "Vampiri salons! How charming! Do you discuss vampiri art and poetry?"

This topic provided a welcome distraction, and they chatted about the vampiri poet Gale, who apparently wrote popular romantic epics. Only after Aldreda had ordered seven new gowns did Elinor risk another question.

"Lady Denier, may I ask what happened to the other French vampiri? The ones who were left behind in the Troubles? We still know so little."

The duchessel busied herself, folding some cloth. "They were burned, Miss Avely. Left out in the sun to die. So be thankful your friend was asleep."

Aldreda went even more pale than usual. A shiver ran over Elinor's own skin.

Lady Denier gathered up her cloths and nodded briskly, blinking something out of her eyes. "I will set my seamstresses to work on these gowns immediately." She paused. "I have only a little assistance, so it may take a while."

Aldreda responded to the hint. "Could I help also? My stitches are neat, and I can follow instructions."

Her gracel nodded approvingly. "Certainly. Return in an hour, and the work will begin."

"Quick," said Elinor, as they left. "Undress, Aldreda."

Perry let out a yelp and turned away as Elinor opened up the reticule. He needn't have worried, for when Aldreda appeared, she was a bat.

Elinor smiled. "Have a look at that notorious ducal library for us!"

Aldreda hovered for a moment and then sped away into the dark.

Elinor and Perry ordered the carriage to beyond the mews archway, to avoid provoking any suspicion, and waited for Aldreda to return. It seemed to take a rather long time, but finally, she reappeared, swooping into the carriage and dropping onto the seat as a tiny, naked woman.

This time Perry's yelp was louder. "Zounds, Aldreda! *Must* you do that?"

Elinor handed over Aldreda's clothes. "Bats land upside-down, Perry. Do you want Aldreda to transform into a woman as she is hanging from the roof?"

Perry paled at this image and shook his head vehemently.

"Certainly not," agreed Aldreda. "That would be *most* improper." She dressed quickly. "The library is certainly set up for vampiri company. There are curtained bookshelves that contain no books, but Vember furniture, like you saw in the mews hayloft. And they are not dusty."

"So well-used then," observed Elinor. "And well set-up, as befits a Musor household. Perhaps we should do something like that at our own residence," she reflected. "How charming that would be! I wonder if James would countenance it."

"Stay on point, Elinor," grumbled Perry. "Did you see anything suspicious, Aldreda?"

"My investigations were interrupted," she replied. "The Duchess of Planx came into the library. At least I assume it was the duchess." Aldreda proceeded to describe the slender, brown-haired woman with a jaded expression, whom Elinor confirmed to be the duchess.

"What did she do?" asked Elinor curiously. "Did she look for evidence of bats also?"

"No, she sank into a chair and put her head in her hands," said Aldreda.

"Ooh, is she guilty?" speculated Elinor. "Could the duchess have killed Lord Rapp for some reason?"

Perry frowned. "Don't be silly. More likely, she is worried the duke killed him."

"I cannot guess at her emotions," said Aldreda. "I used the opportunity to leave."

Elinor leaned back against the seat. "Could *the duchess* be a Musor?" For some reason, she did not like the idea. "Did you sense any magic?"

"No," said Aldreda. "However, it is unlikely she was Musing." She finished doing up her ties. "I have to return to Lady Denier soon to help with the sewing."

Elinor sighed. "Yes, Lady Denier will be a good source of information. You can use the opportunity to ask her if the Duchess of Planx is a Musor. And enquire about Lord Rapp and his companion Lordel Tildenhall."

Aldreda nodded. "True, she will know everyone and hear all the gossip, no doubt, though I am not certain she will be willing to share it."

Perry folded his arms, recovering his composure now that Aldreda was once more clothed. "Lordel Tildenhall? A vampiri, I take it?"

"He was the vampiri companion to Lord Rapp,"

explained Elinor. "He has been missing since Lord Rapp died."

Perry frowned. "I hope he has his clothes with him."

Elinor giggled. "You can carry a spare set around for him too, Perry."

"Hmph," said Perry. "Next, you will want me to carry a reticule."

11

IN WHICH THE ROYAL CONTINGENT IS MET

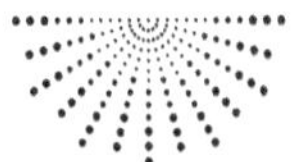

Aldreda

ldreda spent the next few nights sewing, while Elinor spent the days shopping. With the days and nights filled with these imperative undertakings, there was not much opportunity to investigate further for other Musors. Aldreda tried to gain some names from Lady Denier, but in fact, she did not see much of the ducal dressmaker. The duchessel showed her what to do and then left her, no doubt busy with more important matters.

The other vampiri, sewing alongside Aldreda, was a little more talkative.

"Is the Duchess of Planx a Musor also?" asked Aldreda, at the first opportunity.

Miss Tallier, a pale-skinned, fine-boned vampiri who had very nimble fingers, shook her head. "No, much as she regrets it."

"What do you mean?"

"The duchess recently discovered her husband's Gift. She is jealous of it and wishes she had the Musing also."

Aldreda reflected it was usually wise for Musors to marry one another or to keep their Gift secret from their spouses – or so it had been in France when she was young. She wondered how the duchess had discovered the duke's secret, and she asked Miss Tallier.

Miss Tallier looked up from her sewing and cast a furtive glance around. "Her grace saw the duke with Lady Denier. It all came out after that."

Aldreda was thoughtful. Elinor had told her the duchess had received intelligence from her old lover, Lord Treffler, possibly informing her of the existence of Aldreda. Had it been this information that piqued the duchess's investigation?

Miss Tallier did not want to add much to that, perhaps fearing Lady Denier would hear her discussing the duke. So Aldreda asked next about the Prince of Wales.

"Oooh, he's terrible, he is," said Miss Tallier, complacently sewing. "He wants nothing to do with us vampiri, even though he looks so delicious."

"Mary!" said Lady Denier, coming in at that moment. "Don't be so vulgar! As if the prince would consider you as a companion."

"He does not have a vampiri companion?" asked Aldreda.

"No, indeed not," said Lady Denier, inspecting Miss Tallier's seam. "He is head of the Helicon set. Wastrels, the lot of them."

"Indulgent and foolish," nodded Miss Tallier. "Yet, the prince can be charming."

"A Diplomacor?" asked Aldreda.

"Like his father."

This was news. Aldreda pricked her finger and almost drew blood. "Really? The king is a Diplomacor?"

Lady Denier nodded. "It is how he led this country through such troubled times: using great tact and care, as well as the laws that were passed, of course. Everyone underestimates how much our king did to maintain the equilibrium – with my lord duke's help as well."

"It is a pity the king suffers so much for it," said Miss Tallier, sympathetically. "And well that the duke can help with his Healing."

"Suffers?" asked Aldreda.

Both women looked up at her. "You do not know?"

Aldreda shook her head.

The other vampiri glanced at each other. Miss Tallier spoke carefully. "The Gift is not strong with the king. He suffers greatly from Bemusement."

Aldreda looked at Lady Denier to confirm this, and the duchessel ducked her head stiffly in acknowledgment.

"Oh, dear," said Alreda. "Is he allied with a vampiri?"

"Yes, but she is young still," explained Lady Denier, "and she does not seem to temper it much. Or perhaps it is simply that His Majesty overdoes it in his royal duties. He has long stretches of Bemusement, sometimes lasting for days."

Aldreda frowned. That sounded like Bewilderment: the lifelong state of Bemusement that could result from pushing too far into Musing. Yet it appeared the king was able to pull himself back from the chasm, which was rare after whole days of Bemusement. Perhaps it was with the help of his Healor, the duke, who must be Gifted indeed.

Aldreda continued sewing. "So, in a way, the king is not much better than his son?"

"Oh, King George is very responsible when he is himself," said Lady Denier. "And they keep him cloistered when he is not. Unlike the son, who is always kicking up a lark, whether Bemused or no."

This was worrying news. Aldreda did not like to think of Henri's pearls in the safekeeping of a king so disturbed. "It seems a pity the prince does not use his charm for better ends," said Aldreda. "Is he not heir to the throne?"

"Yes, but Prince George and his father do not see eye to eye," said Miss Tallier. "So different, the two of them, though both with the same Gift."

Aldreda risked another question. "Does anyone know what happened to Lord Rapp?"

The seamstress became absorbed in her stitches, and Lady Denier bent her eyes to inspect a hem. After a moment, Aldreda cleared her throat in a question. She wasn't going to be put off so easily.

Miss Tallier looked up and shivered. "I don't know anything. It is frightening that someone can be murdered in his own home, and no one the wiser."

"Oh?" asked Aldreda. "So, you do not think Lord Rapp took his own life?" There was silence. "If it were murder, surely the servants knew who came to the house?"

Lady Denier shook her head. "If they do, they are not saying."

Aldreda paused at her own needlework. "What of his vampiri?"

The duchessel frowned. "I haven't seen Lordel Tildenhall since our last roost revel, two weeks ago. Even then, he seemed preoccupied and worried."

Aldreda returned to her sewing thoughtfully. "You

think he might have known something was about to happen?"

Lady Denier's face shuttered. "Lordel Tildenhall was distracted. Usually, he is very much the gentleman: shy but polite. He ignored me once or twice that night. Most irregular."

Aldreda had to repress the quirk of her lips. Clearly, to ignore Lady Denier was shocking behaviour indeed. "Do you know where he would go to seek shelter?"

"Lordel Tildenhall lives at Lord Rapp's residence, of course," said the duchessel. "But he is not there now. I do not know where else he could have gone. No doubt he will turn up." She gave Aldreda an enquiring glance. "Why are you so interested, Miss Zooth?"

Miss Tallier giggled. "Lordel Tildenhall is an eligible bachelor. Perhaps you are hoping for an introduction, Miss Zooth?"

"I am not interested in bachelors," said Aldreda with a smile. "I am determined to remain a spinster."

"Why is that?" asked Lady Denier. "You would have no trouble finding a mate, I am certain."

Aldreda flushed slightly. "I – er – value the Musor bond, and a vampiri husband would complicate matters." She shook her head. "I beg you, do not match-make me with Lordel Tildenhall. I am simply concerned that he is missing after his companion died."

Lady Denier nodded. "He will be grieving, no doubt. When he is ready to face society again, you will meet him, Miss Zooth."

Aldreda bent back to her sewing. Tildenhall sounded as if he was more civilised than Pags. Shy, polite, and a gentleman. Quite Pags's opposite, in fact. For some reason, the thought made Aldreda smile.

She had not heard from Pags over the last few days.

Not that it mattered. She had quite enough to do without a naked dukel hassling her.

Lady Beresford took Elinor along with her to attend Mademoiselle Laberche's royal court presentation a few days later. It was a resounding success, Elinor told Aldreda, in that it was just as grand and boring as Elinor had warned Mademoiselle Laberche it would be. The young Frenchwoman was now launched into society properly, with her second aunt to escort her around town.

The important thing was that Lady Beresford had gained an opportunity to speak to the king. His Majesty had received the Beresford letter, and the upshot was that their royal highnesses would be pleased to invite the Countess of Beresford and Miss Avely to a private audience the following night.

Elinor was all of a twitter. A royal audience! This would give the scandal-mongers food for thought! Her success in returning to London was now assured. Lady Beresford was smug. After all, it was more comfortable for everyone if Elinor wasn't a social pariah.

More importantly, they were only one night away from regaining the Moria Pearls.

"You must come with me," said Elinor to Aldreda. "I know you have not been formally invited, but where I go, you must go. His highness will understand that. You have the greatest interest in the pearls, after all."

So they both dressed in their finest gowns – Aldreda's newly finished at Lady Denier's – and were borne away in the Beresford's crested carriage after dinner. Mrs Avely, not invited, saw them off with a frown on her face.

It was a pity she could not come, thought Aldreda. A Truth Discernor would be useful at the royal palace.

The carriage took them to Buckingham House, in which Queen Charlotte had borne so many children. Aldreda, peeking out of the reticule, saw it was not as grandiose as the columned house of the prince, which she had since learned was named Carlton House. However, the king's residence was large enough and built with sturdy brown brick that reached three floors.

Aldreda stayed in Elinor's reticule for the disembarkation, though it creased her gown a little. She leaned against the silk, feeling the reticule swing through the air. Eventually, it stilled, and she heard introductions being made. The king's voice was mild and quiet, Queen Charlotte's gentle, and Lady Beresford's and Elinor's remarkably calm. Aldreda listened carefully to the niceties, though they were just as expected.

The mouth of the reticule opened. Candlelight poured in, and Aldreda saw Elinor's anxious eye peering in.

"Your Highness, if I may introduce Miss Zooth?"

Elinor pulled the cloth down so Aldreda could step out. Taking a breath, she did so, smoothing down her skirts, finding herself on Elinor's lap. There was no convenient table upon which to stand. So Aldreda curtsied where she stood, as deeply and gracefully as she could manage in the folds of Elinor's skirts.

Gasps hissed around the room.

Surely her efforts were not so inadequate? Aldreda looked up. The king was staring at her with a look of consternation. He was slightly corpulent, with lines of age and worry etched upon his gentle face. Pinned to his coat was the largest blue lace agate Aldreda had seen: the Talisman Stone of the Diplomacors. No doubt, the stone was so large in the hope it would mitigate His Majesty's Bemusement.

Next to the king was the man she had seen muse-drunk – Prince George – looking a bit more respectable this time, though with a warm flush still on his cheeks. He wore no Talisman Stone. On the other side of the king was an elegant but frail-looking woman with large eyes and a concerned expression: presumably Queen Charlotte, who also wore no stone that Aldreda could see. They were all seated in ornate chairs in a large drawing room.

Lady Beresford stepped into the breach. "Miss Zooth, I present you to His Royal Highness, King George of England, his wife, Queen Charlotte, and his son, Prince George of Wales." Lady Beresford spoke with suitable gravity, but even her tone faltered at the sight of each member of the royal family staring at Aldreda as if she were a leprechaun.

There was a long, outraged silence.

The prince broke it with a laugh. "You do not appear to be familiar with our laws and customs, Lady Beres-ford." He stretched his feet out before him. "Vampiri are not permitted to consort with Musors in public, on pain of banishment."

Aldreda felt a flush rise over her face and did not even know if it was shame or anger.

"Not permitted?" asked Elinor.

King George cleared his throat. "I am afraid not. It was deemed unwise after what happened in France. Any vampiri found openly consorting with Musors is black-listed as a companion and banished."

Lady Beresford looked from one to the other. "What happened in France?"

"The vampiri became too open," explained the king.

"The Musors flaunted them, kept them by their sides, fed them at their own tables. By doing so, the Musors marked themselves out – making themselves a target of fear and suspicion. Hence, we have ruled against it in order to keep the peace."

Aldreda did not know where to look. "I will depart, Your Majesty. I deeply apologise for my breach of your laws and etiquette." She dropped another deep curtsy and looked at Elinor in an agony of embarrassment.

"Miss Zooth did not know," put in Elinor desperately. "Please excuse our ignorance, Your Majesty. I beg you to allow her a short audience. Miss Zooth is the one who knows the most about the Moria Pearls, which is the subject of our discussion."

After a tense silence, the king nodded. "Very well. Miss Zooth may join us briefly. I am sorry I cannot allow more, but as king, I must lead by example." He gestured to the three footmen standing by the door, asking them to leave. "No one is to disturb us until I ring the bell."

The footmen retreated without expressions, but Aldreda could sense the tension in the air. She inclined her head deeply in gratitude, and Queen Charlotte added a veneer of welcome by inviting her to sit. Aldreda clambered across to a side-table (with Elinor's help) and sat primly with her legs tucked over the edge and her back straight.

"Well," said King George. "Begin. I take it from this letter that you claim the right to the pearls which have recently come into my possession."

Aldreda, on the back foot, sought for the right words. "Yes, Your Majesty. They belonged to my late companion, Mr Henri Vernet, a Musor gifted in Memory. He asked me to safeguard them." Aldreda was suddenly doubly glad Elinor had agreed to keep the last pearl a secret and not mention it to the king.

Frown lines showed between the king's eyes. "Do you not consider that the pearls would be guarded safely here?"

"I do not doubt your good intention," said Aldreda carefully. "Yet, as you see, I am not acquainted with the prevailing culture and politics of your kingdom. I fear there may be danger here in the metropolis, to Musors and their magical artefacts."

Elinor bit her lip.

The prince raised a brow. "We can assure you, Miss Zooth; we are able to keep this precious necklace safe."

"That may be so," said Aldreda, directing her comments to the father. "Yet, as king, I am sure you would not deprive someone of their property on a whim."

"Usually, that would be for the parliament to do," agreed his highness. "Yet on matters of Musing, I determine what is to be done, in consultation with my advisors, who are also Gifted. And this decision is scarcely a whim, if you don't mind me saying, Miss Zooth. That necklace contains much of what was lost in the Troubles. We have not had a chance to master even part of its contents. And it appears some of the necklace was destroyed while it was languishing in Devonshire."

Aldreda winced. The knowledge of that sacrilege was still painful to her, and truth be known, she *did* feel guilty that it had occurred on her watch.

Queen Charlotte spoke. "My husband's library is the foremost collection of Musor knowledge in the land. If the necklace belongs anywhere, I assure you, it is here."

Aldreda found herself in an untenable position. She did not wish to give offence to their majesties. Yet there was something here that she did not trust. Perhaps it was the sardonic look in the prince's eyes or the worry in the queen's.

"Also," added the king, "It has come to my attention that there is someone else who claims a right to the Moria Pearls." He rang the bell. Aldreda, her stomach tightening, listened in growing anxiety as the king ordered the visitor from the Green Room to be shown in.

IN WHICH ELINOR DIVINES
SOME JEWELS

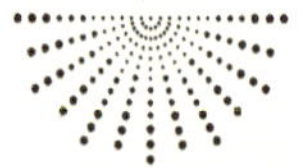

Aldreda

It was Jaq who appeared in the doorway. A strained silence held sway as the butler introduced His Royal Highness, the High Prince of Skerry, Jaq Everen Malleker Glowdon.

Jaq bowed, deep and flourishing: a better attempt than Aldreda had made, she noted crossly. He was dressed very richly, in tight pantaloons, and a coat of fine velvet. His black locks were tied back, and he wore a lofty expression. He must have come straight from his sailing trip with Beresford.

Aldreda attempted to hold back a snarl. Elinor stiffened beside her, looking, no doubt, for Beresford. However, Jaq was alone. Nonetheless, Beresford must have known that Jaq was here and had allowed him to petition the king.

As was proper, everyone made their curtsies and

bows, though Aldreda made hers minimal. Selkie royalty would make no liege of hers.

The king nodded at Jaq. "You are all acquainted, I believe?"

"Indeed." Yet Jaq avoided everyone's eyes. "My queen's waters border near the Beresford estate."

Elinor interposed anxiously. "Is Lord Beresford safe and well?"

Jaq gave Elinor a reassuring smile. "He is, and he returns to London tomorrow."

Aldreda gritted her teeth. How dare Jaq act friendly when he was here to oppose her interests!

The king nodded. "We are glad to hear of Lord Beresford's safety – and look forward to his report – yet we have other business to discuss now. Lord Malleker, would you oblige us by describing your claim to this necklace?"

Jaq did so, his voice only slightly hesitant under the various censorious gazes now upon him. He explained how Henri had been given the pearls on the condition of tutoring the selkies in the knowledge contained within them. "Having betrayed that trust, Henri lost the right to the pearls, which revert to us," said Jaq, finishing in his most pompous tone.

Aldreda, with difficulty, refrained from grinding her fangs.

"What is your reply, Miss Zooth?" enquired the Prince of Wales, at his father's side.

"Henri left Skerry under duress," said Aldreda. "He was driven away by the selkies. Therefore, you cannot blame him for the failure of the bargain."

Aldreda did not want to go into the betrayals that had occurred. But it seemed it was unnecessary. The king spoke with sudden authority. "This all happened eighty years ago, which makes it difficult to determine the true right of it. In the interests of fairness, I will offer you both generous compensation for the necklace, equally. The pearls themselves must be requisitioned by the Crown, in order to safeguard the teachings held within them."

Aldreda frowned. She could scarcely argue with the king. The only good thing was that she could see Jaq was equally unimpressed. But he bowed his acquiescence, and Aldreda could do naught but the same.

"Very well," said the king, with a note of relief. "Now, I shall call for some refreshments. I believe you have brought us a gift of the Beresford jam?"

Lady Beresford bustled forwards, relieving the tension by presenting two large jars of the Beresford nectar. "I present you with our finest, Your Majesty."

The king reached for the bell, then looked at Aldreda. "If I may request that you now observe our customs, Miss Zooth?"

Aldreda flushed at this delicate hint to remove her unlawful person. Elinor stiffened beside her. But they received help from an unlikely quarter.

Queen Charlotte spoke gently. "There may be some difficulty in Miss Zooth leaving unescorted. Perhaps we can find someplace for her to abide, my king?"

Perhaps the queen did not want Aldreda to strip off her clothes so she could fly off as a bat. Or, possibly worse, stalk off through the door beneath the noses of the footmen.

"I suppose so," said the king, but he frowned at his wife.

"Perhaps Miss Zooth could wait upon the mantlepiece," suggested Queen Charlotte. "The bowl there should provide a modicum of shelter."

The king agreed reluctantly. Aldreda also nodded her acceptance, though she was galled at such treatment – to be hidden away behind a bowl! This was not how the old Musor circles conducted themselves. Elinor carried Aldreda across and put her down with an apologetic whisper. "So sorry, my dear."

"I do not enjoy the jam anyway," said Aldreda, in an attempt to reassure her. "I can watch from here."

Elinor did not look happy, but she resumed her place at Lady Beresford's side. The king rang the bell once more, and they chatted about the Season and the war. Jaq gave them the worrying news of large naval forces gathering under Napoleon, seen at close quarters in his mission with Beresford, but he assured them that the rumours of a tunnel under the Channel were completely false.

When the butler returned with refreshments – reverently bearing the jam on a tray with bread and butter – he also brought with him another man, who was introduced as Lord Olliot.

Lord Olliot was tall and slender, with thinning blonde hair and blue eyes. He was perhaps in his fourth decade, with faint lines around his mouth and eyes. He bowed and smiled. "I am lucky indeed, to be in time for the Beresford jam. Its reputation precedes it."

Aldreda peered around the bowl to look at Elinor, but Elinor shook her head slightly. Knowledge of the jam's healing (and libidinous) properties was still secret. Lord Olliot could only be referring to the jam's reputation for deliciousness.

"Ah yes," said Lady Beresford (who, in fact, was oblivious, as far as Aldreda knew). "Our little orchards do well."

The queen began pouring tea. "Is it true, Miss Avely, that you are a Discernor? Lady Beresford's letter hinted as much."

Elinor's eyes widened. Aldreda also looked on anxiously: they had not warned Lady Beresford to keep Elinor's Gift secret. Yet Elinor nodded slowly, perhaps realising that her association with Aldreda implicated herself as a Musor. "I am untutored, I am afraid, Your Majesty. I have a knack for divining the presence of jewels, but I am only slowly learning to extend it to other subjects."

"What of your brother?" enquired the king. "Mr Peregrine Avely? Is he Gifted as well?"

Elinor was amused. "As far as I know, Peregrine is perfectly ordinary."

Jaq looked as if he might say something, but he closed his mouth on the words. Aldreda frowned.

Lady Beresford, however, was happy to defend Perry. "Oh, I would not say ordinary! Mr Avely is a charming young man."

"Yet not a Discernor like his sister," smiled the king. "A rare thing it is to be Gifted."

Lord Olliot clapped his hands together. "How wonderful to have a Discernor among us! We have so few of you. I am a Heightenor myself."

Elinor looked at him in mute question. However, Aldreda was not surprised. She had noticed a faint air of magic emanating from Lord Olliot as the tea was poured, and he had waved his thin hands over the jam. The ring on his hand was adorned with a large citrine stone, the Talisman of the Heightenors. Aldreda only hoped he had not Heightened the *zestful* properties of the said jam, only the deliciousness.

"I can Heighten almost anything," said Lord Olliot, with a modest cough. "Hence I serve the king."

"Indeed, you are indispensable," said His Majesty. "Our guests will see what I mean when they try the tea."

Thus abjured, the collected company obediently sipped their tea and let out exclamations of delight. Aldreda knew it was not forced, for even she enjoyed Heightened tea. The delicious aroma wafted through the room, somehow intoxicating and soothing at the same time. With a start, Aldreda noticed the king too was exerting his power: that of Diplomacy. Elinor and Lady Beresford looked very happy indeed, tossing back their tea, and even Jaq had relaxed a little. Aldreda, however, tried to resist the subtle feeling of acceptance and friendship that wove around the company.

"Oh, it is divine," Elinor sighed. "Truly divine."

"The tea served at Buckingham House is the best in the country," said Lord Olliot modestly. "I do not have to do much to Heighten it."

Aldreda rolled her eyes from the shadow of the bowl. Humans and their tea!

Jaq had not spoken for a while and was sipping rather mournfully. Lady Beresford made an effort to include him in the conversation. The queen took advantage of the discussion of the state of Napoleon's fleet to ask Elinor if she knew much about the effects of Musing.

"A little," said Elinor. She gestured to Aldreda on her shelf. "Miss Zooth has supplemented what I know from my own experience. Bemusement can be quite disorientating, but my alliance with her has mitigated the effects somewhat."

The queen leaned a little closer. "Do you or Miss Zooth know of any other way to mitigate it? My husband suffers greatly. Especially since he has followed his own decree and no longer allows vampiri in the same room as him."

Elinor shot an apprehensive look at the king. He was listening, but he smiled a little vaguely. "My wife worries. I would be grateful if you can tell her that Bemusement is not a curse."

"No, indeed, a mere discomfort," said Elinor. "I believe Benko tea also assists in reducing the effects. Miss Zooth, do I have the name right? Apparently, it has a grassy taste."

Aldreda appreciated Elinor's attempts to include her in the conversation, but she merely nodded and withdrew a little further. She did not want Lord Olliot to be offended by the sight of her and cause a diplomatic incident.

"Benko tea, do you say?" The queen was thoughtful. "We must command its acquisition at once, my dear. You must henceforth drink it every day."

The king patted her hand. "You are overly anxious, dear Charlotte. Yet if my drinking grassy tea every day will please you, I will do it."

The queen sighed, a look of bitterness passing across her face. "Sometimes, I wish there was no such thing as Musing. I do not want him to become Bewildered," she explained to Elinor.

"And, indeed, I will not," said the king, though to Aldreda's practiced eye, he looked a little befuddled, even from the little Diplomacy he had woven. Aldreda tutted behind her bowl. His Majesty would greatly benefit from having his vampiri companion at his side, as it should be.

The queen might be bitter about her son too, Aldreda reflected: another victim of Bemusement, though in a different way. Regardless of how many chests of Benko tea she ordered, she would not be able to make Prince George drink it.

Aldreda saw Lord Olliot's eyes find her on the mantlepiece. However, he looked away quickly and turned to Elinor with a smile, changing the subject. "If you can Discern jewels, Miss Avely, no doubt you are aware of the king's special collection nearby."

Elinor hesitated and smiled. "Yes, I can sense a large group of jewels in a neighbouring room. Sapphires, if I am not mistaken?"

Aldreda pursed her lips. It was not wise to show off in front of these people. Better they thought Elinor's ability was minimal.

The king nodded. "Yes, very special sapphires."

Elinor looked a question.

The prince smiled. "Perhaps if you give us a demon-stration of your ability, we can show them to you," he suggested.

Everyone turned to look at Elinor. She blushed faintly. "Very well." She cocked her head, then paused. "May I request that my vampiri companion assists me? I do not want to become Bemused in the royal presence."

Aldreda bit her lip, touched at Elinor's staunch inclu-sion of herself. Before the king could object, Queen Charlotte spoke. "Of course, you must have Miss Zooth with you. Tonight is an exception to the Vampiri Edicts."

So Elinor came over to the mantlepiece, and Aldreda stepped onto her hand, trying to maintain an impassive facade. Lord Olliot's eyebrows rose, but he stood politely with everyone else.

Elinor closed her eyes briefly, then led the way, with everyone trooping after her through the long length of the opulent drawing room. At the end of it, Elinor pulled a drape aside, showing a door behind it.

Prince George quirked his lips and opened the door, allowing the party through. Elinor led the way in.

Somehow, Aldreda had expected a small room, hidden away. However, another grand space met her eyes, furnished with elegant chairs and thick carpets. Only this chamber did not have any windows: perhaps it was the domain of vampiri as well as Musors. The walls were covered with long, embroidered hangings, as well as bookshelves and several low tables set against them. A fireplace stood empty at the far wall.

Lord Olliot set about lighting candles. However, even in the dark, Elinor had walked over to the largest table without hesitation. Aldreda's superior eyes could see it was covered in a red velvet cloth. Elinor put her hand upon it.

At a nod from King George, Elinor lifted the cloth.

It was not a table. A large, glass case met Aldreda's eyes: the size of two tea trays joined. The wooden backing was inlaid with a white cloth upon which lay rows of sapphires.

Aldreda, on Elinor's other hand, had the best view. There were tiny sapphires and fat ones; some in a light colour, a sparkling sky blue that caught in the candle-light, and some such a deep blue to be almost black.

All were stunningly beautiful, and oddly, unattached. Not one was strung into a piece of jewellery. Each jewel sat alone in all its splendour, nestled on the white cloth.

The rest of the company crowded around Elinor and Aldreda, though the king and queen stood back. Lady Beresford uttered a gasp. "Goodness me, how beautiful."

"They are not ordinary sapphires," said the king. "They have been enchanted with Memories. Specifically, Memories of the Gifts and how to use them."

As he said it, Aldreda looked around. The other tables

must be cases, too, also covered. Sapphires were not as flexible as pearls for such work and were limited in how many memories they could hold. Yet if every case had ten sapphires, that meant there were about fifty jewels here and twice as many spells.

Aldreda would bet her right wing that one of the cases now contained the Moria Pearls. She looked up to see the same thought cross Elinor's mind. Elinor's eyes glazed, and she turned, finding the sense of the pearls. She walked towards a smaller case opposite the door.

"What lies within this one?" Elinor asked. "I sense something special."

"Ah, I see you have found the pearls," admitted King George. "Impressive Discernment, Miss Avely." He went over to draw off the cloth.

The Moria Pearls – what was left of them – lay in a line upon deep blue velvet, shimmering and beautiful under the glass. The sturdy case had an iron lock upon it.

There was silence. Aldreda did not throw herself bodily upon the case. Jaq drew in a breath. The king cleared his throat. "As you can see, the Vernet necklace has found a worthy resting place."

Elinor turned and cast a glance down at Aldreda. "All these jewels here contain Memories?"

"Not just any memories," said the king. "Memories of spells. Each sapphire holds about three spells. They are not as suitable as Laroshin pearls for the task, which can contain hundreds. However, the sapphires are long-lasting in the enchantment. You see before you the largest collection of spellwork in England."

"In all of Europe, perhaps," added Lord Olliot proudly.

"Many were retrieved in the exodus from France," put in Queen Charlotte. "But many lost. You can see now why we are so glad to have the Vernet pearls to add to the collection."

Elinor frowned, but Aldreda kept her face impassive. It was time to ask some pointed questions, regardless of the etiquette. "Do you know of any hostile Mundanes – those who might attempt to destroy them?"

The king turned, stiff and courteous. "Any likely dissidents are under observation. I do not regard them as a threat."

"What about Lord Rapp? What happened to him?"

The polite veneer slipped a little as His Majesty's face showed a twist of grief. "That was a private matter. Deeply saddening, but nothing political, I assure you."

Aldreda thought back to what Elinor had told her about Lord Rapp and the Duke of Planx's final disastrous bet. In the light of the king's edicts limiting vampiri interactions, the bet now became more explicable.

"With respect, Your Majesty," said Aldreda, "Did Lord Rapp accuse the Duke of Planx of publicly entertaining vampiri, in defiance of your customs?"

The king did not speak, his face pained; it was left to his wife to answer. "Lord Rapp was Bemused the night before his death; he had been overzealous in his duties," said Queen Charlotte. "We do not suspect the Duke of Planx of any misdemeanour."

Aldreda watched the royal family narrowly. The king and queen looked sad, but the son was unreadable. Lord Olliot shifted uncomfortably next to Lady Beresford, whose eyes were wide with interest.

"If I may beg one more question," asked Elinor. The king met her gaze, frowning slightly. "Do you know where Lordel Tildenhall might be? He was Lord Rapp's vampiri companion."

"No," said the king. "If you see him, Miss Zooth, or

indeed Miss Avely, kindly tell Lordel Tildenhall to report to me at once. In complete privacy, of course."

Aldreda dropped her own gaze, irked at being turned aside so neatly. The king's answer also implied he knew nothing of Tildenhall – unless the king was lying.

His Majesty refused to discuss it further. To Aldreda's chagrin, they were all led back out into the drawing room. She spent the remaining quarter-hour perched on the mantlepiece, ignored and seething.

13

IN WHICH THERE ARE TEA AND TEARS

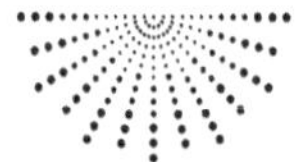

Elinor

An hour later, they were back home. Elinor was relieved to be divested of royal company. Jaq had gone his own way, after an awkward farewell at the palace. Elinor had taken a moment to ask him again about Beresford, but Jaq had only repeated that Beresford would arrive in London on the morrow.

Now Elinor, Aldreda, and Lady Beresford had repaired to the drawing room to discuss the events of the evening. Elinor walked restlessly about the room, mulling over the implications of all that had been said.

Lady Beresford sank onto a couch. "Well, are you satisfied, Miss Zooth?" she asked. "Are you happy to leave the pearls in royal safekeeping?"

Aldreda shook her head. "I want to know more about these Vampiri Edicts."

Elinor stripped off her gloves and turned over a cup

as a seat for Aldreda. "Yes, how terrible – banishing you to the mantlepiece! Such dreadful manners."

"No doubt they have good reason for it," said Lady Beresford. "You must admit that the general populace might take it amiss if they saw Miss Zooth without any explanation."

Elinor took objection to that. "Why should they take her amiss? Aldreda is perfectly respectable!"

"Do not forget her diet is human blood, my dear. Not *perfectly* respectable."

Elinor sat down with a huff. She saw Aldreda was twisting her hands together, and she felt another stab of anger that her friend had been so mistreated.

Aldreda spoke. "Indeed, vampiri have always been kept secret from the Mundanes. However, in the company of Musors, we are accustomed to being treated as equals."

Lady Beresford looked sympathetic. "I am sure the edict against publicly consorting with vampiri is not intended as an insult. It is merely a precaution to keep you safe, Miss Zooth."

Elinor was not so sure. "Not only to keep vampiri safe but to protect the king's precious skin. Publicly *consorting* with the vampiri in France led to the guillotine, by the sounds of it."

"The king is trying to keep the peace," argued Lady Beresford. "And to keep the knowledge of these Musors intact. I think we can trust that his intentions are good."

Aldreda looked sceptical, pursing her lips. "His highness was rather close-mouthed about Lord Rapp. It seemed to me as if he were hiding something."

"It could simply be grief, if His Majesty was close to Lord Rapp," suggested Lady Beresford.

Elinor coughed. "I attempted a bit of Truth Discernment while we were there." Her companions turned to stare at her, and she smiled. "I *think* I might be growing better at it – I can hear a kind of shallow sound to the voice when someone lies. It was in the king's voice when he said Lord Rapp's death was 'nothing political.'"

"Oh?" Aldreda sat up. "What about his other statements?"

Elinor sighed. "The king spoke the truth when he said he did not know where Tildenhall was, and when he claimed he did not regard dissidents as a threat. Unless my Discernment was off, which is possible. I shall have to ask Mother how she does it so well."

Aldreda made an observation. "Also, as a Diplomacor, the king might be more adept at lying."

Lady Beresford was thoughtful. "Interesting their majesties did not question the Duke of Planx's conduct. I wonder if they might think differently if they had heard Lord Rapp's version of the events that night – it sounded as if the duke ignored the Vampiri Edicts."

Aldreda nodded. "I wonder if that provides a motive for Rapp's death? Would the Duke of Planx have wanted to prevent the king from hearing the full details of his disobedience?"

The countess tapped a finger on her chair. "It scarcely seems to warrant murder."

"Mm," agreed Elinor. "And the queen said Lord Rapp was Bemused at the Planxes' card party. Perhaps that is why everyone thought he was drunk; strong Bemusement can seem that way, and it could be used to undercut his story. I wonder if he was Musing that night."

"We must find out what kind of Musor he was," stated Aldreda.

Lady Beresford tilted her head. "What are all the types again? I cannot remember."

Elinor launched into a list. "Discernment, Memory, Illusion, Heightening, Travel, Diplomacy, Healing, and Impacting."

"Oh, Healing? I wonder if you could find someone to help my arthritis," remarked the countess.

At that moment, their discussion was interrupted. The butler opened the door and announced Lord Malleker and Mr Avely.

All eyes turned to see Jaq standing there, still in his royal finery. Perry leaned against him. Or rather, he lolled. Elinor raised her brows, smiling.

Jaq was stiffly courteous in his greeting. "I found Peregrine at a gaming hall. He was playing too deep. I thought you would like me to bring him home."

"Only a pound a piece!" objected Perry, a slight slur to his voice. "Not that deep!"

"Perry, are you drunk?" demanded Elinor.

Perry grinned at her, a blond lock falling over his brow. "Course I am! What else is a man to do in London?"

Jaq led him forward, but Perry seemed reluctant to let go of the selkie's arm.

Lady Beresford shook her head reprovingly. "I suggest you obtain a voucher to Almacks, though of course they are only open on Wednesdays. Far more respectable to go there and do your duty."

"I would not go even if it were Wednesday," declared Perry. "All those frilly girls looking for a husband. Phah."

He launched himself off Jaq and sprawled onto a settee. "Let us try some mermaid tears, Jaq. You told me about them. I want to try them."

Elinor raised her brows again. "Isn't that the liquor in which you have previously over-indulged, Jaq?"

Jaq looked embarrassed. "It is not a drink, Miss Avely.

It is a concoction imbued with Heightening qualities. It might even be of assistance to Perry if combined with the sobering effects of a cup of tea."

Lady Beresford leaned forward, intrigued. "Oh, that sounds interesting. Do you have some on your person, Lord Malleker?"

Jaq, slightly shamefaced, pulled out a flask from his inner pocket after casting a glance at Aldreda. Elinor also looked to see what the vampiri would say about it.

Aldreda crossed her arms and shook her head. "I do not recommend it. Mermaid tears are very strong and can have uncertain effects depending on the person."

"How do you know?" queried Lady Beresford. Elinor saw Aldreda flush. Lady Beresford smiled. "Ah, I thought as much. You have already partaken. Well, I insist on trying them also. I am parched. We can all sample some together. For Mr Avely's benefit, of course." She rang for the butler.

"Indeed," said Perry, smiling widely. "For my benefit. Thank you, Jaq, dear fellow."

Jaq grinned at him.

"I must say I am intrigued," admitted Elinor. "Is this brewed on Skerry, Jaq?"

Jaq shook his head. Aldreda frowned with disapproval and ducked behind her cup to hide from the impending butler. Elinor decided to ignore her. Aldreda's experience of mermaid tears was no doubt extreme, given her size.

The butler appeared. Elinor thought it best to intervene in Lady Beresford's instructions and change it to teacakes rather than the Beresford Jam. Goodness knew what would happen if mermaid tears were added to the jam.

While they waited for the victuals to arrive, Elinor did her best to soothe the tension between Jaq and the rest of the company, and she asked again after Beresford. Elinor felt rather sorry for Jaq; he was only acting out of loyalty to his people, and Beresford must have given him permission to seek the Moria Pearls in London. Yet Aldreda pointedly ignored the selkie, furious with him after his attempt to negotiate for the necklace.

One thing to be glad of was that at least Perry wasn't being rude to Jaq anymore. He was smiling and chatting to Jaq, oblivious to any other tensions, and only faintly slurring his words.

Elinor saw Aldreda tilt her head as if listening to something. Elinor bent down to question her.

Aldreda spoke in a low tone. "I can hear something rustling behind the curtain – by the window that looks out onto the street."

It was too quiet for Elinor's human ears. "A rat? Should I fetch Samuel?"

'Better not. It might be ... a vampiri."

"Hm."

Elinor glided over to the curtain and twitched it aside. She was not surprised to see Pags, though she *was* pleasantly surprised to see he was tying up some boots and was otherwise fully clothed.

"Miss Avely!" Pags stood and bowed. He was attired in the height of London fashion, in tight breeches with a golden yellow waistcoat, complete with a hastily tied cravat. His beard was gone! and his long hair had been cut back to an unruly mop. Now that Pags's face was visible, Elinor could see a strong jawline, sensual lips, and a nose that seemed to jut out for all that it was in miniature. Elinor turned slightly to see Aldreda staring at Pags with surprise, a faint flush to her cheeks.

"Er – Your Gracel," murmured Elinor. "So pleased to see you – er – clothed."

Pags lips quirked. "I took pity on you all, especially Miss Zooth. May I beg an introduction to the company?"

"Hm," said Elinor. "I am not certain you deserve it. Your reception may be cool. We are all Aldreda's friends here."

Pags nodded. "I have information which I wish to share, as a recompense."

Elinor was curious, as no doubt he intended. "Very well." She stood aside, defiant of any Vampiri Edicts that would frown upon such introductions. This was a private drawing room, after all.

Pags pushed past her, striding across the carpet, his masculine jaw thrust forward and his nose leading the way. Lady Beresford was the first to see him, and she let out a shriek. Elinor grinned. If only the countess had met Pags a week ago.

Elinor made the introductions as requested. Far from pouring out recriminations, Perry was loud in his enthusiasm. "By Jove, I say! Wonderful to see you in breeches, dear fellow," he said. "Where did you find your tailor? I wonder if it is the same place I frequent."

Pags lifted an arrogant brow. "I doubt it."

"I have some togs you could borrow if you wanted," said Perry generously. "But you don't appear to need them anymore."

Pags coughed. "I hear the butler approaching. Perhaps if I may shelter behind a cup also, like Miss Zooth?"

Elinor promptly picked him up. The butler was too quick, so she held Pags behind her back. It *was* rather difficult to keep a private parlour private, with servants always gliding around. Pags stayed still in her palm, and Elinor only hoped Aldreda did not mind such familiar behaviour with another vampiri.

The butler retreated, not seeming to notice the

sudden silence that greeted his entrance. Letting out a breath, Elinor carefully placed Pags on Aldreda's table. After all, he was properly dressed now, so Aldreda need not look as if a barbaric savage had been set down in her vicinity to threaten her virtue.

Pags winked at Aldreda, to her apparent outrage.

The countess proceeded to pour the tea, her face alight with curiosity. "So you are the scallywag who stole our pearls? You have much effrontery to turn up here, I must say."

Aldreda folded her arms in agreement.

Pags cleared his throat. "I do apologise most earnestly for my presumption. I trust you are pleased now you have seen the resting place of the pearls? The Sapphire Library is renowned among certain circles. It is almost as famous as the Rothet Tea Set."

Elinor refused to be distracted by this intriguing reference – a magical teapot? – and she wagged a finger at Pags. "We have some concerns as to what happened to Lord Rapp. Have you discovered anything, Your Grace?"

Pags shifted slightly. "Indeed, that is why I have come here today."

"Oh?" asked Aldreda, looking curious despite herself.

"I have found out Lord Rapp's gift, as you indicated you wished to know, Miss Zooth." Pags bowed in her direction. "He was a Discernor."

"Like Elinor?" Lady Beresford paused mid-pour.

"Indeed."

There was a silence, and Elinor sat up straighter.

"I do not like it," pronounced Aldreda.

"Nor do I," said Lady Beresford, frowning.

Elinor had to admit she felt a trickle of fear. If Lord Rapp was a Discernor and now dead, did that mean she could be in danger too?

Jaq spoke from where he leaned against the mantlepiece. "It could be completely irrelevant. I heard Lord Rapp committed suicide after losing a vast sum of money to the Duke of Planx."

"So it is being said," agreed Aldreda. "Yet, this information does cast a new light on the matter."

Lady Beresford put down the pot with a clatter. "Are you suggesting Lord Rapp was killed because he was a Discernor?" She looked anxiously at Elinor. "You must keep quiet about your ability, Elinor."

"Too late for that," said Aldreda dryly. "We just announced it to the royal household."

"They will not bandy it about," said Jaq.

Perry interrupted. "How about you bandy those mermaid things about? I am desperate for a drink here."

The countess finished pouring the tea, and Jaq did the honours of adding a drop from his flask to each cup. Elinor fished some thimbles out of her sewing basket for Aldreda and Pags, and she poured some of her own doctored tea into them. Aldreda murmured something about them not being Vember glasses. Pags told her not to be so fussy, which only succeeded in obtaining him a scathing look and the observation that no cups at all were to be found in the stables.

Everyone raised their vessels.

"To a successful London Season," proclaimed Lady Beresford.

"To ensuring the safety of the Moria Pearls," added Elinor for Aldreda's benefit.

Perry lifted his teacup with a grin. "To kicking up a lark in London."

Pags spoke slowly. "To discovering the truth of Lord Rapp's death."

So, reflected Elinor, Pags had come over to their way

of thinking: that there was indeed something amiss in the Musor circles of London. It appeared he was now assisting their enquiries; well, she would take help where it was offered if she could be certain they could trust him.

They all took a sip, and an appreciative silence fell around the room. The tea was, if possible, even more refreshing and fragrant than it had been at the palace. Lord Olliot's Gift of Heightening did not compare with mermaid tears, thought Elinor.

"How does Heightening work?" she asked Aldreda. "Is it like Illusion?"

"No," said Aldreda. "Illusion is a visual trick. Heightening affects the actual qualities of the object, increasing their strength. Mermaid tears are a special type of Heightening which works to directly intensify your mind-state, which is why they are so volatile. It depends on your own state of mind to begin with."

"Supplies are limited," said Jaq. "So enjoy it while it lasts."

Pags grinned. "I must say I have missed the trappings of civilisation. Thank you for allowing me to join you."

Aldreda gave him a narrow look, but Perry smirked, and Lady Beresford smiled indulgently.

Elinor took another ecstatic sip, as did everyone else except Aldreda. The vampiri put her thimble down carefully and frowned at everyone. "Mermaid tears are best consumed when you are in a happy frame of mind, with all your needs met."

"Oh pooh," said Perry. "Don't be so stuffy, Miss Zooth. Now I see why you like tea so much, Ellie. Fabulous stuff." He took another long swallow.

Elinor giggled and took a bite of teacake.

IN WHICH DESIRES ARE HEIGHTENED

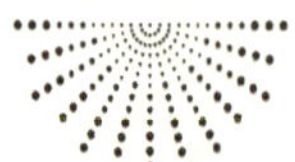

Aldreda

*A*ldreda was annoyed and anxious with the advent of Jaq and the mermaid tears. Jaq was looking at Perry speculatively, no doubt wondering what tears might do to him. Then, when Perry next caught his gaze, Jaq casually loosened his cravat, his long fingers lingering at the task.

Perry's eyes fixed upon Jaq's hands, and he gulped.

Aldreda sighed. Selkies were always so damned attractive. Poor Perry didn't stand a chance unless she could intervene somehow. She looked around at the rest of the company. The countess was dreamy, staring with a faint smile at the flame of a candle. Elinor was lost in divine communion with her teacake.

Beside Aldreda, Pags interrupted her survey. "Miss Zooth, I am glad to see you are decently attired at last."

The effrontery! Aldreda repressed a smile despite herself. "That is *my* line, Your Grace!"

Pags's eyes swept appreciatively over Aldreda's demure gown. "I warrant it was more difficult for me."

"What do you mean?"

"To endure our previous states of undress," explained Pags. "You seem to have no trouble in resisting my charms."

Aldreda realised she was blushing and hastily picked up her own thimble of tea. "I am pleased to see you visited a barber."

Pags leaned forward. "You laid down the gauntlet, Miss Zooth. I realised you were right – I have to make polite enquiries in polite society, and I need to look the part." He paused. "There is a Roost Revel two nights from now. You must accompany me."

Aldreda stared at him. "Excuse me?" That was a bold invitation, marking them as a pair. Not to mention his autocratic assumption that she would accept.

A faint red stained his cheeks. "Apologies, Miss Zooth. I meant: I would be honoured if you would join us there. I have obtained your invitation from the Duchessel of Planx, Lady Denier. Can you arrange for Miss Avely to transport you to the Willis Rooms on Wednesday night?"

"Perhaps Elinor will oblige me." Aldreda was suddenly curious, even desperate, to go. "Will all the London vampiri be there?"

"I believe so."

Aldreda was surprised at the pang of loneliness that struck her. Oh, to go to a Roost Revel again, with her own people! But surely it would not be like the old days in Paris. It was bound to be a terrible disappointment. She looked askance at her thimble of tea and tears. It was playing havoc with her sensibilities. She glanced back at Pags, wondering how the mermaid tears were affecting him. One hoped he would not attempt a bat mating dance with her again.

However, Aldreda was slightly piqued to see Pags was watching the countess, who was now lost in wondrous contemplation of the chandelier. Her head was tilted upwards, exposing her neck, and her throbbing pulse could be seen.

A look of deep hunger passed across Pags's face. Of course, thought Aldreda, he has not had much proper sustenance lately, feeding as he does upon the lower beasts. He really ought to find himself a Musor and settle down.

"My lord dukel." Aldreda tried to distract him. She did not want him to launch himself onto Lady Beresford in the middle of polite company. "Do you think there is a chance Lordel Tildenhall will be there?"

Pags turned to her, shaking himself slightly and hardening his gaze. "Where? Oh, at the Roost Revel? I doubt it. Tildenhall hasn't shown his face at any social function in the last three weeks."

"We can ask some questions," said Aldreda. "What reason shall we give for our interest?"

The mocking look returned. "I am glad it is *our* interest now, Miss Zooth. We shall simply say Tildenhall is a distant cousin of mine, and I wish to be reunited with him."

"Why don't we say he is *my* cousin?" objected Aldreda.

"Because I am a dukel," said Pags smugly. He folded his arms, which made his coat stretch rather nicely across his shoulders.

Aldreda sniffed. Unfortunately, Pags was right; he was more likely to obtain results with his title. She ignored him and looked around at everyone else.

Elinor was still savouring her teacake blissfully. Jaq,

however, had migrated and was now sitting next to Perry on the settee. Perry did not move away; their legs were touching, and he was admiring Jaq's velvet waistcoat.

"Visiting the king, were you?" Perry murmured. "Demned fine waistcoat, that is." He fingered the cloth and smiled dreamily at Jaq. The selkie prince grinned at him and said something in an undertone.

Perry blushed and snuggled in a bit closer.

Aldreda raised her brows. "Elinor," she said quietly, drawing Elinor's rapt attention from her food. "Perhaps someone ought to intervene with Jaq. Before Perry does something he regrets."

Elinor's eyes widened as she took in the intimate picture on the settee. "What shall I do?"

"Take me over there," said Aldreda. "Let us send Perry to bed."

Elinor lifted Aldreda and carried her across to the two young men, who were now gazing into each other's eyes.

Aldreda coughed as loudly as she could. Elinor had to cough also before the tableau was broken.

Perry looked up, rather dazed.

"Perry, it is time for bed," said Elinor.

His cheeks flushed. "Oh, is it? Now?"

As Perry lurched to his feet, Aldreda took the opportunity to hiss at Jaq. "Don't take advantage of Perry like this!"

Jaq grinned and leaned back. "Of course not! He is leading the ship, not I. I cannot help it if I am particularly charming."

Aldreda glared in scepticism. "Well, do not charm Perry into an indiscretion while he is drunk. Or on mermaid tears."

"Fine." Jaq looked sulky. "I will charm him when he is sober."

"Sober already?" asked Lady Beresford, suddenly withdrawing her attention from the chandelier's flickering lights. "These mermaid tears are quite scintillating, I must say. Where are you going, Miss Avely?"

"Perry needs to sleep off his indulgences, Lady Beresford," said Elinor. "Come, Perry." She pulled at his elbow, and he staggered slightly.

Jaq leaned back into the couch and smiled up at them. "Sweet dreams, Perry. See you tomorrow ... when you are sober."

~

Elinor escorted Aldreda to her room, left her there, and dragged Perry off to tuck him in.

Aldreda was wound up and somehow lonely, so she took care to leave the door open a crack should Samuel wish to visit. She curled up on the huge yellow bed, tucking her bare feet into her gown and heaving a sigh. Sometimes it felt as if she was the only sensible person in the room. Elinor would have kept dreamily munching on teacake, oblivious to her brother's predicament if Aldreda had not pointed it out.

Without realising it, Aldreda's ears were pricked, so she heard the scraping at the window as soon as it started.

Turning her head quickly, she saw Pags's form in the aperture. He was still clothed; he must have climbed with his bare hands up the side of the house to avoid transforming into a bat. His hair was dishevelled, and his cravat undone. Aldreda rather suspected he wasn't much of a dab hand with cravats. She wondered what he *was* a dab hand at and then frowned at the thought.

Pags slipped through the window and stood panting on the sill. "That was a tough climb. See the lengths I must take to remain decently attired for you, Miss Zooth?"

"If you call that decent," Aldreda retorted. She stayed on the bed, though she sat up more primly. "How dare you call upon me alone in my bedchamber, my lord dukel? Especially after you have stolen from me once already."

"Ha," said Pags. He leapt off the sill and sauntered forward, his cravat loose around his neck. "You know vampiri have more lax rules than these poor humans. We are more flexible creatures. And I thought you had forgiven me for my other sin?"

Aldreda sniffed and forbore to point out that she had not invited him inside. She tried not to stare at his freshly shaven face, which was oddly attractive despite its imperious nose. "What do you want, Pags?"

"Merely to converse with you, of course," he replied with a gleam in his eye that suggested he would like to do a little more than *converse*. Aldreda again recalled the mating dance he had attempted on first seeing her, and she became rather cross with herself. Those mermaid tears had tampered with her sensibilities. They were both civilised bats now, even if for Pags it was only a thin veneer. He still fed from horses and Helicons, after all.

"May I?" asked Pags, gesturing towards the bed.

Aldreda thought for a moment, then nodded. She had questions; it was nothing to do with a desire for his company. Pags vaulted up and sat leaning against the wooden bedhead.

"Please," said Aldreda. "Can you tell me more about what happened in the Troubles?"

Pags's face shuttered. "What is it you want to know?"

"Who led the revolutionaries? Mundanes?"

He heaved a sigh. "Yes. They called themselves the Quotidians, those who honoured the commonplace over the magical."

"What happened to the leaders?"

"They were later executed when they overreached themselves."

Aldreda considered this for a moment. "Are you not concerned that any of their compatriots – other Quotidians – could be in England, stirring up trouble?"

"No." Pags was firm. "King George's strategy has worked: there is nothing to stir up trouble over. The vampiri are kept secret, and so are the Musors. There is no revolution to be had."

Aldreda traced a pattern on the quilt, thoughtful. "Yet, if a Quotidian was motivated by hatred towards Musors, he might choose a more direct method of extermination than revolution."

Pags's lips compressed. "I have seen no sign of any of the French Quotidians in England. You think there is one lurking around, eliminating Musors one by one?"

"I don't know," said Aldreda. "I simply do not believe Lord Rapp's death was suicide. And Elinor is a Discernor, so I am worried."

Pags slouched down against the board, frowning. "You care too much about Miss Avely."

"It is only natural, given we are bonded companions."

"Which is why you should abandon the bond."

Aldreda shook her head reprovingly. "There is nothing wrong with interdependence, my lord dukel, even if it sometimes causes worry and grief."

A dark look passed across his face. Aldreda felt a stab of remorse for provoking his painful memories, but she pressed on. "Were you forced to turn in your own companion?" she asked bluntly, wanting to know the truth of it.

His eyes hardened. "I did no such thing."

Aldreda was relieved, even though she knew she shouldn't blame him if he had. It sounded as if the Aubadesol rope was akin to torture by sunlight.

Pags continued. "I held out. Refused to tell them anything, even after days tied in that rope." Aldreda felt as if he repressed a shudder, though he kept still against the board. "Then my companion, the young Duke of Demontaine, offered himself up to save me."

Aldreda swallowed. In a way, that was worse. "What happened?"

"His head was chopped off," said Pags brutally. "And the Quotidians did not free me."

Aldreda was startled by the sudden rush of pain she felt on Pags's behalf. "How did you escape?"

"I played dead." Pags scowled. "They believed me, for I probably should have been dead by then, after three days in the Aubadesol. My captors untied me, and I fought my way out."

Aldreda knew it must have taken more than supernatural strength to do so, weakened as Pags must have been. But perhaps he had been fuelled by the rage that now flashed in his eyes.

"And you flew to England?"

The rage dimmed. "First, I fought to release my friends. Most of the Musors I had known were already killed, so perhaps the rebels did not see the need to keep the vampiri anymore. I helped about twenty of us escape. Then I left. There wasn't anything left in France to keep me. And it was still unsafe."

Aldreda imagined he had wanted to leave the scene of his grief. It was something she understood. "I have lost a human companion to betrayal, too," she said tentatively. "After the selkies stole Henri's wife, he died of a broken heart. There was nothing I could do."

Pags was sympathetic. "The seal folk are not to be trusted. I am sorry, Miss Zooth, for your loss."

Aldreda blinked back a tear and pressed her lips tightly together.

"Though, to my mind," added Pags, "it also demonstrates that the Musor bond is to be avoided. Don't you agree, Miss Zooth?"

Aldreda frowned. "I deeply value human companionship. I would be lonely without it."

"Why not vampiri companionship?" suggested Pags. He leaned forward slightly on the bed.

Aldreda avoided his gaze. She did not want to explain that, to her mind, the Musor-Vampiri alliance was a matter of clear rules and defined duties, with plenty of space for each in their own hours of the day. A vampiri relationship was more ... messy. But Pags was waiting for an answer.

"I don't want to have to renounce my Musor bond," she said at last. "If I marry, I must leave my title and residence to live with my husband. Let us say I am a creature of habit."

"Afraid of change?"

"Don't be impertinent," she snapped. "I am fortunate I can remain independent of male patronage, unlike the human women who must depend on it. I would rather depend on Elinor."

"Elinor cannot dance with you," said Pags.

Aldreda did not allow Pags to see he had scored a point: she did love to dance. "I dance at revels. I don't need a husband for that."

"Yet you have not attended a revel for a while. Do I take it you will accompany me two nights from now, Miss Zooth?"

Aldreda bit her lip, feeling he had somehow manoeuvred her into accepting. "I suppose so."

Pags sat up straighter. "And do you indeed know the dances?"

She was struck with sudden doubt. "Perhaps not. There must be new arrangements. I was in hibernation for eighty years, after all."

"Ah, indeed, there are new arrangements," said Pags triumphantly. "You must allow me to teach you." He stood up and held out his hand. "We can start with the Lace and Glove."

Aldreda kept her hands tucked in her gown. "I doubt that will be necessary, my lord dukel."

"Oh, stop calling me 'my lord dukel,'" he said irritably. "And it is necessary, for I don't want you to disgrace me on the dance floor when you are accompanying *me* to the revel."

"Heaven forbid you appear slightly uncouth!" she exclaimed.

He grinned again, but his hand remained imperiously extended.

Aldreda was tempted, despite herself. It was true she did not want to embarrass herself at the Revel. She ought to find a dance master, but maybe Pags would do in the meanwhile.

"How do you know the dances if you have been on the moors for years?" she asked.

"Only nine years, my dear, which is a sight shorter than your eighty-five years out of circulation."

Aldreda ignored the appellation. "Very well. But not on the bed." She leaped gracefully down to the carpet and paused. "I should fetch Elinor as a chaperone."

"Nonsense." Pags landed beside her. "Now, the Lace and Glove is a lively dance, but we will start slow. Face me."

Aldreda frowned at his autocratic tone, but she turned to face him. At least he was properly clothed and a suitable distance away. His golden eyes gleamed in the dim light of the room.

"First, the bow and curtsy. Then rest your fingertips on mine."

Aldreda did so. A shiver ran through her when their hands touched. She took in a quick breath and remembered she was possibly still overwrought with mermaid tears. And Pags too, by the intent look in his eye and the way his thumb rubbed over her knuckles.

Aldreda gave him a repressive look, and he withdrew the offending digit.

"Very well, Miss Zooth," he said unrepentantly. "Let us begin. Can you hear that music from down the street?"

Aldreda listened and could indeed hear the faint strains of a string quartet providing music for some party. She nodded.

Pags proceeded to show her the steps, which were much in the way of the old minuets. It included the light skipping three-step she so loved, in complex circles and turns. Pags explained where the other couples would be as he weaved around her.

If there was one thing vampiri were good at, it was dancing. This explained why Pags was so light on his feet, so sure in his movements, and so graceful and strong. It wasn't him, in particular. Any vampiri could dance that well. Including herself, of course. Aldreda found she was enjoying herself. And she certainly was not thinking of another kind of dance, out in the moors.

There were a few missteps, but she picked it up quickly, and they passed onto the next one, a cotillion.

By the end of that one, they were smiling at each other from the pure enjoyment of it. Then she recollected herself and nodded a gracious thanks, stepping back slightly. "Will I pass, do you think, my lord dukel?"

Pags nodded, his own face a little flushed. "Admirably."

There was a short silence. He coughed. "You must listen out for the leader of the set as she calls the steps. You know a good few of them now."

"I thank you."

"My pleasure," he replied, and the roguish gleam was back. "Now I can rest assured you will not behave like a savage two nights from now."

She laughed. "I wish I could say the same of you."

"Remember, we are there to quest after my long-lost cousin Tildenhall," he said. "Not merely to dance the night away."

"If I do find Tildenhall, I can dance with him and find out his secrets."

Pags took a step closer, drawing her hand to his lips. "Only if you give me the same treatment first."

"Of course," said Aldreda evenly, though her heart still raced. "Do you have very many secrets, my lord dukel?"

"Call me Pagrilliard," said his lord dukel, still holding her hand. "I have already told you too many of my secrets, my dear Miss Zooth."

"You may rely upon my discretion." Aldreda did not offer her own name in return. She did not trust the desire that swirled through her at his touch. Those cursed mermaid tears! Withdrawing her hand, she curtsied, marking the end of the lesson. "Now, if it pleases Your Gracel, I must retire."

"It does not please me." Nonetheless, he stepped back with a bow. "The night is young. What are you going to do with it?"

"Finish my gown," said Aldreda primly.

"Oh, if that is all ..." said Pags. "I can pay someone to do that for you; I have access to the old Duke of Demontaine's bank account in London. Why don't we explore the city instead?"

Aldreda fought with herself, for the invitation was tempting. Her distrust of Pags had softened into something that resembled friendship – in part from the intimacy of dancing, but also due to the confidences they had exchanged. Would it do any harm to fly around London with him and see the sights? Yet this was the vampiri who had arrogantly taken her pearls and remained conceited and uncivilised.

Pags's proffered hand, strong and inviting, lay awaiting her decision. He raised a provocative eyebrow.

However, at that moment, Aldreda was saved by Samuel. The door creaked open, and the cat shouldered his way inside.

A look of shock and utter disdain transformed the feline face. Then Samuel leapt forward.

Pags let out a yell and sprinted for the window. He was faster than the cat, thank goodness, and hauled himself up the curtains. Samuel hissed and clawed at the fabric from below.

"Samuel!" chided Aldreda. "Leave his gracel alone! He is my visitor!"

The cat cast a betrayed look back at Aldreda. He

clearly refused to leave his post, much in the manner of guarding a mouse hole. He glared up at Pags with his green eyes.

Pags was now perched on the curtain rail. He pushed his unruly hair out of his face. "Pet of yours?"

"Not a pet, a friend." Aldreda walked over to stroke Samuel's ruffled fur. In spite of himself, Samuel gave a purr.

"Yet another bond," said Pags, without inflection.

"Another friend, yes."

"Well, I can see I am not welcome anymore."

Aldreda smiled. Was Pags jealous of a cat? "Samuel is a good chaperone."

"Hmph," said Pags. "Perhaps I should bite him too, so he allows my company."

"Planning many visits, are you?" said Aldreda, trying not to feel pleased. "Yet, I can't imagine you would want to *bond* yourself to anyone, even a cat."

Pags grumbled something beneath his breath that she could not catch. "No, Miss Zooth. I bid you adieu. I will see you at the revel in two nights."

Without waiting for an answer, he swung himself down through the window and disappeared.

Aldreda sighed, running a hand over Samuel. "I have a gown to finish. Will you keep me company, dear Samuel?"

Samuel purred loudly and proceeded to clean himself most thoroughly.

IN WHICH LOVERS DISAGREE

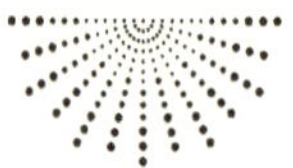

Elinor

*I*n the morning, Elinor woke early; restless and impatient. When was Beresford going to be home? Jaq said he was already in London, so perhaps James was in the townhouse right now.

The thought propelled Elinor out of bed to dress hurriedly and go below. Yet only her mother was at the breakfast table; Perry and the countess, it seemed, were still sleeping off the night's excesses. Upon enquiry, the butler informed Elinor that Beresford still had not returned. Elinor tried to ignore the worry that suddenly shook her.

"Well?" asked Mrs Avely, as Elinor took her place at the table. "How did the royal visit go?"

"It was fascinating," said Elinor, and proceeded to tell her mother about the Sapphire Library. She also reluctantly explained the matter of Lord Rapp's death; after all, the countess knew of their interest in it, and Elinor did not want to exclude her mother again. "The night Lord Rapp died, it appears he may have been Bemused, which might explain his behaviour in challenging the duke."

Mrs Avely was frowning. "Lord Rapp was a Musor? That is concerning."

Elinor hesitated. "Lord Rapp was a Discernor."

Mrs Avely put down her fork. "A Discernor? The king's Discernor? That is not good news."

"Why do you say that?"

"It is the Royal Discernor's role to scry dangers to the king. Perhaps someone wanted any possible warning silenced."

Elinor reflected. "I quite like that theory. It means the murder was aimed specifically at the Royal Discernor, not just *any* Discernor."

Her mother's finger tapped on the table. "Hm. Perhaps it is better we remove from London, after all."

"Oh, no!" said Elinor. "We've only just arrived!"

"You have established that the pearls are cared for."

"We have seen them, but I am not convinced they are in safe hands." Elinor then explained about the Vampiri Edicts. She was not surprised when Mrs Avely nodded her approval. Elinor wrinkled her nose and asked a question that had woken her in the middle of the night. "By the way, Mother, the king asked if Perry was Gifted. Do you think it is possible he could have a Gift and not know it?"

Mrs Avely shook her head. "I have never seen any signs of it. Usually, it manifests around nine years old, as you remember in your case. I'm afraid Perry is perfectly ordinary."

"That is the way I like him," said Elinor. She

wondered how Perry was feeling after his night's adventures.

Perhaps it was the memory of staring into Jaq's dark eyes that caused Perry to eventually emerge after Mrs Avely left. He groaned and cast himself down at the table with an oath. "Oh God," he said. "I drank far too much last night."

"That you did," said Elinor cheerily. "Did the late cup of tea help, assisted by those mermaid tears?"

Perry raised his head and glowered at her. "No."

"It was kind of Jaq to bring you home."

"Mmmgh," said Perry. He returned to his contemplation of the table, perhaps recalling Jaq's arm around his waist.

Elinor pressed on. "It sounds as if Jaq saved you from some embarrassing gambling bets."

This assertion provoked a sulky response. "I might have won it back. Jaq need not have intervened. Besides, I am meant to be showing *him* the sights. Can't do that if he is going to act like a nanny."

"I cannot see Jaq as *anyone's* nanny," observed Elinor. "It is sweet he was watching out for you."

"Mmmgh," said Perry.

"Have some chocolate," suggested Elinor kindly.

Elinor herself finished breakfast slowly, hoping to hear Beresford's step in the hall. But it did not come.

She spent the best part of the day in the library, waiting, for she could not bear to go out shopping or visiting when there was a chance Beresford might arrive. What if he did not return? The Duchess of Planx's little orchestration mattered nil now.

Her patience was eventually rewarded mid-afternoon when at last, she heard Beresford's beloved voice, deep and calm in the entrance hall.

Elinor leapt up from her chair and rushed out. Careless of the watching servants, she flung herself into his arms.

"My love!" she said. "You have been gone too long!"

Beresford laughed and placed a kiss on her lips, pulling her close. "Yes, far too long."

She pulled back and saw there were shadows under his eyes and stubble on his cheeks. "You must rest."

"First, tell me all that has happened in my absence," he said, leading her back into the library.

Elinor went gladly, her arm still tucked in his. "Did you give Jaq permission to approach the king?" she asked. "For he intruded upon our royal audience last night."

"Well, in a sense, I did." Beresford let her go, shrugging off his coat. "I've released Jaq. I returned his seal star, so he is now free to do as he pleases."

Elinor looked a wide-eyed question. "Truly?"

"He proved himself on this last trip to France – he saved my life, at great personal risk to himself, when I found myself in a rather compromising situation with Napoleon's first commander," said Beresford. "I owe him his freedom. And I believe he has reformed the more reckless tendencies which his mother was so concerned about."

"But don't you need Jaq?" asked Elinor. "What of your crew?"

"He says he still wants to assist me on my forays, so I shan't lose my shipmate just yet. I think he enjoys it. God knows he is useful, but I didn't like having him there under any sort of duress."

Elinor thought it best not to mention the reappearance of mermaid tears the night before. She cleared her throat. "Well, I suppose it was only fair Jaq had a chance to present his case for the pearls."

"I hope Miss Zooth wasn't too cross?"

"She was a *little* cross."

"And King George decided to reimburse them equally?"

"It probably will satisfy neither. After all, Jaq wants the knowledge within the pearls, and money means little to Aldreda."

"Does it not?" asked Beresford. He kicked off his boots and sat down in an armchair, smiling wearily.

"Well, Aldreda's needs are small, and I have been able to purchase her a new wardrobe from a vampiri modiste," explained Elinor. "Vampiri rely upon their human companion's wealth."

"And I suppose you have good expectations now you are engaged to an earl," teased Beresford.

Elinor blushed. "Oh, my own pin money was quite sufficient," she said, though in fact, it was true she had little left for her own gloves after outlaying several pounds for Aldreda's gowns.

"Vampiri do not live independently?"

"Not often," said Elinor, though she wondered about Pags. How was he funding his return to society? "I must tell you all about the Vampiri Edicts – I am certain *you* will agree they are offensive and prejudicial."

However, irksomely, Beresford was loath to criticise the king's laws. "Don't forget the vampiri habit of appearing naked," he pointed out. "Perhaps they are best kept behind closed doors, after all."

"Aldreda only does that when it is unavoidable!" objected Elinor. "She now has an unexceptionable wardrobe."

"What about Pags? Is he still … wild?"

"He has become quite civilised," said Elinor. "I think

Aldreda is having a good influence on him." She paused. "I take it you have been to see your superiors in London?"

A shadow crossed Beresford's face. "Indeed."

"Did you manage to discover anything about Lord Rapp? King George was rather reluctant to discuss the matter."

Beresford sighed. "My superiors were also closed-mouthed. They informed me it is not my concern and to concentrate on Devon." He hesitated. "They tried to imply Lord Rapp was sadly not himself in the last few weeks. But I knew his lordship, and I doubt he would resort to suicide, no matter how deep in debt he may have been."

"You knew Lord Rapp?" asked Elinor, curious. "What was he like?"

"He was twenty years older than me, so I didn't know him particularly well. A sparse, intellectual type of man: always buried in his books."

"Hm," said Elinor. She had wondered if Lord Rapp was having an affair with the Duchess of Planx, but he didn't sound the type to interest her grace. "Unfortunately, the thought of suicide does occur when one hears of a 'shooting accident.' Yet, there is more to it, I am certain."

She told Beresford of the strange gamble that Lord Rapp had with the Duke of Planx. Beresford was intrigued.

Elinor continued. "And we have discovered that Lord Rapp was a Discernor! So it could be that he did Discern vampiri at the Planx residence, though I do not know why he should wantonly accuse the duke of it." She paused as a new thought struck her. "I wonder if he Discerned something else ... oh! I have it!"

"What?" asked Beresford, somewhat apprehensively. "I beg you not to speculate too far, Elinor."

"No, listen! It could have been Truth Discernment! Lord Rapp was a Discernor – so he might have known how to Discern a lie! If he uncovered a treasonous plot, it would have led to his death." She paused for dramatic effect. "So all I have to do is Discern the same lie, and we will know who the murderer is!"

She looked eagerly at Beresford, but he frowned. "Elinor, please do not attempt it. In fact, the more I think on it, the more I believe we should return to Devon immediately. I did not realise that Lord Rapp was a Discernor like you."

"You are as bad as my mother!" she exclaimed. "We cannot leave now!"

"We do not want to show too much interest in the matter. You have seen the pearls are well guarded – let us return to Devon and be married."

Elinor leaned her head on his shoulder, admitting to herself that perhaps it was dangerous to seek out a murderer, even if she was uniquely fitted to the task. Yet she was unwilling to retreat just yet and renounce her enquiries. How could she convince Beresford to stay in London?

She smoothed the shirt over his admirable shoulders. "My love, I want nothing more than to return to Devon, but we must at least satisfy the gossips first. We should attend a few events, dance a few dances ... If we run back to Devon now, it will cause more speculation."

Beresford sighed. "How many events?"

"Just a few balls – the Yannows are holding one on the morrow." Elinor lifted her chin. "Besides, I am assured of success. Even the Duchess of Planx called upon me last week."

She watched Beresford carefully. His expression showed no change, remaining concerned. "The duchess?" he said. "That was good of her, after the garden party debacle."

"Was it not?" said Elinor lightly, though she felt a stab of irritation, remembering the conversation. "In fact, her grace informed me that she has previously intervened on my behalf."

"Oh?" said Beresford, with a preoccupied air.

"Yes," said Elinor sharply. "She said she instructed you to offer for me."

Beresford's eyes came into focus on Elinor's face. "Yes, now that I think of it, she did suggest it." He paused. "I wouldn't say she *instructed* me."

Elinor sat up rather straight. "Yet, you immediately obeyed."

"Elinor," Beresford sighed, rubbing his eyes. "I was going to offer for you regardless. If you recall, I did so *before* the Duchess of Planx suggested it – at the garden party."

"Why didn't you tell me she sent you afterwards?"

Beresford's eyes held her own. "Well, truth be told, I did not think you would want to know of her meddling."

"And why do you suppose that was?" Elinor snapped.

Beresford exhaled sharply. "Don't be nonsensical, Elinor. It is all past and done, which is why I did not mention it."

Elinor tried not to look mutinous. For Beresford was right, and she was being exceedingly silly. If only he would sweep her into his arms and kiss away her concerns, and passionately declare that he adored her.

Instead, he frowned. "We have more important things to worry about. I do not like that Lord Rapp was a Discernor, nor do I like your theory of a treasonous plot.

You must be very careful from now on. Do not tell anyone you have the same ability. Or indeed any ability."

Elinor bit her lip. Pags had said the same thing weeks ago, and her mother had always held by it. Yet it was too late now; at least four people in the royal court knew her secret, and heaven knew how many more. Especially if the vampiri talked among themselves ...

"Yes, James," she said, repressing her sense of pique regarding the duchess, for it was unworthy of her. "But you will be there at the Yannow ball tomorrow, won't you? It will be my first ball since we have returned."

"Of course," said Beresford. "Yet now I am desperate to sleep. You must excuse me, my love."

With that, he put Elinor aside with a chaste kiss and trudged off to bed.

Elinor watched him go wistfully.

IN WHICH ELINOR LISTENS
FOR TRUTH

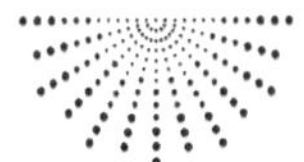

Elinor

The following night the Avelys made their first appearance at a large social event. Announced to a crowded room, Mrs Avely, Elinor, and Perry paused on the threshold to the Yannow ball.

A multitude of gazes turned to examine them, and a tiny hush rippled through the crowd. Elinor pasted on a small, cheerful smile and gripped Perry's arm rather tightly.

"Over we go," said Perry underneath his breath, sticking his chin out pugnaciously.

Carefully they trod down the stairs, Elinor lifting her new blue gown so she would not step on the hem and fall flat on her face.

"Look, there is Beresford." Elinor caught the eye of her beloved. The Beresfords had arrived before them and were nestled in the bosom of the crowd. Beresford looked very dashing in his evening wear, and no longer so exhausted as he had earlier. However, his expression was still slightly strained.

"Hold tight, and I'll sail you over there," said Perry. He guided Elinor through the crowd, though inevitably they were slowed as people turned to greet them and exchange pleasantries.

It seemed that even before she reached Beresford's side, Elinor was being accorded civility and smiles: even the new Viscountess Moonton (previously Miss Dardley) showed only a smiling and respectful face. Elinor let out a sigh of relief: clearly, the duchess and Lady Beresford had done their work well, and she was welcome once more among the upper crust.

When they reached the side of the Beresfords, Perry mopped his brow. "Good Gad, that was the longest room I've ever had to cross."

Lady Beresford smiled. "You both look charming."

Beresford bowed over Elinor's hand, a smile in his eyes. "Beautiful, I would say."

Elinor smiled back, aware of glances coming their way. The last time she and Beresford had appeared in public together, she had thrown his proposal back in his face. Now she hoped to show everyone how much she adored him.

Before she could say a word, however, the Duchess of Planx appeared at Beresford's elbow.

The duchess was richly dressed in a striking outfit of ivory and black, which made Elinor's pale blue gown seem rather girlish. Her grace also had an expanse of decolletage on display and a lacy fan in one white-gloved hand.

"Lord Beresford!" The duchess cooed; her dark eyes were bright. "So pleased to see you here; likewise, the Avely contingent!"

Curtsies and bows were exchanged. Elinor tried to feel glad that the duchess, so high, was putting the seal on the night's success. Instead, she succeeded only in feeling annoyed.

After a brief, trivial discussion on the turnout of the ball, the duchess continued, lowering her voice a little. "Lord Beresford, I must ask – do you indeed have acquaintance with the handsome Lord Malleker? If so, I do beg you will introduce me."

The duchess fluttered her eyes in a direction over Elinor's shoulder. Elinor turned to see Jaq standing on the other side of the room, his striking masculine beauty quite apparent under the glittering chandeliers. Jaq was talking to Lord Worthing, who was an old friend of Beresford's.

Elinor pursed her lips. Lord Worthing, a handsome dandy who sported a cane, was decidedly partial towards gentlemen. She looked over to see how Perry received the sight – Perry knew of Worthing's inclinations, having once caught him in an intimate embrace with a footman.

Perry hadn't seemed to notice Lord Worthing: his eyes were fixed on Jaq with a mixture of admiration and trepidation.

Elinor cleared her throat. "Lord Malleker? What is he doing here?"

The duchess waved her lacy fan as if she were over-heating. "That is what we *all* wish to know, my dear Mr Avely."

"Lord Malleker is my ward," said Beresford. He cast a glance at Elinor; that must be the story he and Jaq had decided upon, even though Jaq no longer was bound under Beresford's guardianship. "He is the younger son of an old friend in Devonshire. I brought him along tonight to gain a little town bronze. You see, I have introduced him to my friend Lord Worthing. I will be happy to introduce Your Grace, as well."

The duchess licked her lips, with obvious plans for issuing her own particular version of town bronze. A pity she did not know that Jaq was sometimes a seal, almost twice her age, and already quite polished.

Elinor reflected that Lord Treffler had obviously not made a lasting impression. And she really hoped that Perry beat the duchess to the chase.

She glanced over at Perry, to see he was still staring at Jaq, as if he was seeing him for the first time. A line appeared between Perry's brow, and he took an unconscious step in that direction.

However, Perry and the duchess were not the only ones who sought Jaq's side that night. Soon the beautiful selkie prince was surrounded by interested parties claiming introductions, and he was the subject of whispered speculation around the room.

Elinor was glad of it. It meant she could relax a little, knowing the eye of the ton had shifted away from her. She danced with Beresford, whirling around the floor, happy in his arms, feeling her heart lighten.

But she did not forget her other object: to find the lie that led to Lord Rapp's death. She wondered whom she should question first, and the answer came in the form of the Duke of Planx, who sought Beresford out.

The duke appeared at Beresford's elbow, much like his wife had done earlier, but with a lot less flair than the duchess. Surprisingly for one of his size, the duke moved quietly. Perhaps he was used to everyone hopping out of his way, reflected Elinor.

She examined his grace closely: he was well dressed but did not seem particularly conscious of it. He had brown eyes and hair, and he wore his usual jovial expression. His hands were clasped behind his back, and he spoke in a low friendly tone to Beresford, making the obligatory remarks.

Elinor found him a strange contradiction: seemingly cheerful and unremarkable except for his size, yet one who had made a ruthless bet to win the house of Lord Rapp.

She strained to listen to the conversation. The duke tilted his head in Jaq's direction (as so many others were doing) and spoke with a false note of cheer.

"A ward of yours, I hear, this Lord Malleker?"

Beresford glanced over. "Not officially. Lord Malleker is the younger son of an old friend in Devon." He repeated his story.

"Haven't heard of the Mallekers," remarked the duke.

Elinor tensed, but Beresford smiled. "Oh, no, they keep to themselves."

"I wish he would keep to himself," said the duke quietly, his cheerful tone slipping, and his eyes fixing on Jaq with a frown.

Elinor turned to see the Duchess of Planx clinging to Jaq's arm and fluttering her fan before her lace-adorned bosom. Jaq smiled down in appreciation.

They made a striking couple.

Beresford cleared his throat. "I can have a word in Lord Malleker's ear if you like, Your Grace."

The duke nodded, his eyes now on his wife.

Elinor made a startling realisation: the duke was in love.

She did not know why it was startling. Of course, the duchess was very attractive, and the duke must have married her because he loved her. Only, Elinor had always thought it was somehow a marriage of convenience. And for the duchess, it was. But the duke's eyes were pained as they rested on her vibrant face, and he looked away, pressing his lips together.

As he did so, he saw Elinor watching him. "Miss Avely. Happy to see you back in London."

"I thank you, Your Grace," said Elinor, blushing slightly. It was in the duke's own garden that her disgrace had unfolded.

"I hear you are making friends in high places," the duke added, smiling with encouragement. Elinor made another startling discovery: that the duke could be quite attractive when smiling at her with his full attention. And she remembered suddenly that the duke was a Musor like herself: the king's Healor, no less. She noticed he had a rose quartz nestled in his neckcloth and wondered if that was the Talisman Stone of the Healors.

"Oh," Elinor stuttered. "Indeed. I have been lucky enough to attend their royal highnesses."

Beresford cut in. "Yes, Miss Avely is climbing high now: she does not even need me."

"No, indeed, women only pretend to need us, don't they?" said the duke, but his joke was undercut by a note of bitterness. He seemed to hear it himself and laughed with a return of his jovial smile. "Did you enjoy meeting our king, Miss Avely?"

Elinor considered her reply, as this was an opportunity to gauge the duke's political leanings in the matter of vampiri. "King George seems a wise and gentle man," she offered. "Yet very cautious when it comes to certain *little things*."

The duke raised his brows at Elinor's coded reference to vampiri. He nodded slowly. "Yes, and hence we must all be cautious too. Though I wish, for his own sake, that the king would reconsider his position."

Elinor dipped her head in agreement. The king's

own health was at risk from his refusal to countenance the vampiri. Or was the duke railing against the Edicts for some other reason? Elinor opened her inner senses wide, belatedly trying for Truth Discernment.

Beresford coughed. "Of course, we all respect the king's edicts."

Elinor saw that Beresford was frowning at her, but this was too good an opportunity to miss. She sought out words while maintaining the Discernment. "Your Grace, I am still trying to determine what is proper or not in regards to the *little things*. Perhaps you can help me? Is it true you were entertaining such little things in your library?"

She fixed her eyes on the duke's face with entreaty.

Beresford's brows shot up in consternation, but the duke smiled leniently. "Yes, but please do not follow my example, Miss Avely. I was betrayed into an impropriety by my fondness for my wife."

Elinor blinked at him. It sounded as if he were speaking the truth, though she could not be certain. "The duchess?"

The duke lowered his voice. "I allowed her to have a little salon with the vampiri. It was in breach of the rules: harmless, I thought. Of course, it shall not happen again, as much as my wife may beg me."

The truth again. Elinor turned once more to stare at the duchess, who was still laughing up at Jaq. So her grace had begged her husband to include her in the Musor secrets.

No doubt, the duke had found it hard to resist her appeals, aware of something he possessed that these younger gentlemen did not: a Musor Gift. And harmless it may have been if Lord Rapp had not insisted on exposing the indiscretion and the breach of the Vampiri Edicts.

Still, it hardly seemed enough to murder poor Lord Rapp for it – unless the salon had been less innocent than it sounded.

Elinor turned back to the duke. "Your Grace, are you much concerned with the plight of the vampiri?"

Beresford interrupted, grasping her elbow. "Elinor, I see your mother is looking for you; perhaps you should go to her." And he gave her a tiny shove in that direction.

Elinor turned to frown direfully at her fiancé. What a high-handed dismissal! Was Beresford afraid she was going to overstep the mark? Feeling more than a little cross, Elinor curtsied and left, after one very speaking glance.

The next half-hour passed in a blur of dancing and gossip, for in fact, Elinor was a little Bemused from her attempt at Truth Discerning. Such a shame it was not as easy as jewel divining! It had not appeared to her that the duke was lying, but if she were entirely honest with herself, she would not rest her life upon it.

Lord Olliot, the court Heightenor, was at the ball too and petitioned Elinor for a dance. Elinor agreed, eager to test him as well. However, it was almost impossible to concentrate in the ebb and swirl of the dance, so she allowed him to fetch her a drink afterwards.

Lord Olliot was more reticent – or more cautious – than the duke, and he admonished Elinor for raising the subject of vampiri in a public place. His concern appeared genuine, both in his voice and his frowning blue eyes.

Elinor protested. "No one can hear us over the music, my lord, and I am so glad of the opportunity to talk to another Musor at last. I am curious as to whether any others defend the rights of the vampiri."

Lord Olliot shook his head slightly. "If they do, they would be wise to keep their opinions quiet, Miss Avely, as I beg you to do also. The events in France are still too recent for us to relax our guard. I do not think you realise how threatening Musor magic and the vampiri can appear to the Mundanes." He lowered his voice as he spoke and glanced around anxiously at the teeming ballroom.

It was true Elinor had been accustomed to her Gift since she was nine, so perhaps it had become common-place for her. And she also had a more lenient view of people's differences. She glanced over Lord Olliot's shoulder to see Perry leaning moodily against a wall. Yet, it was true that differences could also be dangerous if people took them amiss.

Lord Olliot smiled and waved a thin hand, his citrine ring glittering. "Though we may not talk of it, I could demonstrate a Heightening spell for you, Miss Avely."

As his lordship spoke, the music seemed to swell in Elinor's ears, becoming more heady and vibrant. She raised her brows. "How delightful, my lord."

Lord Olliot smiled smugly. "Forgive me for showing off, but it is nice to have a new face in the royal court."

Elinor marvelled at the play of the music. But Lord Olliot refused to talk any more of magic, kissed her hand lingeringly, and went off to talk to the host. Elinor surreptitiously wiped her hand, staring after him. This Truth Discernment lark was harder than she first thought. Soon afterwards, she went to dance with Perry, if only to stop him from glowering at the floor or frowning at Jaq.

After a while, Beresford returned to her side. Before

Elinor could even say a word, he apologised most humbly for sending her off.

"Well!" she said crossly, forgetting her resolution to show only an affectionate face to him in public. "As you should be sorry! I did not say anything too bad, and I discovered a very salient fact: that the duchess was involved that night. I know, for I was Truth Discerning!"

"I know you were," said Beresford grimly. "Your eyes went all vague, and you started blinking like an owl."

Elinor drew herself up. "I did not!"

"It was quite apparent," said Beresford. "What if the duke is the murderer? You will set him onto you next!"

"I believe he is too kind to be a murderer." Elinor remembered the anguished look on the duke's face as he watched his errant wife.

"Well," said Beresford, pulling Elinor into an alcove. "I did ask him about the bet with Lord Rapp."

"Oh?" Elinor forgot her chagrin in curiosity. "What did he say?"

"He claimed he made the bet to lose it. He was trying to let Lord Rapp regain some of his losses, and he knew that the vampiri were in the library. However, when they arrived, the vampiri were too quick to disappear."

"How curious," said Elinor. "Did you believe him?"

"I'm not certain," said Beresford thoughtfully. "It is a convenient story. He says he won't claim Rapp's house."

"Well! If I had been there, I would have been able to tell you if the duke was lying! It is abominable that you sent me off like that!"

"Elinor, I want you to be careful." Beresford drew her into his arms and petitioned for a kiss, which she reluctantly gave him. "Besides, this evening was meant to re-establish you in society, not put you in the path of a murderer."

Elinor sighed. "Very well. Then you must dance with me again."

"Only if you have forgiven me."

"Of course." She took his arm, smiling up at him, unable to feel angry with him for long.

Dancing, Elinor ignored the melee around Jaq, Perry's withdrawn look, and the duchess's flirtatious siege of the selkie. For the moment, all was well in her world again. The only thing that marred her enjoyment was the fact that Aldreda, her dear friend, was not able to be present as well.

17

IN WHICH ALDREDA ATTENDS
A ROOST REVEL

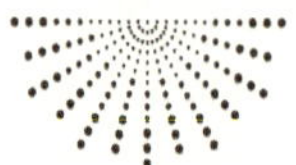

Aldreda

*A*ldreda put the time to good use while Elinor was out. After all, it was advantageous being able to fly, and the brimming night of London begged for exploration. It was better if she did not have Pags to accompany her, she told herself – Pags would simply distract her and possibly insist on another dance lesson.

After some searching, Aldreda located the Rapp residence. She flew around the attic, but she could see no sign of life. The windows were all locked, and no one responded to her tapping, which was probably just as well, as she had no clothes with her. She did not want to follow Pags's precedent and announce herself naked.

Giving up on Tildenhall for the moment, Aldreda followed the throb of magic again to the Helicons and saw the prince once more in a languid stupor. This time, however, there was no sign of Pags indulging in barbaric behaviour.

Thoughtful, Aldreda then flew to the palace to spy on the king. But there was nothing to see; His Majesty was only occupied in a cosy family scene with Queen Charlotte and their younger daughters, tucked away in their private quarters. No aura of magic drifted from them, and they looked the picture of innocence.

Despondent, Aldreda eventually flew home again. She might as well put the finishing touches on her gown instead. It was nothing to do with the hope that Pags might turn up at her bedroom window again. But only Samuel came to keep her company.

Elinor returned in the very early hours, with news of her successful appearance at the Yannow ball and the information that the Duchess of Planx had attended the suspicious vampiri salon in the ducal library.

"Furthermore," announced Elinor, "I have a plan." She proceeded to outline her theory that Truth Discernment would uncover the killer.

Aldreda had to admit it was a possible avenue of investigation, but, like Beresford, she was reluctant for Elinor to pursue it.

"At least practice a little more before interrogating any suspects," Aldreda begged. "I can tell when you are Truth Discerning – your eyes become wide and unfocused, and you tilt your head as if listening. We don't want anyone to guess what you are doing."

"Hmph," said Elinor. "Are you suggesting I look like an owl, perchance?"

Aldreda raised her brows. "Well, yes, that is a good description."

Elinor hmphed again. "Very well, I shall ask Mother how to do it properly, and I will practice." She yawned. "Now, I must sleep – as must you. It is past dawn."

Aldreda slept long but fitfully through the day. When

she awoke, it was with a sense of excitement. Tonight was the Roost Revel!

She carefully dressed in the deep red silk gown, which looked lovely against her white skin and black hair. She even had a beautiful pair of red velvet slippers to match.

Just as Aldreda was perched on the human dressing table, arranging her hair, Elinor came into the room. Elinor also looked lovely, her pale green gown suiting her honey-blonde hair. She, too, had a glow of excitement to her cheeks.

"Almacks tonight!" said Elinor. "I'm still exhausted from the Yannows. Yet I am intrigued that your Roost Revel is at the same address as the Willis's rooms."

"We will be in the ceiling, dancing right above you," said Aldreda, artfully pulling a few more black curls to lay upon her cheek. "There, do I look respectable?"

"You look stunning, as you very well know," said Elinor. "It is lucky my voucher has been restored, thanks to the conniving of Lady Beresford. Otherwise, I would not be able to escort you there." She let out a sigh of relief. "I am glad, for James's sake, that I am no longer tainted by scandal."

"Speaking of scandalous, how is Perry after his drunken night about town the other night?"

Elinor grinned. "Still a bit subdued after his foray into mermaid tears. Also, to make matters worse, Jaq caused quite a stir last night with his introduction to polite society. The Duchess of Planx wanted to know all about him. It is to be expected: a handsome, dark-haired, mysterious stranger suddenly in London. All the girls were aflutter, and probably a few of the gentlemen too."

"I imagine they were," said Aldreda dourly. It was vastly irritating.

"Jaq obtained a voucher to Almacks for tonight as

well," said Elinor. "So, you will see firsthand how many faint at the sight of him."

"I am sure some will prefer Perry's blond good looks," said Aldreda. "Perhaps there will even be a pretty girl to distract him from Jaq's charms."

"What about you?" asked Elinor. "The Dukel of Demontaine looked rather attractive in his new attire."

"That was merely the effect of good tailoring," said Aldreda. "Pags is still wild underneath."

Elinor raised her brows but did not comment.

Aldreda changed the subject. "Did you ask your mother how to practice Truth Discernment?"

Elinor frowned. "Yes. She was most unhelpful at first, but I convinced her to give me a lesson. Apparently, it helps to listen from the left ear only. I would never have thought of that."

"I believe you were doing that intuitively," remarked Aldreda. "You tilt your head to the right when you try it."

Elinor sniffed. "Well, I practiced with Perry to try to be more discreet." Then she giggled. "I asked him if he was taken with Jaq, but of course, I already knew his answer was a lie."

It was Aldreda's turn to sniff. "Don't encourage him. Especially given English laws are not very accepting of such liaisons; you must think of his safety."

Elinor sighed. "Yet on Skerry, it is a different story. And Perry has always loved the sea."

Aldreda shook her head but did not argue. Elinor was prone to be lenient towards selkies; she did not have Aldreda's first-hand experience of how deceitful they could be.

Soon they descended and piled into the Beresford crested carriage. It was crowded, with Mrs Avely, Perry, and Lady Beresford seated with Elinor. Beresford said he would walk. "To King's Street," he instructed the driver, and the carriage rumbled off.

Aldreda was tingling with anticipation. Her first ball in eighty-five years! She was concerned she would not remember the dances Pags had taught her or unknowingly breach some new etiquette. She was hiding once more in Elinor's reticule, so it was difficult to determine what to do, keeping in mind the new edicts that prevented any display of vampiri in polite company, even among Musors.

"I shall take you into Almacks with us," whispered Elinor. "Then we will see where you must go."

"Egad," said Perry. "Are you trying to land us in trouble? No bat antics, Aldreda, I beg of you. We have only just recovered our reputation."

From her peek hole, Aldreda could see Elinor frowning at him. "You watch your own behaviour, brother, instead of criticising ours. And I hope you are carrying that spare pair of vampiri clothes if your sensibilities are so delicate."

Perry scowled and turned away.

The rooms were buzzing with chatter and music. Aldreda listened as Elinor made her greetings to Lady Sefton, one of the patronesses, and chatted with another young woman, Lady Margaret Reeves, a good friend of Elinor's.

Soon, however, Elinor made her excuses for some fresh air and found a balcony on the side of the house. Aldreda's reticule opened, and Elinor helped her out onto the balcony rail, shielding her from sight.

Aldreda brushed down her red gown, her heart beating a little faster than she would have liked. Perhaps it was from feeding on Elinor's wrist that evening when the young woman was so excited herself.

"What now?" Elinor asked. "How are you to gain entrance? I cannot see anything except a ceiling up there. Yet this balcony has a black and white ribbon. I thought that might indicate vampiri admittance."

A cough from the shadows heralded the arrival of Pags. Aldreda turned to see him immaculately clad in evening wear, his face freshly shaved. However, his golden eyes still gleamed with a rather uncivilised appreciation of Aldreda's red silk dress.

"Good evening, my lord dukel." Aldreda dropped a deep curtsy, lowering her eyes modestly. It was nice to have some male attention, even if she was a confirmed spinster. "Do you know the way upward?"

Pags bowed and produced two small pieces of card. "These vouchers are cast with small Travelling spells. It is enough to transport us to the Revel."

Aldreda took one gratefully; Travel vouchers were a luxury, though, of course, it was easier to make a small vampiri Travel than a large human, so the cost to the Musor would not have been so great. She turned to smile at Elinor. "Enjoy your evening. Shall we meet back here at midnight, when the rooms close?"

Elinor nodded and watched avidly as Aldreda breathed on the card and whispered the words written there.

Aldreda looked up and winked as she felt the sudden whoosh that indicated she was vanishing from sight. Pleased, she reappeared twenty feet overhead in the ceiling, with Pags by her side.

She drew in a deep breath.

The scene that met her eyes was similar to that below, except in miniature. About fifty vampiri – almost the entire London population of aristocratic companions – stood talking in groups, around a room that was sparsely but elegantly furnished with Vember pieces. Much of the space was cleared for dancing, where ten couples now turned and dipped. Small tables lined the left walls, with plates of human food and even some vital-punch.

"Here we are," said Pags from her side. "I have to confess to a slight feeling of nerves."

Aldreda turned. "You, nervous? I can scarcely believe it. You have nothing to worry about. Your arrogance and title will gain you acceptance."

Pags glinted at her. "It is not the assembled company I am apprehensive about. However, at least I do not have to face down a pesky cat here."

Before she could reply to this disconcerting remark, Lady Denier bustled forward to greet them. She was clad in a stunning green gown that complemented her bronze skin, and subtly announced her high status. "Miss Zooth! So glad you could attend! And my lord dukel! Allow me to introduce you to everyone. We are so pleased to have new faces among us."

The next half hour was a whirl of introductions and examining looks. Aldreda tried to act with as much dignity and charm as possible, aware that it was crucial to make a good first impression. Not that she need worry too much, associated as she was with the Dukel of Demontaine. That practically guaranteed her success. However, they were soon separated, and Aldreda had to make her own way through the milieu.

About a quarter of the vampiri present were from Paris, refugees from the Troubles. The others were Londoners, and it was soon explained to Aldreda that the London population had never been high, for reasons unknown. France was where the vampiri had flourished, along with their Musors – but it had all ended in tragedy.

"We were right to keep things quiet here," said one

Viscountel Yannow, another dark-skinned vampiri who had come to England from the West Indies, by way of France. "Now the laws enforce the secrecy, but it is for the best." He gave Aldreda a charming smile. "You are safe here, Miss Zooth."

"When were the Vampiri Edicts passed?" asked Aldreda.

"Fifteen years ago," replied the viscountel. "When King George realised what was happening in France, he tried to prevent a similar trajectory here and ensured that Musors and vampiri stayed hidden."

Aldreda looked around at the half-empty ballroom. "Is it possible there are more vampiri in England, who simply keep to themselves? Lordel Tildenhall, I hear, is missing tonight."

The Viscountel Yannow's black eyes sharpened on her. "Lordel Tildenhall, I fear, is not simply hiding away at home."

"What can you mean?"

"Tildenhall himself discovered the body, or so I heard." The other vampiri looked away. "The shock may have sent him wild, or perhaps he is afraid." Then the viscountel caught himself and shook his head. "Yet, this talk is not suited for a lady. Please, may I be honoured to have the next dance, Miss Zooth?" He held out a friendly hand and smiled.

Aldreda inclined her head graciously and accepted his escort onto the floor. It would not do to pursue the subject of Tildenhall too closely, though that was an interesting bit of news. She gave herself up to the enjoyment of the dance, which thankfully was very similar to the cotillion Pags had taught her. She repressed a passing wish that it was Pags dancing with her instead and allowed herself to enjoy

Viscountel Yannow's amicable smiles and compliments.

At the end of the set, nonetheless, she found Pags at her elbow.

"Miss Zooth, that should have been my dance," said Pags. He put his arm out peremptorily. The viscountel relinquished her with a bow.

Aldreda took Pags's arm, but she shook her head. "I am not certain I will know the next dance."

They listened as the La Boulanger was called.

"I know it," he said. "I can lead you through it."

"We have more important things to do, Your Gracel."

He sighed petulantly. "Very well. A drink?"

Pags led her to the refreshments. He poured himself a liberal glass of vital-punch and a small glass of champagne for her.

Aldreda accepted the drink. "Have you discovered anything about Lordel Tildenhall?"

"My 'cousin', you mean?" Pags took a long gulp of punch, the red liquid swirling. "No, though I did receive a frightened look from at least one vampiri. I think some might know more than they are saying."

"Perhaps it is enough that they know he is missing. The Viscountel Yannow told me that Tildenhall found Lord Rapp's body. Yannow gave it as his opinion that Tildenhall has gone mad with grief."

Pags frowned. "It is possible. Even so, Tildenhall might have seen or heard something that would be useful in understanding Lord Rapp's death."

Aldreda looked around at the Revel, which was now a little busier with vampiri. "I wonder how Elinor is doing down below."

"You can see for yourself," said Pags. "There are handy viewing apertures above the chandelier."

Aldreda admitted she would like to see, so Pags escorted her to the right side of the ballroom, which was, in fact, the centreline for the room below. The viewing platform was cleverly constructed, hidden behind a candelabrum. Any human eyes glancing their way would not see past the bright flickering flames, yet small gaps allowed Pags and Aldreda a clear view of the ballroom below. When Aldreda put her eye to one, she could see the hectic, human scene of Almacks below.

It was far more rollicking than the vampiri Revel. People crammed together at the room's edges, and a dance of many was underway: the same quadrille that the vampiri mirrored above.

Aldreda soon made out the Duke of Planx. His large personage was stationed by the food table. At the other end of the ballroom was his lady wife, the duchess, flirting with some young gentleman. Elinor had informed Aldreda that was the lay of the land.

It took longer to find Elinor's blonde head, hidden as it was by a crowd of people. She was sitting by the wall, with her friend Margaret by her side, and several others claiming her attention. Obviously, Elinor had been fully reinstated. Those who had snubbed her before probably now claimed to have believed in her innocence all along.

Aldreda hoped Elinor was too clever to turn those people away. For Beresford's sake, if nothing else, she should graciously accept her new rise in status, ignoring the falsity which lay behind it. And, Aldreda prayed, Elinor wasn't Truth Discerning for a murderer, as she had threatened to do.

At least, from what Aldreda could see, Elinor's head wasn't tilted to the right, nor was she blinking like an owl. Aldreda searched a little further and saw Perry in a small crowd of people, apparently well accepted too.

In fact, as Aldreda sharpened her gaze, she saw Perry was flirting desperately with a pretty, golden-haired girl, giving his best lopsided smile and pinning his big hazel eyes upon her in admiration.

Even better. It was about time Perry found himself a nice girl and forgot about a certain dangerously handsome selkie. Even a strapping stablehand would be preferable if it came to that.

Then, to Aldreda's dismay, she saw Jaq seated on the other side of the blonde girl. Jaq's dark head was bent in interest towards her, and his black eyes appeared to be full of some unfathomable mystery. Aldreda was not surprised when, at the start of the next dance, the young lady accepted his escort onto the floor. Perhaps it was merely that her golden hair would look to advantage next to Jaq's black, as opposed to the uniformity of dancing with Perry.

Perry watched them go, keeping his countenance. Only his eyes hinted at the scowl that threatened.

Aldreda sighed.

"All well?" enquired Pags.

She nodded, turning away from her viewing point. She wasn't going to share her concerns with Pags.

"You worry yourself overly much about your humans."

"I rely upon them," pointed out Aldreda.

"Too much," said Pags. "You should wean yourself off Musor blood."

Aldreda raised her brows at the vulgar turn of the conversation. However, it was an opportunity to chastise Pags in return. "What do you suggest? That I become wild and hungry like you? I saw the way you were looking at the Countess of Beresford the other night."

Pags shrugged. "That was merely the effect of the tears."

"You should find a Musor and become civilised again."

"You do not think I appear civilised enough?" Pags swept a hand down his smartly tailored person. "Why, Miss Zooth, you wound me. After all this effort I made, especially for you."

Aldreda shook her head dismissively. It certainly was not only for her. However, before she could retort, she was distracted by the duchessel, Lady Denier, suddenly at her elbow.

"My lord dukel," said her gracel, her voice low with a strange air of import. "I have news that will interest you."

18

IN WHICH ITEMS OF
CLOTHING ARE LACKING

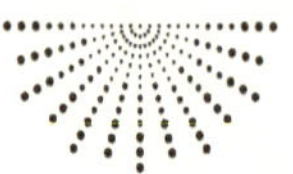

Aldreda

*P*ags and Aldreda turned as one. "Yes?" asked Pags, in his best lordly manner.

"I can take you to your cousin, Lordel Tildenhall."

Pags raised his brows. "Tildenhall is here?"

Lady Denier leaned forward, a light of excitement in her eyes. "Not in this room. He waits below in the back gardens."

Aldreda felt a rush of relief. Tildenhall was not dead, then, or captive. "That is wonderful," she said. "How did you find him?"

"He heard the Dukel of Demontaine was making enquiries," replied her grace. "He seems to know your name and is eager to claim the connection. However," she lowered her gaze, "I am afraid he is not in a fit state for company."

"If he is in the gardens now, I wish to speak to him immediately," said Pags. "I am able to withstand a certain amount of indecency." He flashed a laughing look at Aldreda, then his gaze sobered. "Will you escort me below, Your Gracel?"

The duchessel rose a hand to her breast. "Oh, I cannot abandon the Revel. I can give you another Travel voucher back down to the human ballroom. You will have to make your own way from there to the gardens."

"May I request one, too?" put in Aldreda.

Pags interrupted before Lady Denier could answer. "That will not be necessary," he said. "I will see my cousin alone, Miss Zooth. Especially if Tildenhall is indecent."

Aldreda bridled at the irony of this order. But she dared not object in front of the duchessel. She bowed her head meekly and seethed as Pags stalked off to the balcony with his token.

She looked around the room. Within minutes she had stationed herself next to the sturdy Viscountel Yannow and wrangled his spare token from him, claiming a headache and a dire need to return to her carriage. Gripping it between her fingers, Aldreda hurried to the balcony, hoping she would not be too late to hear the import of the meeting between Pags and Tildenhall.

When she uttered the words for Travel, she found herself on the balcony below where Elinor had shielded her. It was at the side of the house, however. Grimacing to herself, Aldreda slipped behind the curtain and stripped off her beautiful red gown. She folded it quickly and neatly, placing it next to Pags's own pile of clothes. What was he thinking, to meet Tildenhall stark naked? Who knew who might be waiting and watching from the shadows?

Well, she, for one, would be. Aldreda shivered into her bat form and crept to the edge of the balcony. Then she winged her way up and around the building.

The back gardens were not large. Hiding in the branches of a poplar, she soon saw the movement of small figures by a rosemary hedge. Straining her ears, she heard the faint murmur of lowered vampiri voices. Certainly, those deep tones were Pags's.

Quietly Aldreda flew down to hang from the other side of the rosemary hedge.

Staying as a bat, she peered through the thick leaves, wrinkling her nose against the strong scent of the herb.

Pags stood in full view, completely naked, standing with as much ease and arrogance as if he were clad in royal garb. Aldreda did not allow her eyes to linger in disapprobation. She turned her gaze quickly to Tildenhall.

The other vampiri, despite the duchessel's warning, was at least clad in a long cloak and cast a much more respectable appearance than Pags. No doubt, underneath, he was bare, but the brown cloth went to Tildenhall's ankles and came up around his throat. Aldreda could not see his face but could hear his voice, low and earnest. Not mad with grief, then.

He was speaking now. "When I heard you were in England, I was so relieved, my lord dukel. I have heard tell of you – that you dealt with the French Quotidians firsthand. Would you recognise any if you saw them in London?"

Aldreda tilted her head, straining to hear Pags's reply, for this was exactly the concern she had raised.

"I have not seen any," said Pags.

"How certain can you be?"

Pags shrugged. "I would have noticed. They are rather engraved upon my memory."

Tildenhall turned away, and Aldreda saw his face for the first time. It was long with sensitive features, his thin brows in a deep frown. A gentleman's face, just as Lady Denier had said.

Tildenhall sighed. "Did you know Lord Rapp was the king's Discernor?"

"Yes," replied Pags, and waited. His eyes shot to the rosemary hedge, and Aldreda resisted the urge to fidget. Surely Pags had not heard her approach?

Tildenhall continued slowly. "Lord Rapp spent some time in the royal court. I have come to believe the king is not what he seems. His Majesty claims he wants to protect the Musors and the Vampiri as his reason for these restrictive laws. However, I suspect that the political necessity matches his own inclinations."

"His own inclinations? asked Pags. "Are you suggesting the king himself is a Quotidian?"

"Not exactly." Tildenhall swung around, revealing a flash of a long, pale body. "The king suffers greatly from the practice of Musing – he is Bemused for days after."

"But that would be Bewilderment," argued Pags. "No one can recover after days of Bemusement. Usually, it indicates irreparable damage."

Tildenhall nodded sombrely. "The Duke of Planx is the royal Healor. He must be very Gifted, to hold back the tide of Bewilderment for His Majesty. Yet the king is afraid for himself and for his children, who are also Gifted. I think he wants to repress Musor magic entirely."

Pags looked unconvinced. "And you think Lord Rapp realised this and died for it?"

"Yes." However, Tildenhall could not tell Pags much more than that. Indeed, Aldreda began to think it was only Tildenhall's personal theory, born from a disordered imagination and a grieving wish to lay blame.

Pags shrugged his shoulders, which rippled with muscles in the moonlight. Aldreda reflected that all his time as a wild bat on the moors had certainly done a lot for his physique. Then she chastised herself for being distracted.

"May I ask –" said Pags. "Did you find Lord Rapp's body?"

"No," said Tildenhall, a shudder passing through his slender frame. "The human footman, Creel, found him soon after he heard the shot. But Creel says he saw no one else."

Pags shifted, staring once more into the shadows of the rosemary bush where Aldreda hid. "Lordel Tildenhall, perhaps we can repair to somewhere more convivial? Can I take you indoors, find you some vitalpunch, where we can continue our discussion?"

"I am hungry," admitted Tildenhall. "I have only fed on horses for weeks."

"Ah, a kindred spirit," said Pags, winking at the rosemary bush. Aldreda frowned. "Well, then, I invite you to join me at Carlton House, where I can guarantee you a good feed."

Aldreda gasped in disapproval. Was Pags going to involve Tildenhall in his barbaric habit of drinking from Helicons? She could not intervene, however. Before her affronted gaze, Pags transformed into a bat, lurching into the air. The cloak around Tildenhall also collapsed, and a brown bat crawled out from underneath it. Tildenhall took off into the skies, winging his way after the dukel.

Aldreda grumbled to herself. The conversation was being taken away from her! She flew over the hedge and landed next to the cloak, sniffing at it. Yes, it smelled of horses; perhaps Pags had found a friend. Shifting into her human form, she went through the pockets but found nothing. Of course, when Tildenhall was flying, he would want his cloak to be as light as possible.

The fabric was fine and soft. Obviously, Lord Rapp had ensured his vampiri was well looked after.

Aldreda sighed and flew slowly back to the balcony. It was time to dress herself again. She wasn't going to demean herself by following those two vampiri to the Helicons. Besides, she had some dancing to do.

However, when she landed on the edge of the balcony, Aldreda found it was already occupied. Jaq and Perry were there, arguing.

"What are you playing at?" Perry's voice sounded sharp and angry above Aldreda. "You stole Miss Peaches and Cream from right under my nose!"

"She was not worthy of you." Jaq's tone was teasing. "I saved you a boring dance full of giggles and fluttering eyelashes."

"Sounds good to me," said Perry sulkily.

"My eyelashes are quite good at fluttering," said Jaq.

Aldreda peered around the curtain. Sure enough, Jaq was fluttering his long dark lashes at Perry.

"Don't be ridiculous," snapped Perry. "And choose some other conquest this time. Not the *one* girl I had my eye on. Isn't it enough for you that the rest of London's women are at your feet?"

"No."

Perry gave him a sharp look. "Well, for God's sake, learn some restraint."

"I am."

"I don't see how."

Jaq leaned in a little. "Are you drunk, Perry? Your Miss Zooth told me I must wait until you aren't drunk."

"I am not drunk," snapped Perry. "And she is not my Miss Zooth."

"Oh good," said Jaq. "May I kiss you then?"

Perry's mouth opened, and he blinked, but he did not demur. Jaq leaned forward and kissed him.

After one startled second, Perry responded, allowing their lips to meld together. His hand even came up and pulled Jaq a little closer.

It was time to intervene.

Aldreda coughed as loudly as she could. Unfortunately, it seemed both men were deaf. Luckily, she was still a bat. She flew at Jaq's head, squeaking loudly into his ear.

The two leapt apart. Jaq clutched at his head and swung around angrily. "What the hell was that?"

Aldreda hovered before him, putting as much venomous disapproval into her gaze as possible.

"I do believe it is Miss Zooth," said Perry. His tone was low and husky, and his blond hair dishevelled. He cleared his throat. "She seems to have appointed herself chaperone to me as well as my sister."

Jaq snorted. "Not much of a chaperone without her clothes," he said and twitched the curtain up. He let out a satisfied huff. "Here is her little frock. I will take that, thank you very much."

Aldreda flew at him in a fury, but she was no match for his human size. Jaq stuffed her precious red gown into his waistcoat pocket – the sacrilege! – and gave Aldreda a severe look. "You can have that back when you promise to leave us alone."

"Us?" asked Perry.

Aldreda became human and landed on the balcony. Perry raised his hand to cover his eyes, and Jaq put his hands on his hips, unfazed by her miniature, womanly form.

"Do not dally with him, Perry!" said Aldreda. "He is a selkie. Treacherous and lecherous."

"Not all selkies are treacherous," said Jaq coldly. "Do not heed her, Perry."

"You don't deny the lecherous," pointed out Aldreda sharply.

Jaq quirked his lips. "I am hot-blooded in human form; what can I say? It needn't be a bad thing."

"Not only that, you are a prince," said Aldreda. "A spoiled one, accustomed to doing as you please and having what you want."

"That is true, too," acknowledged Jaq with a grin. He patted his pocket where Aldreda's gown lay.

His grin faded when he saw Perry drop his hand, showing a deeply furrowed brow.

"Aldreda's right," said Perry slowly. "You are royalty. And you are a man."

"Neither matters!"

"You should find someone from your own class," said Aldreda. "Not to mention species."

Perry nodded. He pressed his lips together and looked away from Jaq.

The selkie's face shuttered. "Fine. Have it your way, Perry. Marry a silly female. I won't try to stop you next time." He loosened his cravat with an angry gesture. "I need a swim. I'm going to dip into the Serpentine. So you know where to find me after this stupid ball, Perry. If you want."

Perry shook his head slightly; his face still turned away.

Jaq clenched his jaw. He turned and swung his way out of the balcony. Unfortunately, he also took Aldreda's clothes with him.

Perry crumpled slightly and covered his face with both hands.

"Cursed sea mammal," said Aldreda with great feeling.

After a short while, Perry dropped his hands, though he avoided looking at Aldreda. "Miss Zooth, would you like that spare pair of clothes I have in my pocket?"

Aldreda drew herself up. "Gentleman's clothes? Certainly not." She paused, for she was in rather an exposed situation. "Do you have a handkerchief?"

"Indeed." Perry pulled it out with alacrity. He escorted Aldreda, wrapped up in the soft linen, to the carriage. Then he went to fetch Elinor and Beresford from the ballroom.

"What is wrong with Perry?" asked Elinor as Beresford handed her into the carriage. "He looks like he's eaten a snail, and he declares he is walking home. Goodness, Aldreda! Where are your clothes?" Elinor stopped, blocking the carriage door, and she stared at Aldreda in consternation.

"Jaq took them."

"Heavens! Why?"

Aldreda scowled. "Because he is a sneaky seal."

"There must be some other reason."

"He was kissing Perry. I interrupted."

"Oh." Elinor sat down with a bump, opposite from Aldreda. "They kissed, did they? At last. Why did you interrupt?"

"Perry doesn't want Jaq!"

Elinor quirked her lips. "I would say he *does*, rather."

"Not if he knows what is good for him."

Beresford had taken one look in the carriage and averted his gaze to the street. His voice could now be heard. "Miss Zooth, I know Jaq has a troubled history, but his character has improved lately." Beresford coughed. "Under my influence."

"Nonsense," snapped Aldreda. "Even two nights ago, Jaq was convincing us all to imbibe mermaid tears."

"Was he?" There was a thoughtful silence, and then Beresford's voice sounded concerned. "I acknowledge that was foolish. Jaq had an over-fondness for such libations, but I believed he had overcome it."

Elinor defended the selkie. "It was only a few drops of tears."

Aldreda twitched her handkerchief in annoyance. "Quite apart from his vices, Jaq is royalty. Too high for Perry."

"Perry can look where he likes," said Elinor loyally. Then she paused. "I suppose Jaq cannot, however. Is male – er – alliance even possible on Skerry?"

"Yes, they have different orders of union," said Beresford. "However, perhaps you should just let them have a little – er – affair, and clear it out of their systems, Miss Zooth. I'm certain you needn't worry that Jaq's intentions are serious."

"Exactly," said Aldreda, huddling into her handkerchief. "I don't want Perry hurt by a selkie."

"Perhaps I can see if Lord Worthing can distract Jaq," said Beresford. "Lord Worthing is practiced in such affairs, and I'm sure will be happy to oblige."

Elinor sighed. Lord Worthing was elegant and handsome, but he didn't have the boyish charm of Perry. "I doubt Jaq will be so easily distracted." She shivered in the cold night air. "Now – let us go home and find Aldreda some clothes."

19

IN WHICH THE RAPP RESIDENCE IS VISITED

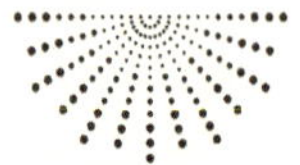

Elinor

On the way home, Elinor was fascinated to hear about the re-emergence of Tildenhall and the vampiri's warning about the king.

"The king is the murderer? Goodness, I didn't think of that!" she exclaimed.

"I personally do not believe it," said Aldreda. "It could be someone else – perhaps that Heightenor, Lord Olliot. Maybe Lord Olliot was planning to steal the sapphires. I saw him looking at them with great avarice."

"*Everyone* was looking at those sapphires with avarice," remarked Elinor. "Even you, Aldreda. If we are going to make accusations based on avarice, we should probably accuse Lady Beresford."

Beresford spoke dryly. "If there is an opportunity to accuse my mother, I am sure you will avail yourself of it."

Elinor smiled sweetly at him. They were on good

terms once more. She had much enjoyed swirling around the dance floor in his arms, under the envious gaze of all Almacks. Yet, it sounded as if Aldreda had had a more exciting evening.

Elinor turned to her friend. "Tell us more about these Quotidians."

Aldreda shrugged. "Quotidian is the name given to Mundanes who revolted against the Musor nobles. Tildenhall suggested there are some hiding in London, plotting against the king, or indeed trying to convert him."

Beresford leaned back against the seat. "I cannot see it. I rather think it is the king's own son who we should suspect of lies. From what you have told me, Prince George revels in magic, unlike his father. Perhaps the prince wants to overturn his father's laws and herald a new order."

"Yes," said Elinor thoughtfully. "The prince would want that kept secret. He is powerful enough to buy the silence of any witnesses. Perhaps Lord Rapp was not amenable to the prince's bribes and so had to be killed."

"Regardless, Prince George is equally hostile to vampiri," said Aldreda. "He has no reason to change those edicts against our fraternisation."

"So rude," said Elinor. "And so uncivilised. Don't they know they would *benefit* from your acquaintance, Aldreda?"

Aldreda huffed, but she gave Elinor a grateful look for the attempt to cheer her up. "Indeed."

"All this talk of motive is rather speculative," said Beresford. "We should rather look for opportunity. Who called on Lord Rapp that night and had a chance to kill him? The servants must have seen someone."

"Ah, yes," said Elinor eagerly. "Surely the butler or a footman must know who had the opportunity to shoot Lord Rapp. And what of this footman who discovered the body? He might have seen someone."

Aldreda was doubtful. "If the prince came calling, he would be able to buy their silence," she observed. "Or, as a Diplomacor, manage to obtain their co-operation in a more subtle way."

"Even with a murder charge hanging in the balance?" objected Elinor.

"Even then," said Beresford. "Wealth and power often provide immunity against justice, even without magic. Still, I will make enquiries tomorrow to see what I can learn."

Elinor sat up eagerly. "I will come with you," she announced. "I have been practicing Truth Discernment, and I am better at it now.

"Elinor!" said Beresford. "I told you: I forbid you from doing any such thing!"

She widened her eyes. "Forbid me, my lord?"

Beresford saw his error and tried to retract a little. "At least beg you most earnestly, my love. Especially if Discerning lies is what landed Lord Rapp in trouble."

"No one need know I am attempting it," she argued. "I admit Truth Discernment taxes me a little, but I need not speak, just observe. I won't say anything – I promise. And I won't blink like an owl." She glared around at both of them. "I cannot stay at home when there is a chance my Gift can help solve this injustice."

She stuck her chin out and defiantly crossed her arms in front of her.

"It will be daytime," said Beresford. "Miss Zooth won't be there to accompany you and temper your Bemusement."

"It matters not," insisted Elinor. "I will conduct myself carefully."

Beresford heaved a sigh. "You are being very difficult. Why won't you listen? It is dangerous. I plan to visit the Rapp residence itself tomorrow. The house may be watched."

"Why won't you listen to *me*?" she returned. "I shan't be in danger; I shall be meek and quiet and melt into the wall."

"Ha," said Beresford. "More like you will rush in where vampiri fear to tread and start asking all manner of unfortunate questions."

Elinor let out a gasp of outrage. "Well, you can't simply order me away again, my lord. I won't have it."

"Then I will simply leave without you," snapped her beloved. "I won't have you in danger, and that is that."

They glared at each other, then looked away. The sound of the rattling carriage was suddenly loud.

Aldreda cleared her throat from her handkerchief. "Perhaps you should both sleep on the matter. It may look different in the morning."

Elinor kept her eyes fixed on the window. "I am not going to abandon my duty simply because someone orders me to do so."

"Nor will I, you can be certain of that," said Beresford coldly.

Elinor remained stubbornly silent, but even when they arrived home, Beresford did not retract his dictatorial stance. Crossly, Elinor disembarked and stalked through the front door with her nose in the air and Aldreda wrapped in her hands.

"I will tend to Aldreda now," Elinor said over her shoulder to Beresford. "Goodnight, my lord."

"Goodnight," said Beresford. "I will look for Jaq."

"Very well," said Elinor.

"Very well," said Beresford and left.

"Irksome, bothersome man!" Elinor exclaimed to Aldreda.

Elinor spent a restless night feeling very out of sorts. How dare Beresford order her around like that? How dare he suggest that she was 'difficult' and asked 'unfortunate questions'? How else, pray, was one to solve a murder?

Even if the vexatious man had a point, being all high and mighty was not the way to convince her of it!

Of course, Beresford had inherited the earldom very young: he was used to everyone agreeing with everything he said. However, he must learn that his soon-to-be-wife would be an exception to that – or else he would not have a wife!

So Elinor told herself, but she was, in truth, feeling nervous and miserable as she lay in wait for him in the foyer just after dawn, fully dressed and ready to attend his expedition. She was momentarily distracted by the sight of Perry coming through the front door, still wearing his clothes from Almacks, his shoulders in a dejected stoop, and his hair dishevelled.

"Perry!" she said. "You are home late! Where have you been?"

Perry started and then sank back into his gloomy posture. "I went for a long walk, that's all. I'm fed up with this London lark. I think we should go back to Devon and be done with it."

"Oh?" Elinor remembered, suddenly, that Perry had

kissed Jaq. Obviously, it was causing her brother some consternation.

However, Perry did not want to discuss the matter. He heaved a sigh and trudged past her. Elinor saw his boots were sodden and wondered why. She did not have time to think on it long, for soon after, Beresford came into the hall, dressed for walking with a cloak thrown over his shoulders.

Elinor stepped forward tentatively. "Good morning," she said quietly.

Beresford pulled up short, then gave a deep sigh. "Good morning, Elinor. I suppose you still want to come with me?"

"Yes."

"You are a tiresome wretch," said Beresford, but the bite had gone out of his voice.

He glanced over his shoulder to see the butler following him. Elinor knew he would not make a scene in front of the servants, so it was perhaps unfair of her to confront the issue right then and there. Beresford nodded brusquely and marched past her. "Very well, then. You may walk with me."

Both triumphant and deflated, Elinor trailed after him.

As they walked to the Rapp residence, Elinor broke the silence by insisting they come up with a suitable ploy for their questions. He agreed reluctantly and extracted a promise from her that she would allow him to do the talking. Elinor sighed and nodded, and Beresford looked relieved. Then they discussed a possible ploy to broach the Rapp servants, and the tension between them gradually eased. By the time they reached the house, they were on more amicable terms.

Beresford squeezed her arm, which was now tucked into his elbow. "Ready? You keep silent, remember?"

Elinor nodded. "Yes, my dear. I will be Truth Discerning."

"Well, try not to be obvious."

Beresford knocked on the door and adopted his most quelling air of authority.

The butler who appeared was rather wan and thin, with sparse brown hair and nervously clenched hands. Elinor reflected it must have been a difficult few weeks for the Rapp servants.

The butler looked at Beresford with a frown between his pale brown eyes. "My lord, I am sorry to inform you that Lord Rapp passed away two weeks ago."

Beresford pulled himself to his rather impressive height. "I am well aware of that, my good man. I am here to collect my property."

The butler's frown deepened. "Your property, my lord? I do not recall ..."

"I loaned a book to Lord Rapp – in fact, on the very night he died. You do not recall my visit?"

Elinor was pleased to notice that she could tell that Beresford was lying. Of course, she knew that anyway (she had helped concoct the lie), but her open senses could also hear a tinny sound in his words. Perhaps it was easier if one knew someone very well – which would explain why Elinor's mother was so good at catching Elinor and Perry out.

The butler shook his head slowly. "I do not recall, my lord."

"It was very late," asserted Beresford. "Were you on duty?"

The butler swallowed. "I went to bed at midnight, my lord."

Elinor rather thought this was the truth. She gave a tiny nod to Beresford.

"Well, someone will remember me." Beresford stepped forward, insisting on entry. The butler fell back. Beresford continued, brooking no argument. "I will wait in the foyer while you look for my book. *The Eight Humours and their Application to Agricultural Yields.*"

"*Eight Humours*, my lord?" The butler became a little flustered. "Certainly, I will look."

"And while you're at it, send me the footman who was on duty that night. He might remember what Lord Rapp did with my book."

The butler froze like a pale rabbit under Beresford's penetrating stare. He wrung his hands together. "I am very sorry, my lord, but I cannot do that."

Beresford raised his brows haughtily. "Why not?"

"The footman, Creel, passed away in his sleep two nights ago."

Elinor stared aghast. The butler's words rang with sincerity and fear. Her own mind felt a little Bemused from the Discernment, but she spoke up carefully. "The footman is dead?"

The butler nodded mutely.

"Do you suspect foul play?" demanded Beresford.

The butler shook his head. Elinor frowned. Such actions were impenetrable to her Discernment. But she could see the butler looked nervous – or perhaps that was simply because he was facing down Beresford's autocratic questions and broad shoulders.

"What was the cause of death?" asked Beresford.

"An unreliable heart, we believe, my lord," replied the butler. Elinor didn't need her inner senses to see his doubt about this.

Beresford continued. "Did Creel tell you if he saw

anyone call on the night Lord Rapp died? Or indeed, after the shot was fired?"

"No, my lord," said the butler. This was the truth, thought Elinor. But it did not mean that Creel had not seen anyone. The butler backed away. "I will look for your book, my lord."

Elinor and Beresford stared at each other silently in the entrance hall. Elinor felt a little dizzy. "Dead?" she whispered.

Beresford did not say anything, but his grey eyes were hard, and he put out a hand to take hers.

At that moment, the door sounded with a loud knock. Elinor jumped, and Beresford swung around. He marched to the door, opening it before the butler could return.

On the step stood the Duchess of Planx.

She was elegantly clad for morning calls and wore a fetching bonnet of pink and mauve atop her glossy, brown ringlets. She held a bag between her hands, but when she saw Beresford, she took a tiny step backwards, her eyes widening.

"Lord Beresford?"

Beresford bowed. "Your Grace."

"What are you doing here?"

"I might ask the same of you," returned Beresford, folding his arms. Elinor was pleased to see he was giving no quarter.

The duchess gave a little laugh. "Oh, I came to see if I could be of assistance, after what happened ..." She trailed off, then rallied. "You must come to visit me, my lord; we have not spoken properly for so long! I must congratulate you on your engagement. I always hoped you would sort it out with Miss Avely." She gave Beresford a wink.

Elinor stiffened. How dare she wink at him!? Elinor cleared her throat loudly.

Beresford turned, and the duchess saw her for the first time.

"Miss Avely! You too! How extraordinary." The bright eyes narrowed. "Why are you both here, did you say, my lord?"

"Fetching a book," said Beresford. "One I loaned to Lord Rapp."

The duchess looked from one to the other, and Elinor gave Beresford an adoring glance to lend credence to the idea that they were inseparable even in collecting books.

At that opportune moment, the butler appeared again, but with empty hands. "Your Grace! I am sorry I was not here ..." He looked nervously at Beresford. "I could not find your book, my lord."

The butler did not so much as by word or expression suggest the book was entirely fictional. However, Elinor thought he might have his suspicions – and the duchess, too.

"Very well," said Beresford. "If you see it, send it to this address." He handed over a card. "Or if you think of anything that might bear upon Creel's death," he added.

The butler took the card, glancing with apprehension at the duchess.

"Whose death?" demanded her grace. "Don't you mean Lord Rapp's? That was an unfortunate affair, but there is nothing mysterious about it."

Surprisingly, these words rang with sincerity. Elinor frowned. She would rather like to pin the murder on the duchess. Unless the words were true because, for the duchess, there was no mystery? This Truth Discernment was trickier than Elinor had first thought. She was also starting to feel a little dizzy from the attempt.

Beresford turned back to the duchess. "The footman Creel is dead, which, to my mind, makes it more of a mystery."

The duchess paled, and her fingers tightened on her bag. "Rapp's footman?"

"Indeed," put in Elinor, opening her inner senses wide. "Do you know how it happened?"

The duchess drew herself up. "Excuse me?"

Beresford gave Elinor a reproving frown. "We are a little shaken by the news, and we must return home now. Come, Elinor." He put out a peremptory hand.

Elinor frowned back at him but, aware of the duchess watching, took it reluctantly. Unable to help herself, she made one last query. "Your Grace, did you happen to visit Lord Rapp before he died?"

The duchess raised her brows in astonishment. "What a question, Miss Avely! Of course, I used to visit Lord Rapp occasionally …"

Beresford wrenched Elinor's elbow. "Apologies, Your Grace, we will go now. Good day."

The duchess allowed them to pass; her eyes were speculative. Elinor tried not to look as if Beresford was dragging her.

Once in the carriage, Elinor turned furiously to him, all her anger surging back from the previous night.

"How can you haul me out of there like that! One or two little questions would not have done any harm! I would be able to hear if she was lying!"

"Of course the duchess wasn't lying! Don't be ridiculous, Elinor! You were Bemused. I was trying to remove you before you said something unpardonable."

"Unpardonable?" gasped Elinor. "Is that what you think of me?"

Beresford sat up straight against the backing. "You

almost accused the Duchess of Planx of murdering the footman!"

"Well, she might have done so! She has her husband to protect in this sordid matter! We could have found out more if you let me question her."

Beresford heaved a sigh. "Question her!"

"Why ever not? And you did the same thing with the duke – sending me off like a child!"

"Elinor, the last thing we need is to make an enemy of the duke or duchess. *Especially* if either one is a murderer!"

"I think you should trust me to know that." She sniffed. "And it seems as if you are rather too *friendly* with her grace."

"You go too far, Elinor," snapped Beresford.

"So do you, my lord. You must allow me some freedom! It is beyond everything that I must promise you not to speak!"

The carriage drive proceeded in icy silence. Beresford became a stone statue, and Elinor seethed at his high-handed conduct. But, as the wheels rumbled on, she couldn't help but feel that perhaps her Bemusement had led her to say something unfortunate. Perhaps she had been a little too obvious in her questions to the duchess. And perhaps she shouldn't have accused Beresford of being too friendly with her grace …

Just before they reached home, Elinor turned and swallowed the lump in her throat. "I'm sorry, James. Perhaps my tongue led me astray. Please forgive me."

Beresford let out a breath. "There is nothing to forgive." He paused. "You had a right to question the duchess, my love. You are right; I cannot ask you to be silent."

Elinor nodded and sought out words. "I want our union to be a partnership, James, not a dictatorship."

Beresford edged along the seat towards her. "I'm sorry, Elinor. Forgive me; I am accustomed to authority. I will try to be more fair in the future and allow you to make your own decisions."

His grey eyes were serious and apologetic. Without further ado, Elinor scrambled into his arms.

When the footman opened the carriage door, they were most improperly engaged.

20

IN WHICH ELINOR RECIEVES A SPECIAL INVITATION

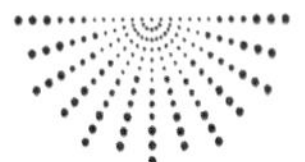

Elinor

*B*eresford left Elinor at home after kissing her one last time and leaving to make some enquiries among his more secretive connections.

Elinor went up to her room, her heart relieved. Now they were reconciled, she could turn her mind to the problem of Creel's death. This, without doubt, meant Lord Rapp had indeed been murdered by someone who visited that night. And the one person who had known it now lay dead.

Who could it be? The duchess's presence there today was suspicious, despite what Beresford might say, or the inconclusive nature of Elinor's Truth Discernment. Was the duchess there to cover up the evidence of Creel's demise? Would anyone have even known or cared had Beresford not enquired? It was a sad truth that servants rated very little attention, and no one would have thought to mention it had Beresford not asked.

Elinor reflected that the duchess seemed quite at home at the Rapp residence – she or her husband could have administered poison to the footman themselves.

Or – more likely – the duke could have sent a vampiri to do it, and perhaps the duchess suspected it. The ducal vampiri companion was the duchessel, Lady Denier. Would Lady Denier do as the Duke of Planx asked, to protect them both from the consequences of breaking the Vampiri Edicts?

Or could Lady Denier have done it herself, for her own reasons? Perhaps she was the one who had hefted a gun at Lord Rapp – Aldreda had said a vampiri had the strength to do so; it was just a little difficult to pull the trigger. Yet perhaps Lady Denier had managed it, in order to stop Lord Rapp from intruding upon her salons.

Elinor sighed. That was ridiculous. And if it could be Lady Denier, it could equally well be Lordel Tildenhall or any number of vampiri. What was missing was a motive. The sanctity of salons was an insufficient reason for killing Lord Rapp.

But then, Lady Denier had much to lose, as the highest-placed vampiri in London. Perhaps if she was found to be breaking the Vampiri Edicts, she would lose her powerful position, so hard won. Elinor suddenly recalled what the king had said: any vampiri found in breach of the Edicts was blacklisted and barred from being a Musor companion at all.

In fact, Elinor suddenly realised, it was indeed Lady Denier who had the most to lose from the fallout of the duke's bet. Being caught socialising with the duchess – a Mundane no less – would mean Lady Denier would go from the highest-ranking vampiri in England to a position even lower than she had occupied before. Her position was already unusual enough, as a dressmaker turned ducal, and she would be well aware that she could ill afford to break the king's edicts.

Elinor marched down to the drawing room to announce her theory to Mother, Perry, and Lady Beresford.

When she arrived there, however, she found something that quite superseded everything else.

A letter had arrived from the king.

It had just been delivered by a very handsomely clad footman, seen by Perry (who was unaccountably lurking by the front windows and watching the street). The letter was stamped with the royal seal, and it contained a flowery request. Or perhaps a demand.

His Royal Highness, King George, humbly requests Miss Elinor Avely to become Royal Discernor in Training, to be appointed as a future Discernor Advisor to the King. An honoured and necessary position, we would be most grateful if Miss Avely would consider this Illustrious Appointment.

Miss Avely is invited to call on the Royal Palace for Luncheon at noon on Saturday to discuss the matter and answer any questions she may have, as well as arrange for Suitable Recompense for placing her gift in Royal Service.

Yours sincerely,

His Majesty, etc

George

Elinor read it over three times before she could fully comprehend its contents. A royal advisor! Suitable recompense! What on earth would that be?

She looked up and waved the thick piece of paper in the air jubilantly. "I'm to become a duchess!"

"A duchess?" Perry was still at his station by the window. "Are you certain?"

"Well, not *certain*. This letter mentions 'Suitable Recompense for Royal Service'. That's a duchy, isn't it?"

Perry looked doubtful. "A barony, more like, or simply lots of money."

Elinor paced around the drawing room, both intrigued and apprehensive. "Lots of money would be good, too. What should I do, Perry? I do not really need to be a duchess, as I will soon be a countess. However, I would like to meet the other Musors who advise the king. Imagine being part of the secret Royal circle of Musors! I would have access to the Sapphire Library and the Moria Pearls. I could help safeguard them."

Yet – Tildenhall had warned them against the royal court: that the king himself was playing a double game. Elinor chewed on her lip, torn between curiosity and fear.

Perry frowned, letting the curtain fall once more. "May I read the letter?"

Elinor gave him the paper and twisted her hands together.

Perry read frowningly. "I do wonder why the king is so quick to extend such an honour to you," he observed with brotherly scepticism. "Surely, there are other Discernors around who would warrant the position first?"

Elinor frowned at him. "Perhaps the king was impressed by my jewel divining. I *am* rather good at it, you know." A new thought occurred to her. "Maybe the king will give me a Talisman Stone; he must have some more."

At that moment, Mrs Avely came into the room, and

Elinor showed her the invitation too. As she might have predicted, her mother was against the whole notion.

"You must not accept," Mrs Avely decreed. "I will accept instead."

Elinor gaped at her mother. "You?"

"You?" stuttered Perry.

"Why not?" Mrs Avely looked around at them both, her chin up. "I am a Discernor as well, and older and wiser than you, and more able to deal with the politics of a royal court."

Elinor drew in an outraged breath. "Only because you are so practiced at hiding and deceiving yourself!"

"Elinor Avely! I have only withheld the truth for your own good. And now you wish to cast all caution aside and put yourself in danger." Mrs Avely put her hands on her hips.

Perry looked on with interest, his head moving from side to side as he watched the interplay. "Will there be danger in the royal court, do you think?"

"Lord Rapp was a Royal Discernor, and now he is dead," snapped Mrs Avely. "Do you want Elinor to end up the same way?"

Elinor gritted her teeth. "Well, I'm certainly not going to let *you* take on that danger, Mother. It is far better no one knows you can Discern. They already know of my Gift. I do not want to expose yours. That is what *vincit prudentia* would counsel, would it not?"

Mrs Avely was silent a moment in the face of this irrefutable argument and the recitation of her oft-repeated motto turned against her. "If you had listened to me, you wouldn't be exposed either!"

Elinor huffed. "We have found no evidence that Lord Rapp's death was related to his Discerning. It is just surmise – wild speculation, in fact."

"Y*our* wild speculation," pointed out Perry.

"I have a new theory," explained Elinor. "I think Lady Denier shot Lord Rapp so she would not be banished when he exposed her breach of the Edicts. She was entertaining the duchess, and that would be enough to have Lady Denier blacklisted as a noble companion."

Perry scoffed. "You think the little dressmaker is the murderer?"

Elinor shrugged. "Why not? She has the most to lose. And if I become Royal Discernor, I will have the opportunity to prove it."

Mrs Avely drew in her breath in a long, impatient sound. "I know the position is tempting, Elinor, but can you not see it is dangerous?"

The echo of Beresford's words was irritating. However, Elinor saw her mother was genuinely concerned, so she dropped her militant stance. "I promise I will be careful, Mother. Can I at least attend this meeting on Saturday, to find out more?" She paused and decided to concede a little. "You can come with me and Discern for lies, for I still haven't mastered the knack of it. It is more difficult than I thought."

Mrs Avely pressed her lips together. "I am reluctant to countenance the scheme at all. Why don't we see what Lord Beresford has to say on the matter?"

However, when Beresford returned that afternoon, Mrs Avely was destined to be surprised. Remembering his earlier promise – to allow Elinor her own agency – Beresford reluctantly accepted that Elinor would attend the royal luncheon. She could tell he was on the brink of forbidding it, but he managed to bite back the words just in time.

Elinor smiled at him, knowing how hard it was for him to refrain from ordering her about. She slipped her hand into his. "I shall be fine, James," she said. "Mother will come along, and she will Discern if there are any lies hiding behind the king's offer."

Beresford did not look happy, but there was nothing he could say.

Elinor claimed she was eager to be a duchess, but secretly, she was aware of a yearning to go back to Devon. The whole investigation was like grappling with a seven-headed monster – there were too many suspects. Was it the Duke of Planx, killing to save his standing with the king? Was it Lord Olliot, another royal advisor plotting something treasonous? Or was it Lady Denier, killing Lord Rapp to keep her secrets safe? And that didn't even account for the notion that the king himself might be lying, or indeed the prince.

Elinor rather liked the theory that the Duchess of Planx was guilty, but try as she might, she could not quite make it fit.

She rubbed her forehead as she went upstairs to find Aldreda that evening. Worse, amid all this – and the threat of murder – her mind kept going back to the Duchess of Planx's patronising smile and the wink she had given Beresford. How dare she wink at him!

Elinor sighed. Never mind that now. She had to turn her mind to this curious invitation and how to convince Aldreda that they should accept the royal position – if only to find out what lay behind it.

IN WHICH MRS AVELY OVER-REACHES HERSELF

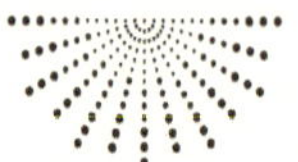

Aldreda

Aldreda awoke to find Elinor in her room and eager to babble about a royal invitation. Hearing the particulars, Aldreda felt a shiver of uneasiness run over her shoulder blades.

She leaned against the bedhead where Pags had sat. "Don't forget what Tildenhall said," said Aldreda carefully. "He suspects King George is against Musing, which would make this invitation spurious."

"Well, the only way to find out is to become closer to the court," argued Elinor. "We can ensure the Moria Pearls are protected if I am part of the inner circle. It is a good opportunity. At the very least, we must attend this Saturday luncheon."

Elinor sat on the bed, with Samuel for once in her lap as a contented bundle. Her hazel eyes were wide and pleading.

Aldreda sighed. "I suppose it gives us an opportunity to find out more."

Elinor beamed. "My thoughts exactly. We can ask a few more questions. And try a little more of that tea." Her face fell. "By the way – I have some bad news."

"What is it?" Aldreda felt a sudden stab of anxiety about Pags. Of course, she told herself, the dukel was well able to look after himself.

"Lord Rapp's footman is dead." A guilty expression crossed Elinor's face. "I should have told you at once, instead of being taken up with this royal position."

Aldreda felt another frisson of alarm. "The footman who might have known who visited on the night of the murder?"

"Yes, by poison, we suspect." Elinor told of her expedition that morning with Beresford and her new theory that it was Lady Denier who administered the poison. "Either on instruction from the Duke of Planx, or to cover her own tracks. Do you really think it is possible a vampiri can shoot a gun, Aldreda?"

Aldreda pursed her lips. "Yes, but you are forgetting something. Why would Lady Denier need to poison the footman? He would not have known if she visited Lord Rapp. She could have slipped in quite unseen."

"Oh! Of course, you are right!" Elinor sighed. "How inconvenient. I thought I had worked it all out."

"Well, the murder of the footman certainly tells us that it was indeed a human caller, not vampiri, on the night of Lord Rapp's death."

"Good point. Unless Lady Denier murdered the footman to throw us off the scent?" said Elinor, hopefully.

"Unlikely."

Elinor grimaced. "I suppose so." She flopped backwards onto the bed and then leaned up on her elbows in a most unladylike pose. "We must ask the royal court if they know of the footman's death to see what they say."

"The invitation is for noon," observed Aldreda. "Difficult for me." She wondered if that was deliberate.

Elinor frowned. "Oh, yes. So impolite. However, Mother insists she attends with me this time."

"Oh?"

"She suspects danger too. She even wanted to take the position of Royal Discernor, instead of me." Elinor twisted her lips in disapproval. "As if I will let her put herself in danger."

"So, you acknowledge there *is* danger."

"Well, if there is, Mother will Discern any lies or subterfuge. So you needn't worry, Aldreda."

"Hm," said Aldreda. "Will you promise to leave the Truth Discerning to your Mother, and keep your own wits about you?"

Elinor considered a moment. "Very well. I promise."

"And I insist on coming also. I will hide in the reticule. No one need even know I am there."

"You will be exhausted," objected Elinor. Then she sighed. "However, I will be glad of your company. It will ameliorate any Bemusement I might suffer if the king puts me to the test."

The evening before the royal visit, Aldreda tried to sleep most of the night away, to save her strength for the morrow. At eleven in the morning, Elinor apologetically woke her and helped her clamber into the double-lined reticule.

Rather foggy, Aldreda didn't bother to change out of

her lacy nightdress. She was to stay hidden, after all. Furthermore, if she had to become a bat, it was easier to divest herself of a nightdress than anything else.

She fell asleep in the warm dark, despite the rattle and rumble of the carriage journey. Fortunately, Elinor bumped the reticule on her dismount, and Aldreda woke up.

Her brain was still murky with dreams – something involving Pags? – and she felt weak from the altitude of the sun. She made herself sit up cross-legged in the curve of the bag and rubbed her hands against her cheeks to wake herself.

Outside, Elinor and her mother were making their deep curtsies. Aldreda could hear the king's quiet voice through the cloth.

"I am so glad you accepted our invitation today, Miss Avely. Very pleased to meet your mother, too. Are you Gifted, Mrs Avely? Perhaps Elinor received some of her Gift from you."

Aldreda raised her brows. The king was more astute than he let on.

Mrs Avely paused for a fraction of a moment. "Oh, I have only an Insignificant Gift, Your Majesty, barely above Mundane. My daughter far surpasses my meagre allotment."

Aldreda's brows went further up. It appeared that Mrs Avely's talent for Discerning untruths meant she was also talented at lying.

The king appeared to accept her statement. "Ah, it was your husband who excelled, was it not? It must be him from whom Elinor received her distinction. The Avely family motto is *Vincit Prudentia*, is it not?"

Mrs Avely spoke stiffly. "Yes, Your Majesty."

King George continued, "*Wisdom Conquers*: an old Discernor motto, of course."

Aldreda wondered why Elinor had never mentioned the family motto before. The reason soon became clear as words tumbled out of Elinor's mouth.

"*Prudence Conquers*, Your Majesty. *That* is our family motto, not a Discernor motto, though I am sorry to disappoint you."

The queen's voice sounded amused. "The Latin word *Prudentia* can also be translated as *Wisdom*, my dear girl. Or *Discernment*."

There was a silence. Aldreda imagined Elinor's mouth falling open, and her eyes swivelling to stare at her mother with accusation. Mrs Avely said nothing, but there was an agitated rustle of fabric.

The king came to the rescue. "Ah, no doubt it was wise to disguise your husband's connection with Discernment. Mrs Avely, you did right to obfuscate the meaning of the phrase."

Inside the reticule, Aldreda bit her lip thoughtfully. So Elinor came from a long line of Discernors, did she? The royal position began to make more sense.

Queen Charlotte spoke kindly. "We are grateful for your late father's military service to the Crown with his Gift. We hope that you, as his daughter, will continue to do so with your prodigious talent."

There was another fraught silence, and Aldreda's eyes widened. Elinor's father had also served the Crown? As far as she could recall, Elinor had told her that Mr Avely had died in battle ten years ago, in an earlier war against France.

Mrs Avely spoke stiffly. "We are flattered by your interest, Your Majesty."

Elinor said nothing.

The king continued, "I was most impressed at Miss Avely's ability to divine the Sapphire Library. Unerring. Am I correct in understanding that jewel divining is the primary manifestation of your Discernment, Miss Avely?"

"Yes, Your Majesty," acknowledged Elinor, finally recovering her composure. "I am not very practiced or capable in any other form of Discernment." Except for where jam and cream might be found, thought Aldreda. Elinor continued. "I am perhaps unworthy of your honoured position."

Another voice spoke. "Your jewel divining shows such talent, however, Miss Avely."

Aldreda had not realised that Lord Olliot was there also. His voice was admiring, and from what she could tell, he was sitting quite close to Elinor.

Lord Olliot continued. "I am sure you will be able to learn other aspects quickly."

"Indeed," said the king. "You will have access to all our secret teachings in the Sapphire Library. And, of course, you will be supplied with refreshments as you pursue the contents."

Very canny. The king offered that which was most likely to bribe Elinor. It was hard to predict which was more tempting: the royal library or the royal tea.

Elinor's mother, however, was not so easily bought. "My daughter is not nobility, Your Majesty. Surely she is not fitted to be such a close member of your court."

Ah, a good move, subtly indicated. The king picked up the hint. "Of course, her station will be elevated. As Royal Discernor she will be endowed with a noble title to match the Musor title. Perhaps you fancy yourself to be a viscountess, Miss Avely?"

Aldreda could hear no response and assumed Elinor

was modestly lowering her eyelashes and nodding. Or perhaps she was giving the king an outraged stare at falling short of a duchy. It was impossible to tell.

Fortunately, Mrs Avely intervened. "Such an honour would be gratefully accepted, Your Majesty. Do tell me, are there any other Royal Discernors?"

The king paused. "No. Not anymore." He cleared his throat. "Our former Royal Discernor sadly passed away recently. That is why we are eager to find a replacement."

"Lord Rapp, I presume?" asked Mrs Avely. "Nothing untoward?"

"A sad accident, I am afraid." The king's voice was cool. "Nothing to do with his royal duties."

Aldreda would give a lot to know what Mrs Avely made of this response.

The Queen intervened, directing them all to a dining room where refreshments awaited. Aldreda was hard put to stay awake as the humans all set about eating royal meats, jellies, and something called a ruffle cake, involving copious amounts of cream, which Elinor pronounced to be amazing. However, some sixth sense woke her when she heard Elinor clear her throat in a portentous manner, and her next words were indeed controversial.

"Were Your Majesties aware that Lord Rapp's footman passed away last week?" asked Elinor loudly.

In the taut silence, a spoon tinkled on a saucer.

"Pardon me?" said the Queen. Confusion sounded in her voice. "The footman?"

"Yes," Elinor's voice was firm. "Dead in his sleep. His name was Creel, and he was on duty the night Lord Rapp died. To my mind it casts a more suspicious light on the whole matter."

The Queen spoke slowly. "You are suggesting the

footman was witness to a murder and therefore was also killed?"

Aldreda could hear nothing but imagined Elinor must have nodded. Another silence stretched.

"How do you know this?" asked Lord Olliot.

"Lord Beresford visited the Rapp residence," said Elinor, leaving out her own attendance at the event.

"Why?" queried the queen.

"To make some enquiries ..." Elinor trailed off, obviously not wanting to mention they were investigating the murder, assisted by her Truth Discernment. And no doubt she was realising that when one asked questions, questions were asked in return.

"Why did you think enquiries were necessary?" asked the king curiously. "Have you Discerned something that provokes suspicion?"

Elinor gulped. "Oh no, nothing like that." Aldreda, inside the reticule, shook her head vigorously. The last thing they needed was everyone thinking Elinor knew something vital. "Truly not. It was simply a precaution to see if it was indeed as it seemed. Beresford and I were concerned for the Moria Pearls."

When the king next spoke, Aldreda sensed Musor magic emanating from him as he tried to soothe the suspicious tension in the air with Diplomacy. "Miss Avely, I assure you, Lord Rapp's death was only a terrible accident. This footman's death must be a coincidence. And surely you are not still worried for the pearls when you yourself are being appointed to their safekeeping?"

The magic worked, or perhaps the king's logic did. Aldreda heard Elinor let out a small sigh. "Yes, Your Majesty. I do trust that you don't intend to put me in a position of danger."

"Indeed not," said the king, and again Aldreda

wondered what the silent Mrs Avely made of this. Elinor's mother so far was simply observing the conversation and drinking tea; Aldreda hoped she was at peak Truth Discernment capacity. And that Diplomacy did not interfere with it.

Elinor spoke again. "Your Majesty, I would feel safer if I might be permitted to have my vampiri companion, Miss Zooth, assist me in my royal service. Is that possible?"

"Well." King George sounded as if he were on the back-foot. "Only in the privacy of your own home, you understand, and completely alone. The Vampiri Edicts forbid open fraternisation with vampiri, even before other Musors."

Elinor protested. "It seems unfair to the vampiri, to be banished into the shadows."

Brave, foolish girl, thought Aldreda. Elinor must not stick her neck out for me. And if the king were against magic, it was better not to press him on the matter.

"It is necessary." The king's voice became pained. "For the good of the country."

"Yet oppressive," said Elinor, then added, "Your Majesty."

Aldreda held her breath.

His Majesty apparently decided to overlook Elinor's treasonous attitude. He gave a little laugh. "You sound like my son, Prince George. He argues our laws are oppressive to Musors too. We also have to stay in the shadows, Miss Avely. Sometimes great power must be wielded discreetly." He waited for that to sink in, then added more kindly, "As you will learn for yourself, as you grow in your own power. I hope you will join us in our pursuit of protecting the Musor Gifts."

"And assisting His Majesty in his decisions," said Lord

Olliot. "You should be honoured, Miss Avely, as a woman, to be granted such privilege."

Perhaps Elinor was giving him the outraged stare now. The king interceded. "Lord Olliot, if Miss Avely has finished her repast, please show her to the Sapphire Library. She can peruse a jewel or two to see if we can tempt her. And show her the Talisman Stones."

Clever again. Aldreda knew Elinor was curious about the Talisman Stones, and the king had probably noticed Elinor did not wear one. Aldreda felt the reticule lift and was glad Elinor had the wit to take it with her. Aldreda swung through the air, still cross-legged and thoughtful. It did seem odd that the king would invite an untried young woman to be his advisor; unless it was to put Elinor where he could keep an eye on her.

2 2

IN WHICH A ROPE SWINGS
TOO CLOSE

Aldreda

A door opened and shut as Elinor followed Lord Olliot. Aldreda could sense they had moved into the hallowed room of the sapphires. There was the sound of a whisk of cloth slithering through the air, and Elinor drew in a breath.

"So these are the Talisman Stones!" she exclaimed. "I didn't realise there was such a variety."

"Yes," said Lord Olliot smugly. "As a Discernor, your Talisman would be a lapis lazuli – the blue one with the golden flecks. Mine, as a Heightenor, is the citrine: the golden-yellow stones you see there."

"Beautiful," breathed Elinor. "They help counter Bemusement, I believe?"

"Yes," said Lord Olliot. "The king, you may have noticed, wears a very large agate of blue lace, which is the stone of the Diplomacors."

"Wonderful," said Elinor.

"You may pick one up," allowed Lord Olliot.

There was a silence as Elinor bent over the tray. After a few minutes, Aldreda could sense her doing a divination, though Talisman Stones were not jewels. Perhaps Elinor was interested to see if the Moria Pearls were still in the Library and how many sapphires surrounded her.

The reticule swung as Elinor turned and paused for a long moment. Did she sense something special? Aldreda sat up a little straighter in the reticule, consumed with curiosity.

"An admirable collection," said Elinor, her voice absentminded. "Could I indeed try to read a sapphire as well, Lord Olliot? I am curious to see if I am able to do it before I properly consider this honourable position."

"Certainly," said Lord Olliot. "Wait a moment, Miss Avely, while I put the Talismans away."

As he fumbled with the tray, Elinor used the opportunity to walk across the room in tentative steps, following a call known only to her. Aldreda, remembering the layout of the library, thought that they might be traversing towards the fireplace.

Elinor stopped. "Such a lovely room," she said distractedly. "As befits such treasures."

Aldreda heard the sound of a lid closing, and a key turn as Lord Olliot tended to the Talismans. At the same time, she felt the motion of Elinor bending over quickly and then straightening. The mouth of the reticule opened, and Elinor dropped something onto Aldreda's lap.

It was a black shard from the fireplace.

Aldreda held it in her own small hands, careful not to cut herself. Her eyes were very good in the dark, but it was hard to tell what she held. It was the size of a Vember wine glass stem: large enough for Aldreda, but it must have been tiny to Elinor's human eyes. It was covered in coal dust, the black smearing Aldreda's fingers. Was it possibly a broken sapphire or another jewel, if Elinor had been able to sense it?

A shattered jewel in the Sapphire Library was a curious find indeed. Aldreda carefully wrapped it in her own tiny handkerchief and placed it next to her. She hoped Elinor had the wit to wipe the coal smears from her own fingers.

Outside, Aldreda heard Lord Olliot's voice. "Here, you may choose a sapphire from this case, Miss Avely."

Elinor walked back to Lord Olliot. Soon, Aldreda felt the divination again and prayed Elinor would not over-reach herself as she read the contents of the sapphire. Even with her vampiri present, it was not wise to overdo it, especially today.

"Ah," said Elinor, after a moment. "It is a spell I have already read from the Moria Pearls: how to imbue an object with an Illusion charm."

Lord Olliot's voice took on his admiring tone. "You find it so easy to read? That must come with your Gift at Discernment."

"Why yes, I suppose it could. Are you not able to read the sapphires?"

"I can," admitted Lord Olliot, "but only with some difficulty."

"Perhaps it is because I have already read it else-where," said Elinor kindly.

"I think you are modest," he said. "You show great ability. Yet you are untutored in the basics, I believe?" Elinor must have nodded because he continued. "I am willing to teach you all I know. That includes general knowledge of the Musor arts, and my little skill in Heightening if you would be pleased."

"That is very kind of you," said Elinor politely. "I am eager to learn."

Aldreda could hear that Lord Olliot had leaned in closer. His voice dropped to a murmur. "With such a Gift as yours, you could make a powerful alliance with another Musor, should you choose to marry in that direction."

Elinor's tone became frosty, and she took a step backwards. Aldreda's reticule swung. "I am already affianced to the Earl of Beresford, Lord Olliot."

"Oh yes." His lordship's tone became patronising. "I believe I read that announcement. Did you make that decision before you knew of your own power and your likely position in the royal court?"

"The best position for me is at Lord Beresford's side," said Elinor coldly. "Our attachment is deep and abiding."

Hm, thought Aldreda, remembering the lovers' quarrel in the carriage. She hoped they had made up.

"Of course," said Lord Olliot. "I do apologise for speaking out of turn. It is simply that we Musors must stick together and advise one another. I beg you, think on my words with an open mind."

Elinor took another step backwards. Aldreda stood, tense with concern, and wondered if she should stick her head out and assert chaperonage over the situation.

Lord Olliot spoke again, seeming to change the subject, his voice more genial as he moved away. "Perhaps if I may show you something, Miss Avely?"

After a pause, Elinor followed him. "What is it?" she asked cautiously.

There was a whisk of another cloth being removed and the click of a case being opened. "Aubadesol rope."

Aldreda drew in a sharp breath. She had not told Elinor about this; she had not wanted to worry her.

Elinor leaned forward. "It is very beautiful. Look, it almost shimmers. Does it have some special quality?"

"Indeed," said Lord Olliot. "It is spun from the sun silk-worms from the New World. Would you like to hold it?"

"May I?" Perhaps sensing a trap, Elinor paused. "Is it dangerous?"

"Oh, no. See, I am quite able to hold it. It feels warm. Quite a pleasant tingle, in fact. I would be interested to know what you make of it."

Aldreda did not feel a pleasant tingle. She felt her skin shudder and fear spread through her. As Elinor took the rope, the tail of it must have swung down. It brushed the reticule, coming within a quarter of an inch of Aldreda. Her blood shrunk within her, with a strange sensation that was almost pain.

Her head swooned. Fortunately, after a brief minute, Elinor must have handed the rope back. "It is warm," she agreed. "I cannot sense any spells within, though it seems magical. What is its purpose, Lord Olliot?"

Elinor's tone was still distant. Through her own blackened vision, Aldreda could also hear a faint note of fear. She wondered if Elinor had divined some of the history of that particular rope. She herself did not want to think on it too closely.

"It can bind and kill vampiri," said Lord Olliot. There was the click of the case as he returned the rope to its resting place.

"Pardon me?" Elinor's voice was muted, and she took a few steps backwards again, for which Aldreda was grateful.

"It was used in the French Troubles. I notice you are keen to champion the rights of the vampiri. I thought you should know that in the Troubles, they were used against

Musors. Vampiri can track our magic, as you know. The Mundanes used this rope to enslave them and lead the Quotidians to our doors – and to our deaths."

"How awful!"

"Yes. So you see, our king has good reason to limit hobnobbing with our little companions."

"It was not their fault!"

"Nevertheless, I beg you, do not display your ignorance on the matter again."

Aldreda heard Elinor swallow. Then, to her relief, another sound came from behind them.

"Miss Avely." It was the gentle voice of Queen Charlotte. Aldreda felt the turn and deep curtsy of Elinor. The queen's voice drew close. "I hope I am not interrupting?"

"Not at all," said Lord Olliot smoothly. "I was just showing Miss Avely the library, on the instruction of His Majesty."

"I am learning much already," said Elinor, with only a slight quaver.

"Good," said the queen. "I have come to ask you for a special favour, Miss Avely."

"Certainly, anything, Your Majesty."

Queen Charlotte carried on smoothly as if she had not noticed any discomfort in the room. "As I said to you on our previous meeting, I am most eager to learn of any cure to Bemusement. Especially any way of warding off Bewilderment. I very much fear my husband will push himself too far one day."

"Surely not." Elinor's voice grew stronger. "His Majesty is wise, and he would not jeopardise England by becoming Bewildered."

Lord Olliot interrupted. "You have not seen the repercussions of his magic. The king is sometimes Bemused for days. Her Majesty is right to worry, I am afraid."

"There must be something we can do." Queen Charlotte's voice became pleading. "I am hoping the knowledge lies somewhere in the pearls."

"Lord Rapp did not find anything?" asked Elinor.

"No," said Her Majesty. "Though he was looking. I am not sure if Lord Rapp managed to read all the jewels. This morning the Duke of Planx visited the library again to look for a Healing spell in the pearls, but it is slow work for him. It will be wonderful to have a talented Discernor among us once more."

Elinor cleared her throat. "Is it possible any of the jewels are missing? Or perhaps broken?"

Aldreda stiffened again. It was not wise for Elinor to mention broken jewels so openly if that was indeed what she had found!

The queen's voice became surprised and a little disapproving. "I should hope not. We guard them well. However, it is possible Lord Rapp or the duke may have missed some Healing spell that might help my husband's Bemusement. And now, of course, there are the Moria Pearls, which have untapped knowledge. I am greatly hopeful, Miss Avely."

"I will do my best," said Elinor. "Though I confess I have not formally accepted the position yet."

Lord Olliot chuckled. "Miss Avely is toying with us," he said. "Of course, such a highly Gifted young woman must serve the court."

"Oh, you simply must accept," said Queen Charlotte. "We need you. I must admit, I quite agree with your stance on the Vampiri Edicts. It seems so *impolite*, besides anything else, in a country where we pride ourselves on our manners! Perhaps with you advising the court, we can manage to sway my husband's opinion towards a more civilised attitude."

Elinor responded eagerly to this, and the reticule swayed as the party moved back into the drawing room. Aldreda relaxed a little once more. Further civilities were exchanged, and the conversation drifted to more trivial matters such as the latest show at the opera.

Finally, it was time to leave. Elinor promised to send the king her decision within the next week. Aldreda was struggling to keep her eyes open, so she was glad when movement suggested Elinor and her mother had left the room.

Back in the carriage, Aldreda was jolted awake by the sound of Elinor's voice as they rumbled onto the street.

Elinor was strident with accusation. "Mother! *Wisdom Conquers*! I cannot believe you did not tell me! All this time, I have belonged to a line of Discernors! Did you not think I would wish to know? I've a good mind to accept the royal position now. And Father! A Discernor! I knew it!"

"Never mind that," said Mrs Avely, her voice a little ruffled. "The king was lying about something."

"About what?" demanded Elinor, distracted.

A strange sound escaped Mrs Avely's lips. Aldreda was almost certain it was a giggle. "I'm not sure. Perhaps about whether he enjoys the opera."

Oh dear. Mrs Avely was Bemused.

"Mother, you overdid it! Were you Discerning the whole time?"

Another giggle trickled out. "Not all the time."

Aldreda dared not stick her head out of the reticule to discuss the matter. She could sense the sky was covered in heavy clouds, but it was still the middle of the afternoon.

"Mother, you need a vampiri," announced Elinor.

"A vampiri!" Mrs Avely tutted. "Always appearing naked! It is not conducive to a civilised atmosphere. No," she added firmly. "I have done without a vampiri for this long; I will continue to manage without one."

"You *knew* about vampiri?" exclaimed Elinor.

"Of course," said her mother. "You are not the only one to have little adventures, my dear."

There was a pregnant silence.

"And," added Mrs Avely, "I still think *I* should become the Royal Discernor. I did not like the atmosphere in there. I don't want you landing into royal trouble."

"Mother! Certainly, you will not become the Discernor! Especially if you are going to become musedrunk like this."

"I am not musedrunk!" Mrs Avely sniffed, then spoiled the effect by giggling again. "Haven't been musedrunk in *years*."

"Well, you are not going to start now," said Elinor. "I will be the Royal Discernor, not you. You'll disgrace us if this is what happens."

"But I can Discern lies," said Mrs Avely. "That is the kind of thing needed in a Royal Discernor."

"But you cannot even tell us what the king was lying about!"

"I can indeed," asserted Mrs Avely. "When he referred to the 'accident' of Lord Rapp's death, his voice was all wrong." She sighed sagely. "Though that could be because he believes it to be suicide."

Elinor frowned. "What about Creel's death? Was the king lying when he said *that* was a coincidence?"

Mrs Avely hummed to herself. "I think so. Perhaps he has suspicions. I'm not sure."

Elinor did not sound impressed. "I must learn to do it. I could have done it today myself if Beresford and Aldreda hadn't ordered against it."

"But I am better than you."

"Well," said Elinor sharply, "I have something you don't."

"What is that?"

"Miss Zooth."

Mrs Avely gave an uncharacteristic harrumph. "We'll discuss this later," she said ominously. "When I'm not … tired." Then she subsided into silence.

"That's right," said Elinor ominously. "We certainly will. I want to know about Father."

Quiet fell over the carriage. Aldreda was glad. She herself was exhausted. She could not endure anymore eavesdropping. In the dark sway of the carriage, she fell fast asleep.

IN WHICH ELINOR FORMS
A PLAN

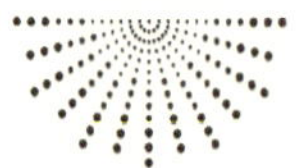

Elinor

Elinor put Aldreda to bed without waking her and left the shard in the reticule on the dresser. There would be plenty of time to discuss it in the evening. She had to hurry back down, as the countess was receiving callers that afternoon. All of London appeared to want to renew Elinor's acquaintance after the Yannow ball – probably because of her possible connection with Jaq through Beresford.

Elinor's mind was only partly on the callers; she was contemplating the mystery of the broken sapphire. She had only just caught its presence as she swept her divination sense over the contents of the room. The flicker of it had called from lower down, at a different level to all the cabinets. Curious, she had turned her mind towards it and followed a scrap of jewel song toward the fireplace.

There, winking from the hearth, Elinor had felt it –

but not seen it. Without her divination, she would not have known it was there: the dark blue of the sapphire hidden in the black of coals.

Elinor was fairly certain Lord Olliot had not seen her as she swooped down to pick it up. Perhaps he had caught sight of her opening her reticule, but he might have guessed Aldreda was there, given it was the vampiri's method of conveyance last time. He would have assumed Elinor was simply ascertaining Aldreda was well – not passing her a broken jewel.

The question was: who had broken it? And why?

Elinor, smiling vaguely at the guests, could not help but feel that there was a good chance it had something to do with Lord Rapp's death. Which meant Aldreda was right: the Moria Pearls were not safe. If only she could discuss the matter with Beresford, instead of having to utter inanities to various callers. Worse, they all kept turning the conversation to Jaq.

Looking across the drawing room, she saw Perry was suffering more than she was. He sat very stiffly as an older matron asked if he were previously acquainted with Lord Malleker and whether Lord Malleker was an eligible bachelor.

"I could not say," said Perry shortly. "You would have to ask him."

Elinor sighed, wishing she could tell the matron that Jaq was a seal. That might frighten her off for her daughters and leave the field clear for Perry. It was time Elinor had a little talk with her brother, for as far as she was concerned, Perry was behaving like an addlepated fool.

After the final callers blessedly left, Elinor asked Perry to accompany her for a walk. Gloomily, he agreed.

It was a relief to leave the house and stretch their legs.

They headed towards Hyde Park, though it was now late in the afternoon. Light streamed through gaps in the clouds, and a brisk wind swept down the streets, carrying with it the inevitable splattering of rain. Elinor put up her parasol.

"Are you attending tonight?" Perry asked Elinor as their strides lengthened. He was referring to the latest ball, to which the Avelys were now invited.

Elinor breathed in the cool, damp air. "I will go fashionably late. I want to have a coze with Aldreda first. We have important things to discuss." Like a broken jewel, and its corollary: some missing spells. And why the Duke of Planx had visited the Sapphire Library that morning before Elinor.

Perry was not curious; he had other things on his mind. "Do you think I should attend? I suppose everyone will be there."

"Jaq will be there," observed Elinor, tucking her hand into Perry's arm. "If that is what you mean."

"That is *not* what I mean," huffed Perry. "Besides, Jaq is too busy revelling with Lord Worthing. Beresford asked *Worthing* to show him around when really it should be me."

"Oh?" asked Elinor. "I wonder what Lord Worthing will think of Jaq? For someone who is also a seal, Jaq can be very charming."

"Ha," said Perry moodily. "Only if you like arrogant wastrels."

"Do you?" asked Elinor innocently.

Perry scowled.

They reached Hyde Park. The wide expanse of green and the huge trees were a welcome change after the narrow confines of the drawing room, even with the drizzling rain.

Elinor squeezed Perry's arm and glanced around to make certain no one could hear them. She tilted her parasol so it covered them both, giving the impression of a small bubble keeping them safe from the rest of the world. "You know, I do believe Lord Worthing and Jaq may have ... matching inclinations."

Perry groaned suddenly. "Oh God. If it is to be Worthing, I don't see why it can't be me." He shot a glance at Elinor. "If you take my meaning."

"I do," said Elinor. "And I don't blame you for taking a fancy to Jaq," she added carefully. "I think he has a chivalrous heart under that rakish exterior."

Perry looked unconvinced. "Well, he seems eager to demonstrate he has forgotten all about me." He groaned again. "Oh, Ellie, I can't believe I kissed him!"

"I can," said Elinor.

"But he's a man!"

"So? You are well aware that such attractions exist."

"Not in me! I didn't know it was in me!" Perry said, rather contradictorily.

"Well, now you do." Elinor paused and then said kindly. "I suppose I have always accepted I am different from everyone else, so it does not faze me if you are a little different also. Why don't you stop fighting it?"

"I did go to the Serpentine after Almacks," admitted Perry, jerking his head at the lake which lay glittering in soft rain. "Jaq was having a swim, and I ... well, we kissed again. But I couldn't continue, Elinor, it was too much. And now, there is no point." Perry hunched his shoulders. "He is pursuing Lord Worthing now."

Elinor pursed her lips. "I don't believe so. I think Jaq still regards you fondly, Perry, and if anything, he is probably just trying to make you jealous." And succeeding. "If you would only give him some sign ..." She trailed off.

Perry looked at her and then sighed wearily. "I won't have the chance. Besides, I wouldn't know what to do."

"Nonsense," said Elinor. "You know exactly what to do. I can give you some pointers if you like. Beresford and I ..."

She leaned towards him mischievously. Perry gave an exclamation of horror and threw up his arm in a warding gesture. "Good Gad, no! Spare me the details!"

The mood shifted, and they both laughed.

"Has the wedding date been set yet?" asked Perry. "It had better be soon."

"Actually, we thought to wait until Christmas," said Elinor. "So that we can be married in Devon." She paused. "By the way, Perry, do you have any secret abilities I don't know about?"

Perry shook his head. "You mean like your jewel divining? No. I wish I did. Then I could divine what in damnation Jaq is thinking."

Elinor refrained from observing that it was quite obvious what Jaq was thinking. "It needn't be Discernment. It could be one of the other Gifts."

Perry shook his head. "Unless you count my uncanny ability to be attracted to the wrong person."

"Jaq is not the wrong person," averred Elinor. "Oh! And you will be interested to know that *Vincit Prudentia* is, in fact, a Discernor motto." She told Perry what she had learned that day at Buckingham House.

Perry was curious about their Father's Discernment and affronted. "*Mother* was musedrunk? That's disgraceful."

"Indeed," said Elinor. "She needs a vampiri, like me."

Perry shuddered. "By Jove, no, that would be far worse."

~

Later that evening, Elinor knocked on Aldreda's door. She entered to see Aldreda fully dressed, pacing on the carpet.

"Elinor! We must talk!"

"I agree." Elinor lifted Aldreda and bore her to the dresser, where the reticule lay. "The little jewel is safe?"

Aldreda unwrapped the shard while Elinor lit some candles. Once uncovered and cleaned, the sliver of jewel glinted on the wood.

"It *is* a sapphire," said Aldreda. "Or the remains of one. What happened to it?"

"It appears someone destroyed it."

"The question is why."

They both stared at the shattered remnant.

Elinor picked it up and opened her mind. Nothing came to her other than the whispering song of the jewel. "I cannot read any spell within it. If it did hold something, it is now lost."

"What spell could it have been?" Aldreda sank down on the edge of a book.

"I have a theory." Elinor put the shard back on the dresser. "I think it contained the very spell that Queen Charlotte is seeking – the one that can help Heal the king."

Aldreda looked up. "Rectify his excessive Bemusement? I don't think there *is* a cure for that, other than a vampiri companion."

"But does the royal court know that? If the knowledge of Musing is lost or limited, then perhaps they still nurture hope for a cure. And I think that is why this sapphire was broken: because it contained memories of Healing spells that might have appeared to work."

"You think someone wants to keep the king indisposed?"

Elinor nodded. "And what is more, the Duke of Planx visited the library this very morning."

"You think the duke destroyed it *today*?"

Elinor explained. "I didn't sense this sliver on our previous visit, though I cannot be sure. I was rather taken up by the pearls. But it seems too great a coincidence that the duke visited the Sapphire Library on the very day that I discover a broken jewel."

Aldreda spoke thoughtfully. "He is in the king's confidence; he would know of your appointment. He might have wanted to destroy it before you had a chance to read it."

"Precisely. And the duke has unrivalled access to the king as long as his highness remains ill."

Aldreda drew a breath. "You think he destroyed evidence of Healing spells, and Lord Rapp discovered it …"

"And the duke killed him," said Elinor, "After setting up a reason to make it look like suicide. Why else go through the pantomime of that awful bet? I don't believe he meant Rapp to win, even if that is what he claims now. And if Lord Rapp discovered the duchess was also implicated, it was another reason to silence him."

"It is a good theory," said Aldreda. "But we have no proof."

"Well," said Elinor. "We have a way to test my theory."

"How?" asked Aldreda sceptically.

"We still have the last pearl, remember."

The first thing Elinor did the following morning was to write a short missive to the king, warning him that she had found a broken sapphire and that the Library was potentially in danger. Elinor sent a post-boy to fetch Jaq. She then gave the letter to Jaq, impressing upon him most earnestly to hand it to the king and no one else.

Jaq – avoiding Perry's gaze in the drawing room – clicked his heels together and promised most faithfully to do so.

Left behind, Perry sighed mournfully. "He won't even look at me."

"Well, you shall have to find a way to make him look at you," said Elinor unsympathetically. "I have more important things to worry about now. I'm laying a trap for the Duke of Planx. Where is Beresford?"

Of course, Beresford didn't like her plan very much, but he had to acknowledge that at least it did not place Elinor in danger. "You want to pretend the last Moria Pearl contains Healing spells?" he demanded. "And see if the duke tries to destroy it?"

"Yes – you must tell his grace that the pearl is safe at Jaq's quarters, but that Jaq intends to present it to the king tomorrow. That will provoke the duke to act quickly before the pearl is under lock and key at the Sapphire Library."

"Mm," said Beresford. "I suppose suspicion is less likely to fall on the duke if the pearl goes missing while it is in Jaq's care."

"Exactly – so he will try to catch it before the king or I have a chance to read its contents. And you will be waiting to catch *him*."

This was the part that Elinor did not like, and she

elicited a promise from Beresford that he would take at least four other men to stake out Jaq's lodgings.

"Jaq can't keep watch with me," said Beresford. "If your suspicions are true, the duke will put someone on to trail him. I'll have to send Jaq out to some public event."

Perry, listening from the window, offered his own services in this regard.

Beresford looked across, a frown between his grey eyes. "I would rather you stay behind and guard Elinor, Perry. I am not convinced there is no danger to her, especially if she has somehow stumbled on the truth. Besides, Lord Worthing has already arranged some entertainment tonight, which will suit the purpose."

Perry looked as if he had swallowed lemon juice, but Elinor ignored him. "And you will be careful, James? I don't like that you will not have Jaq or Lord Worthing or even Perry with you."

"Even Perry?" snapped Perry.

"I will find other men to go with me," Beresford said apologetically. "Though I don't really believe the duke will make any such attempt. By the way, where *is* the last pearl?"

Elinor grinned at him. "It is safe enough."

"Where?"

She glanced across at Perry. "Tucked away in my underthings."

"Your *underthings?*" Beresford went slightly red, and Perry shook his head in disapproval, muttering something about the influence of Miss Zooth.

Elinor lifted her hands. "Can you think of a better place?"

Beresford smiled reluctantly. "Well, keep it there, and don't mention it to anyone. I might try to find another pearl to put in Jaq's room, just to lend verisimilitude to the tale."

So Beresford set out that afternoon, first to purchase a pearl, then to hunt down the duke in his club, and pass on the fabricated story. He returned home satisfied that he had hooked the duke's interest. He had already posted men at Jaq's lodgings, and after an early dinner, Beresford set off to join the watch.

Her beloved seemed energised now that he had something to do, but Elinor waited at home unable to read or sew and twisting her fingers together. She was anxious now she had put events in train. What if Beresford was hurt somehow? She would be the one to blame. It was most irksome being a woman, not able to join in herself to apprehend a murderer. Yet Elinor trusted that Beresford was capable, clever, and strong, and would handle the matter admirably. Didn't she?

She sighed. If she were to ask Beresford to trust her, she had to give him the same courtesy. She simply had to wait, and soon they would have compelling evidence to present to the king of the Duke of Planx's culpability.

The countess went out to a dinner party, but Mrs Avely, Elinor, and Perry dined together at home. Elinor found she didn't have much of an appetite. Perry also was picking at his food. Mrs Avely had been informed of the plan and was a little doubtful. "It might work," she acknowledged. "If indeed the duke is the culprit."

"Of course he is," said Elinor. "Who else would want to keep the king ill? It keeps His Majesty reliant upon the duke."

"You are making an assumption about what that sapphire contained," said Mrs Avely. "We will find out if you are right."

After dinner, they repaired to the drawing room to

occupy themselves. Elinor fetched Aldreda to keep them company in their vigil, despite any Edicts to the contrary. The vampiri sat on the mantlepiece above the fire, reading a tiny book of poetry that Lady Denier had loaned her.

Eventually, Elinor gave up pretending to sew. Even Mrs Avely appeared to be chewing on her lip.

The clock struck nine.

Perry paced around the drawing room. Elinor looked at him crossly. "You're not helping my nerves, Perry, prowling around like that."

Perry kept fidgeting. "Why didn't Beresford let me accompany Jaq? For all we know, the duke might attack Jaq directly. He could be in danger."

"Nonsense," said Elinor. "Beresford told the duke that the pearl is at Jaq's lodgings, not on his person."

Perry started to pace again. "We don't know what the duke will do," he argued. "If he is a murderer, he could do anything."

Mrs Avely spoke calmly. "The duke has no reason to attack Lord Malleker."

Aldreda sniffed from the mantlepiece. "Unless Jaq is seducing the duchess."

"Hmph," said Perry. "Where is Jaq, anyway? Where did Lord Worthing take him?"

Elinor sighed. "I believe they went to the opera."

Perry came to a halt, appalled. "The opera?"

"Yes. What is the matter with that?"

His eyes boggled. "Jaq is alone with Lord Worthing in his opera box?"

Elinor began to gather an inkling of Perry's distress. "Well, yes. I suppose it *is* rather dark and intimate in there."

Perry's hands came up to pull at his blond hair in

agitation. "Anything could happen in that opera box! Anything!"

Mrs Avely frowned. "I don't think the duke will sneak into the opera box and murder Jaq."

Elinor repressed a grin. It was obvious to her that Perry was imagining Jaq's muscled thigh pressed up against Lord Worthing's, and perhaps their hands entwining in the cosy dark. Over on the mantlepiece, Aldreda frowned with disapproval.

"The opera box!" exclaimed Perry again. He closed his eyes in anguish. "Oh God, I wish I was there instead."

Elinor tried not to smile. And then, right before her eyes, Perry vanished.

Elinor started from her seat, aghast.

"Perry?" She blinked, not believing her eyes. "Perry! Where are you?"

Aldreda dropped her book of poetry. It fell with a tiny thump on the floor. "Where did he go?"

Mrs Avely looked up. She stared at the blank space where Perry had been. "Peregrine?"

Elinor circled the spot, warily, where her brother had last stood. The drawing room carpet remained bare. "Mother! One minute he was there, and the next, he winked out of sight!"

Mrs Avely stood, her hands clasped white together. "Good God. Did he ... Travel?"

Elinor stared. "Travel? You mean Travelling? As in Musor Travel? Are you mad? Perry can't Travel!"

Aldreda interrupted. "Don't babble, Elinor. Is it possible someone snatched him?"

"Snatched him!" shouted Elinor, her nerves at breaking point. "How could someone snatch Perry? Where is he? Mother!"

Before Mrs Avely could answer, the front doorbell jangled.

Aldreda and Mrs Avely both swivelled their heads to the door. Elinor leapt over to the window and whipped the curtain aside.

"It is an unmarked carriage," she said. "Could it be Beresford? Why would he ring like that?"

It was not Beresford. The butler entered the drawing room, ushering in the Duchess of Planx.

IN WHICH SEVERAL MISTAKES
ARE REALISED

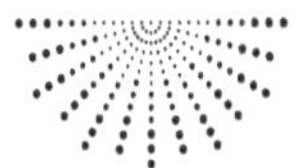

Elinor

"Your Grace!" cried Elinor. "Have you taken my brother?"

The duchess raised a delicate brow. "Miss Avely, no, I have not taken your brother. What a curious question. You do appear to be full of such curious questions."

"Elinor!" said Mrs Avely, dropping a curtsy. Aldreda had vanished behind a small clock on the mantlepiece.

Belatedly, Elinor curtsied also. "Your Grace, I apologise. My brother just – er – went missing."

"Oh?"

Mrs Avely took a step forward. "Perry wasn't outside when you came in?" she demanded.

"No." Her grace shook her head, jingling her ringlets.

Mrs Avely invited the duchess to sit. Elinor stared around the room, hoping Perry would somehow reappear. But no blond head met her eyes.

She realised her heart was beating rather rapidly, which was not surprising given that her brother had just disappeared into thin air.

The duchess declined the offer of a seat. "I won't stay, my dear Mrs Avely. In fact, I came to invite Miss Avely to a little salon this evening. May I whisk her away with me now?"

Elinor's eyes sharpened on the duchess, especially at the words 'whisk away'. Could her grace have anything to do with Perry's disappearance?

For the first time, she observed that the duchess seemed ill-at-ease. Her face was pale, and her hands clasped nervously together.

"A salon?" Elinor asked. "In your … library?"

The duchess gave a tinkle of laughter. "Oh, I see you have guessed my little secret. I do have little salons with the vampiri; very naughty of me, I know, with these silly Edicts." She looked around the room. "Where is your vampiri, Miss Avely? I would *love* to meet her, having heard so much about her. She is invited too, of course. You must both come with me now."

Elinor wondered if Aldreda was really the subject of the invitation and hoped she would stay out of sight on the mantlepiece.

"I thank you, Your Grace, but I must stay home," said Elinor. She did not want to mention it was quite possible she would shortly be making haste to Lord Worthing's opera box if it were true that Perry had *Travelled*. Goodness knew what scene was unfolding there. Elinor repressed a shudder. She had to dispatch the duchess as quickly as possible.

However, the duchess was being obstinate. "Miss Avely, I beg you to accompany me." She came over and took Elinor's hands in her own gloved ones. Lowering her voice, she leaned in to murmur in Elinor's ear. "It is a matter of *grave importance.*"

Elinor stared. "Grave importance? What can you mean?"

Mrs Avely stalked over, wearing a look of suspicion. "What has happened, Your Grace?"

The duchess let go of Elinor's hands. "Oh! I see there are no secrets in this house! If you must know, I come on a royal errand."

"A royal errand?" asked Elinor. She saw that her mother was staring at the duchess in a frowning sort of way, with her head slightly tilted to the right. Elinor's own suspicions were acute. She knew her mother must be Truth Discerning, so she let Mrs Avely bear the burden of that Discernment. Elinor had a feeling she would need her own wits about her. "What errand?"

The duchess twisted her hands together. "A case of the Sapphire Library has gone missing. We need your help to find it."

Elinor drew a breath and glanced at her mother. Mrs Avely nodded slightly in confirmation of her grace's words. Unbelievably, the duchess was telling the truth.

How could a case of the Sapphire Library go missing? It was under royal guard, in a royal palace.

"Who sent you?" demanded Elinor.

"Queen Charlotte," said the duchess, to Elinor's surprise.

Mrs Avely nodded again. This, too, was true.

Her grace's voice quavered a little. "Queen Charlotte suspects my husband has taken the sapphires. We need your Divination to help find them, Miss Avely. You must come with me at once to search my house before the duke returns and destroys them."

Mrs Avely's eyes met Elinor's, and she nodded once more. Again, the duchess only spoke the truth.

Elinor bit her lip, thinking hard. "Lord Beresford is trailing the duke." She ignored the duchess's look of surprise. "There can be no danger in going now to his residence, can there, Mother?"

"I suppose not," said Mrs Avely reluctantly. "Are you certain the queen knows of this jewel hunt, Your Grace?"

The duchess nodded, already turning for the door. "Hurry, Miss Avely."

"Very well, I shall come," said Elinor. "I will be there in a moment, Your Grace. Wait for me in the carriage."

The duchess looked from one to the other. "Be quick," she said and then left the room.

Elinor and her mother stared at each other. Aldreda reappeared from behind the clock. "It seems odd to me. I suspect a trap. You don't really mean to go, do you, Elinor?"

"Mother says the duchess was telling the truth."

Mrs Avely nodded, blinking. "The duchess did not lie. If the queen wishes for your service, Elinor, I think you should go. As you say, Beresford has the duke under his eye."

Elinor turned to her mother. "What of Perry?"

"I will look for him," said Mrs Avely. "Mayhap you know if faerieland is anywhere near here? Did he turn counter-clockwise before he left?"

"You're Bemused, Mother!"

"Only a little," said Mrs Avely, vaguely.

Elinor frowned. "Try Lord Worthing's opera box. If it is true Perry Travelled, then that is the last thing he spoke of."

"Why would he be so set on Lord Worthing's opera box?" asked Mrs Avely.

Elinor sighed, deciding that was for Perry to explain. She strode over to the mantlepiece. "Aldreda, you must come with me. I will need you to keep me from becoming too Bemused. Mother, find Perry at once and ensure he doesn't land us in a pickle!"

"Hm," said Aldreda. "Good luck with that, Mrs Avely."

~

With Aldreda ensconced in her reticule, Elinor climbed into the ducal carriage. The crest had been covered, and Elinor wondered at the need for secrecy.

Inside the carriage, the duchess sat back, still twisting her hands together in her lap. A frown marred the dark eyes.

Elinor placed her reticule carefully beside her as the carriage rumbled into movement. Perhaps she could find out more about what was afoot, with a few careful questions.

"Why does the queen suspect your husband?" Elinor asked and tilted her head to the right, opening her inner sense. It was time she tried some Truth Discernment herself, as much as she trusted her mother.

The duchess sighed. "Apparently, you wrote something to the king. Some warning? My lord duke was there when His Majesty received your message and soon gained the contents of it. The king tells him everything, regardless. And this afternoon, a case of jewels vanished before steps could be taken to safeguard them better."

Elinor, listening closely, felt the duchess was speaking honestly: there was no shallow ring to her voice. Elinor let the divination go, marshalling her energies for the task ahead. Yet, she felt a seed of doubt and suspicion still within her.

The story didn't make sense. Why would the duke steal a case of sapphires? Unless there was some larger plan afoot, to take the spells for his own ends? While he had the king under his thumb, surely there was no need for that.

The duchess interrupted Elinor's thoughts. "I wish I was a Musor. You are lucky to be Gifted, Miss Avely."

"Yes," agreed Elinor.

"And lucky to be marrying Lord Beresford."

Elinor looked across sharply. "Yes."

The duchess sighed. "I can tell that you do not like me, Miss Avely, and I understand. It would irk me too – if you had persuaded my husband to marry me."

Elinor sat up very straight. "I do not believe for a moment that you persuaded Beresford to marry me."

The duchess laughed. "No, nor do I. Shall I tell you something?" She paused, seeming to choose her words carefully. "The only reason I made the suggestion in the first place was to show Beresford I didn't care for him anymore. To demonstrate that I was – er – mistress of the situation, as it were."

"Pardon me?" A trickle of icy rage ran down Elinor's spine. It sounded very much as if the duchess implied Beresford had undertaken an affair with her. But the next words dispelled it.

"Oh, Beresford never touched me," said her grace. "I rather wanted him to – about a year ago, I invited him. However, he would have none of it. I suspect now that he already had his eye on you, Miss Avely."

Elinor found she had nothing to say to this revelation. She stared at the duchess, for once bereft of words.

Her grace continued. "It was a blow to my pride, as you can imagine. I moved on – there are plenty of handsome men in London eager to dally with *me*. But I had to let Beresford know I didn't care, so I told him to marry you after you managed to throw yourself into scandal."

The duchess sat back as if relieved of some burden. She smiled at Elinor. "So now you know."

Eventually, Elinor said, "Thank you for telling me, I suppose."

The duchess gave a wry look. "Well, as is my usual practice, I am only doing it to be selfish."

"What do you mean?" Elinor frowned.

"I am hoping we can be friends, Miss Avely."

An awkward silence ensued. Elinor hardly knew what to make of her grace's confession. She had to admit it changed the complexion of the matter greatly. Poor Beresford, not wanting to betray such an indelicate history!

And now the duchess wanted to be friends? Elinor didn't know what to think. She thought back to her grace's earlier call when Elinor first arrived in London, and she wondered if it were friendship that had been extended all along, not merely an exchange of blackmail. Perhaps the duchess was not very practiced in the art of friendship.

Elinor turned to examine her. "Why were you at the Rapp residence that morning?"

The duchess grimaced. "I was looking for Lord Rapp's vampiri. You know he is missing? I intended to leave a note, offering him protection. In my husband's name, of course, though now I see that might have scared him off."

Elinor did not reply. She didn't want to divulge Tildenhall's reappearance. She was too preoccupied:

worried about Perry, fearing for Beresford, and puzzling over the missing case of sapphires.

Aldreda still hid in the reticule, and Elinor dared not bring her out. The duchess seemed to sympathise with the vampiri, but she had not met Aldreda yet. It was better not to complicate matters. Besides, it was advantageous to have a secret companion who could fly for help if needed.

Why did Elinor feel a sense of foreboding? Her own mother had applied her knack for Truth Discernment to everything the duchess had said. Yet there was something here Elinor did not like. Puzzling over the whole problem, she finally realised what it was.

The duchess herself believed – though reluctantly – the tale she had told Elinor. But whoever told her the story could be lying.

Elinor shook her head. Queen Charlotte had sent the duchess, and why would the queen lie? Unless the queen was also being manipulated.

When they arrived at the Planx town house, the duchess told Elinor to disembark. "I have told my servants to expect you and to assist your search. I will hurry back to the opera and make certain my husband does not surprise you with an early return."

Elinor nodded and clambered down. She wanted to send the duchess to fetch Beresford, but Beresford had his own task this evening. And Elinor would send for Jaq, but she rather suspected he had his hands full right now.

Reluctantly, she stepped away from the carriage, clutching the reticule with Aldreda in it. The sooner she found the missing jewels, the better.

The duchess smiled. "Hurry, Miss Avely! And please think on my offer of friendship." She gave her orders to return to the opera, and the vehicle rumbled away.

The rain from earlier had dissipated, and the night was still, though clouds still hung heavy in the sky. Elinor turned slowly towards the ducal house. Lamps were lit out front, throwing the elegant facade into relief. Only a few windows showed light; the house was quiet, with its master and mistress out. Elinor opened her senses for a preliminary sweep for sapphires. She should know soon enough if they were there.

But before she could take a step towards the house, a slim figure appeared before her, startling her out of her divination. It was Lord Olliot, his hair pale in the lamplight.

Unease once again pricked Elinor's senses.

"Good evening, Miss Avely." Lord Olliot bowed. "I am here to assist you in the search. You have been sent by the queen, I assume?"

"Lord Olliot." Elinor curtsied. "His Majesty sent you as well?" Nervously, she tipped her head and listened for truth, for here she did not have her mother to rely upon.

"Yes." Lord Olliot nodded portentously. "There are sapphires missing from the Library."

No shallow ring coated his voice. Nevertheless, Elinor frowned and started towards the front door, disliking that she was alone in the dark with him. However, Lord Olliot caught at her elbow.

"Miss Avely, I think we should approach from the back of the house."

"Why?" She turned suspiciously, her senses still alert.

"I suspect the jewels are in the vampiri trade quarters."

He spoke the truth. She cocked her head. "You mean Lady Denier's loft? Why?"

Lord Olliot paused. "I think the duke would take care

to keep the jewels out of his house. That way, he could blame his vampiri if it came to it."

Elinor stilled. The sound of his voice had gone tinny.

"You really believe the duke stole the sapphires?" she asked.

"Yes," said Lord Olliot, and it was as if the word was coated in an echo.

Elinor knew, without a doubt, he was lying. She tried to keep the knowledge of it from showing and fumbled with her reticule. If she could somehow let Aldreda know her doubts, the vampiri could fly for help.

But something must have shown in her face or in her jerky movements. Lord Olliot suddenly stepped forward and plucked the reticule out of her grasp.

"Not on the street, Miss Avely," he said smoothly. "We must respect the Edicts and keep our vampiri hidden. Now, let us walk around to the mews entrance."

"Hand me that reticule back at once!" demanded Elinor.

"Once we are in vampiri quarters," repeated Lord Olliot. He turned and walked off along the road that went down the side of the Planx house.

At that moment, Elinor saw a shape flitting past the lamp. It was a familiar shape: that of a large bat. As she watched, it hovered as if staring straight at her.

Pags. Elinor was certain of it. He flicked his wings and followed Lord Olliot.

Elinor drew a sigh of relief. At least Pags was here to help rescue Aldreda. Was his arrogant wing flick intended to send Elinor off? She would not abandon Aldreda so easily. Pags could raise the alarm; as a human, Elinor was more fitted to grabbing the reticule back.

Taking a deep breath, she hurried after Lord Olliot and Pags, feeling angry and a little afraid.

The ducal house was the first in the row, so they soon reached the mews. Lord Olliot glanced back and disappeared under the shadowed arch, and Elinor followed, trying to keep a close eye on Aldreda.

Just on the other side of the arch was the Planx carriage house and stables. The black and white ribbon still hung from the upper floor, and the mews were quiet. The duchess and the duke had their carriages out, and the stable-hands were sleeping while they could, or perhaps had sought their own entertainment.

Lady Denier's loft seemed deserted too. Pags was nowhere to be seen.

However, to her astonishment, Elinor could hear the song of sapphires. It emanated from the third floor, where Lady Denier resided. So Lord Olliot was not lying about that, at least.

His lordship stopped in front of the carriage house. "The duke's vampiri is at the opera," he announced. "However, we can find our way inside the loft if the jewels are there."

Elinor held up a hand, biding for time, hoping that Pags was hurrying. "I can determine it easily enough from the street. Wait a moment while I try a divination."

Lord Olliot folded his arms, still holding Elinor's reticule tightly in his grasp with Aldreda trapped within. Elinor closed her eyes and opened her senses, seeking to confirm what she already knew: that a pile of sapphires and Moria Pearls was in the hayloft. The queen's message had not mentioned the fact that the pearls were missing too, and yet their peculiar song mingled with the call of the sapphires.

How could this be? It must be a trap. Could the duke really have placed them there? But even Olliot did not believe that.

"The sapphires are there." Elinor opened her eyes. "I will wait here while you fetch them, my lord."

She turned. Lord Olliot was fumbling with her reticule. To Elinor's horror, she saw he was wrapping it round and round with a long rope that shimmered gold in the lamplight. The Aubadesol rope, which could bind and kill vampiri.

Aghast, Elinor leapt forward to snatch at his hands. The reticule was wriggling, but he was quick.

"What are you doing?" Elinor shouted. "Stop at once!"

Lord Olliot shouldered her out of the way and tied a quick knot. He swung the reticule up over his shoulder. "A little precaution, Miss Avely, to make certain you fetch the jewels. Such a useful habit you have: carrying your vampiri everywhere."

"How dare you!" Elinor hissed. "That is no way to treat Miss Zooth! I will report this to the king! This is illegal!"

"Will you?" said Olliot. "Into the hayloft, Miss Avely, otherwise I will tighten this rope so much your vampiri cannot breathe. Or I could simply Heighten the qualities of it, which I'm sure your companion will not appreciate."

Furious and frightened, Elinor stared at him. "Aldreda? Can you hear me?"

No sound came from the reticule, and it no longer moved. Elinor gritted her teeth. She marched over to the side door that led to the hayloft, hoping Pags was flying for help with due haste. She also sent an agonised thought to her mother, for Mrs Avely knew where Elinor had gone.

Lord Olliot crowded at her heels and followed her up the narrow staircase, with the reticule still swung over his shoulder.

The key was already in the lock. The door swung open. Elinor saw the empty hayloft with the armchair Perry had sat upon and the deep shelves upon the walls, with their tiny vampiri furniture. Now it was like an abandoned dollhouse. Only the lamps outside provided a dim light, casting shadows on the arched ceiling. The upper window was open, however, and the thick curtains parted.

Elinor stalked in, straight to a corner where the hay was piled deep. She plunged her hand in and pulled out a cloth sack. It was heavy with sapphires and pearls, and the mingled song was loud to her inner senses.

She turned. "Here. Now give me Miss Zooth at once."

Lord Olliot stood at the other side of the room. He dropped the bound reticule onto one of the high shelves and shook his head. Then he took a few menacing steps towards her.

To her shock, Elinor saw he now held a knife in his other hand.

It was pointed at her.

IN WHICH ALDREDA TAKES
MATTERS IN HAND

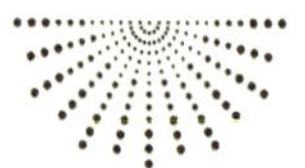

Aldreda

Inside the reticule, Aldreda swooned. She had sensed the Aubadesol rope a moment too late to effect an escape. Now a strange pain emanated from under her skin as if her own blood was starting to simmer.

She could only spare thanks that she had the thin cloth of the reticule between her and the Aubadesol rope. She shuddered, not liking to think of Pags's suffering when he had been bound directly by it. Trying to keep her mind away from the sensation, she turned her attention to what was occurring in the hayloft. She could smell the scent of horses and hay, and she could hear Lord Olliot's voice.

"Miss Avely, I have a little task for you," said Lord Olliot. "I need you to read the pearls for me and tell me which one holds the Heightening spells. I haven't had the chance, in my rush today. I would be much obliged if you can tell me which is the pearl I want before I destroy the rest."

Elinor's voice was cold with anger and maybe a little fear. "I can see I do not have much choice, my lord."

Aldreda tilted her head, hoping Elinor was not going to do anything his lordship asked just because she herself was tied up. But Lord Olliot's next words hinted at a new threat.

"Well, I don't want to kill you yet," he said. "But I will do so if you try to escape. Then the duke will be nicely blamed for your death, and I can be rid of two annoyances in one nice little tableau."

Aldreda rubbed her head, trying to think in spite of the pain that muddied her thoughts. Lord Olliot must intend to kill Elinor regardless, she realised, or else he would not have revealed so much. She pushed against the mouth of the reticule in renewed desperation, but it was no good. Her hands burned, and the reticule remained firmly shut.

Aldreda closed her eyes in despair and listened again, hoping Elinor would not provoke the man. If Elinor could just keep him talking ... but who would rescue them? Mrs Avely had no reason to doubt Elinor's safety, and she was busy hunting down Perry. Beresford was trailing the duke. And Jaq was at the cursed opera. With Perry.

Still, it sounded as if Elinor had the same idea, to bid for time. Her voice now came from the direction of the armchair, as if she had sat down to make herself comfortable – and less of a threat. Aldreda could imagine Elinor folding her hands primly in her lap and staring up at Lord Olliot with a bland expression.

"So it was you who destroyed that sapphire?" said Elinor. "I had thought it was the duke."

Lord Olliot snorted. "I saw you fossicking about in the fireplace. I thought I had swept all the remnants up."

"I found the tiniest piece," said Elinor. "Which spells were contained in that jewel?"

"Heightening spells," snapped Olliot. "Now find the pearl with the same."

There was a silence, then the sound of a bag rustling. Elinor spoke again. "But why would you destroy Heightening spells? It doesn't make sense, my lord. I am cursed with curiosity. Can you please explain it to me?"

Lord Olliot's voice became arrogant. "It makes perfect sense if the spell is how to Heighten Bemusement."

"Oh." Elinor gasped. "The king's Bemusement!"

Aldreda rubbed her hand over her eyes. No wonder the king's malady seemed so strange. And with the king almost Bewildered and secluded in Kew Palace with the duke, Lord Olliot would be left as the most powerful Musor in London.

"Indeed," said Olliot. "I thought it best to destroy evidence of the spell."

"And Lord Rapp suspected what you were doing?" asked Elinor.

At that moment, Aldreda became aware of her reticule shifting slightly. She froze. The sounds of someone grappling with the rope were loud against the fabric of the reticule, but she hoped it was inaudible to Lord Olliot. A hoarse whisper came through the cloth.

"Will you let me rescue you this time, Miss Zooth?"

It was Pags. And unlike when he tried to liberate her from the selkies' tea-chest, this time she was very glad to hear his voice.

"Yes," she murmured in reply. "At all speed, I beg you."

"I suggest you disrobe, as I will be seeing you soon."

Aldreda gave a small huff, amused despite herself. He was outrageous even in this extremity.

She shuddered at the thought of the rope touching her bare skin, but she knew Pags was right. She needed to become a bat, for which she needed to undress.

Aldreda began to take off her clothes. It was difficult in the tight space, and she had to wriggle carefully. Her skin crawled at the thought of further exposing her flesh. All the while, she worried for Pags, who was battling the rope with his bare hands. Aldreda had tried before to untie human knots and failed. It was an impossible task, especially when the knots were in Aubadesol silk. Yet Pags continued to wrestle with it. Aldreda heard a scraping sound and was relieved to realise he had appropriated the dressmaker's scissors to assist him.

There was also the chance that Lord Olliot might turn around and see Pags at his task.

His lordship was replying to Elinor's last question. Aldreda hoped Elinor had seen the rescue underway and was keeping Lord Olliot's attention on herself.

"Lord Rapp didn't know the whole of it," said Lord Olliot. "He never knew how I tinkered with the king's Bemusement. Yet he knew I lied to the king; he was a pesky Discernor, like you."

"Truth Discernment?" asked Elinor.

Olliot sighed. "It was only a matter of time before he worked it out. And somehow, Lord Rapp knew I had taken a sapphire."

"But that could be explained away," said Elinor. "Surely, you didn't need to kill him?"

"Rapp tried to blackmail me, the stupid ass. When he lost his house to the duke, he came to me the following day. As if I would rescue him! He threatened to tell the king everything. I told him I would think about it. Then I visited late that evening and shot him. Easy to make it look like suicide."

"What of the footman, Creel?" asked Elinor, with barely contained fury in her voice.

"Oh, he let me into the house that night, so I had be rid of him," answered Olliot coolly. "He said he would keep his silence at a price, but I couldn't risk it. At our last meeting, I slipped something into his drink."

Lord Olliot's voice was cold. Aldreda shivered, but she had no time to listen anymore. Pags finally wrenched open the mouth of the reticule.

His head and bare shoulders showed in the dim light above Aldreda. He peered in, panting, and jerked his head.

She was already a bat. She crawled out past him and quietly lifted into the air.

Pags didn't follow. She turned, hovering, and saw he was once more grappling with the rope. With her heart in her mouth, she saw him loop it around the reticule again, so it would appear she was still inside.

Aldreda grimaced at the pain that must be searing through his hands. She waited impatiently, keeping a sharp eye on Lord Olliot, her wings quivering as she hovered.

Elinor was staring wide-eyed at his lordship. "But why destroy the pearls?"

"Because I don't want anyone competing with me," said Olliot. "I will be the most eminent Musor if no one else has any spells to cast. Now, find the Heightening pearl, or I will do it myself, without you."

Elinor made a show of holding up a pearl and staring at it. Behind Lord Olliot, Pags, at last, became a bat and lifted into the air.

Quietly, Aldreda and Pags slipped through the crack

of the window and winged their way out. The sensation of cool night air on Aldreda's wings was a blessing, but at the same time, her heart contracted with fear. Her last glimpse of Elinor had shown her sitting in the armchair while Lord Olliot towered over her, holding a long, ugly knife.

Aldreda swooped under the archway of the mews, wondering where to go for help. Then she pulled up in the air, astonished, for there were familiar figures huddling in the shadow of the arch: Mrs Avely, Perry, and Jaq.

Aldreda dove down, transformed, and vaulted to her feet before them.

"What are you all doing here?" she demanded.

Mrs Avely blinked, eyes wide. "Miss Zooth! Where are your clothes? It isn't proper, you know."

"Good Gad!" hissed Perry. "Not again, Aldreda! At least I don't appear naked, Jaq." He grinned at the selkie. Jaq was holding Perry up, for Perry appeared to be drunk.

Jaq grinned back. "I wouldn't mind it if you did."

Perry blushed but smiled dreamily. Perhaps, in fact, he was Bemused and not drunk. Aldreda didn't have time to determine which.

"Quiet!" she said. "Elinor is in grave danger. We must help immediately."

Jaq stared. "What's afoot? And can you tell me what is wrong with Perry?"

At that moment, Pags landed behind Aldreda and collapsed on the ground.

Aldreda spun around. Pags's hands were raw with burn marks, and he had fainted. Foolish bat! This is what came of being heroic, not to mention drinking only from horses and Helicons.

Kneeling beside him, Aldreda took one of his hands and swept a dark wave of hair from his face. He was very pale, and his breathing was shallow. His nose still stuck out prominently.

She looked over her shoulder. "Mrs Avely. Come here at once, and feed Pagrilliard."

"Pardon me?" said Mrs Avely vaguely. "I don't need a vampiri, and so I keep saying."

"At once!" shouted Aldreda. "It will help clear your mind, and it will give him strength. Do it now!"

Mrs Avely wandered over and knelt down beside Pags. Eyeing Aldreda, she stripped off her glove and held her wrist up. The scent of Musor blood must have stirred him, for Pags opened his eyes.

"Drink," ordered Aldreda. "Mrs Avely needs help, and so do you."

"A horse?" asked Pags. "Aren't we near the stables?"

Aldreda glared at him. "Don't be rude. And drink now. We don't have much time."

Pags sighed and did as ordered. A few minutes later, he was standing again, and Mrs Avely put her glove back on with a new briskness. She smiled at Pags. "I thank you for rescuing Miss Zooth," she said. "I don't believe we have been introduced?"

Pags's cheeks were now warmer, and his arrogant posture was back in evidence. He bowed. "The Fifth Dukel of Demontaine, Pagrilliard Deponzel at your service," he said, as naked and cocksure as before.

Aldreda was glad of it, but she wasn't finished with him yet. "Now drink from Perry," she ordered.

"Steady on!" said Perry. "*I'm* not a horse, even if you think my mother is."

Mrs Avely frowned at him. "Aldreda is right, Perry.

You are sadly Bemused. A vampiri bond will help you recover."

"And we need you to Travel again," said Aldreda. "To land inside the hayloft and take Lord Olliot by surprise."

Jaq sighed. "Travel? Is that what it was? Perry just landed on my lap out of nowhere. Not that I'm objecting," he added, squeezing Perry's arm.

Perry blushed. "Sorry about that, dear fellow. Got a little carried away. I was worried about you. Duke on the loose and so forth."

"Duke on the loose?" asked Jaq.

Perry nodded. "Not to mention the opera box."

Jaq looked confused. "The opera box?"

"It's not the duke," said Aldreda. "It is Lord Olliot, and he has Elinor at knife-point."

Mrs Avely drew a breath. "I'll fetch help."

"Yes," said Aldreda. "Find Beresford. We will stay here and storm the hayloft. Pags, drink from Perry now."

Pags shook his head. "I'm not thirsty. Mrs Avely was sufficient for me."

"I don't care," snapped Aldreda, losing her patience. "Perry is our best chance of surprising Olliot. Do you think you can Travel again, Perry?"

Perry stared at Aldreda and giggled. "You want me to land on Elinor's lap this time?"

"No! You have to land behind Olliot, near the window."

Pags sighed. "Give me your wrist, Perry. You need a clear mind."

Perry looked mutinous, but when Jaq seconded the order, he picked up Pags and held him in his hands. "I've got clothes for you too," Perry said, by way of conversation as Pags drank. "Do you want me to pull them out?"

"Never mind that," said Aldreda. "Pags will be a bat again soon enough."

Aldreda watched Mrs Avely set off at a brisk pace to the main street. If only it was easy to locate Beresford – or indeed anyone – to help. And she hoped Elinor was making a theatrical show of divining the contents of each pearl, very slowly.

"Now," said Aldreda, "I need you to listen carefully, Perry. Do you remember Lady Denier's hayloft, where we went for my gown fitting?"

Perry straightened and nodded, his expression clearing a little.

"Remember how you sat in that armchair in the corner? Elinor is sitting there now. Lord Olliot is facing her, with his back to the window. You need to arrive just inside the window and grab him from behind. Can you see the room clearly in your mind's eye?"

Perry stepped a little away from Jaq. "I think I can remember it." He gulped. "You say Olliot has a knife?"

"And probably a gun," said Pags.

Aldreda continued to instruct. "You have to *want* to be there, Perry. Visualise the room and wish with all your might. Elinor is in danger of losing her life, remember."

Jaq spoke. "I don't like this. What if Perry is hurt? We need a better plan."

"Elinor *will* be hurt if we don't do something fast," said Aldreda, her voice sharp. "Pags and I will fly in and distract Olliot, so he doesn't have a chance to pull out a gun. Perry, you bring him to the ground and wrest the knife away from him. You have to wait until we give the signal."

Perry rubbed his forehead, frowning. "What if I can't do it? Travel again, I mean?"

Pags answered him. "Then it will be up to Aldreda

and me. And you will have to come in the normal way: through the door, with Jaq."

Perry's eyes widened. "No, Jaq mustn't go in there! I've only just got him out of the opera box."

Jaq scowled. "I think it is better we go in together, rather than you popping in there like a jack-in-the-box."

"No," said Perry firmly. He screwed his eyes shut, clenched his hands together, and vanished.

Aldreda jumped a few inches. "Damn it!"

"Stupid boy," said Pags. "He's gone."

"Perry!" Jaq looked around wildly. He spun towards Aldreda. "If he comes to any harm, I will kill you," he hissed. "I'm going in!"

At that moment, they all heard a muffled shout from the other side of the arch.

Aldreda's superior hearing could make out that Perry had arrived in the hayloft. She held up a hand, listening, and hoping against hope. Jaq and Pags froze. They all strained their ears.

The shout was followed by a faint thud. And then Elinor screamed.

IN WHICH THERE IS A CONCERTED ATTACK

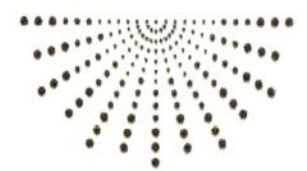

Elinor

Elinor got the fright of her life when she saw Perry materialise behind Lord Olliot. Involuntarily, her eyes widened in shock, and her breath caught. Olliot, seeing her face, spun around.

Perry staggered where he stood. Then he gave a shout and lunged forward.

Olliot was already moving. The knife blade glinted as it flashed through the air. Before Elinor's horrified gaze, it drove into Perry.

Perry turned, somehow slowly, and fell to the floor. Elinor screamed.

"Sorry, Ellie," he said blinking. "Tried my best." Red blood seeped from his shoulder, through his fingers.

Elinor threw herself down at her brother's side. "You're not going to die, Perry!"

Lord Olliot stood over both of them, panting. His

knife was still at the ready. "If either of you move, I strike again."

Elinor snarled up at him. "Don't you dare touch my brother!"

A look of disgust passed over Olliot's face. "One Avely was enough; now I have two? How did you get here, boy?"

Perry looked up, his face pale. "I wished to be where my sister was, and so I arrived."

Olliot frowned. "Does anyone know of it?"

Perry shook his head. "I didn't know where I'd end up, did I?"

"Well, now you will end up dead," replied Olliot coldly.

He jabbed the knife for emphasis, and despite herself, Elinor cowered away. "Perry," she whispered. "Do you think you can Travel back out?"

Perry shook his head slightly. "Don't think so. Besides, I'm not leaving you here."

Elinor pressed her lips tightly together and looked back up at Olliot. "My lord, if you intend to blame our deaths on the Duke of Planx, you must think again."

"Why is that?" Olliot inquired coolly.

"Lord Beresford is watching the duke this very evening. He will be a witness to his grace's innocence."

Olliot's jaw clenched. "Then I might set this place alight, so it seems an accident. The duke will come under suspicion regardless, especially if jewels are found in the wreck." He jerked his head towards the hessian bag. "Open it up, Miss Avely, and spread some sapphires around. And if you try anything, I'll stab your brother again."

The look Elinor gave him should by rights have fried his lordship alive. She crawled over to the bag and gathered it up slowly. Her heart was beating very fast, but she was trying to think. If Perry had made it here, perhaps the others were also near, unless he had Travelled from far away. Elinor wanted to ask him, but she didn't want to alert Lord Olliot. Still, she had to be ready for the moment when help came, if it did.

She reached into the bag and felt the cool gems on her fingers.

"Quickly," rasped Olliot. "Scatter the sapphires."

Elinor pulled out a sapphire and tossed it into the air over her shoulder.

"More," came the order. Elinor glanced at Perry. He lay on the floor, his eyes closed and face pale, blood still seeping through his fingers, and the knife still hovering over him. She stood, holding the bag, with her head bent submissively.

"Hurry," said Olliot. "I want this over and done. And your life's blood will mingle with the flames, make no mistake."

Slowly, Elinor pulled out sapphire after sapphire and dropped them onto the hay. All the while she kept her eyes on Lord Olliot.

Behind him, a black shape fluttered through the window.

Elinor dropped another gem onto the floor, in a mixture of hope and fear. What could a bat do against a knife? Heaven forbid the blade sliced through Aldreda as she flew. Elinor was fairly certain it was Aldreda; the bat wasn't big enough to be Pags. Perhaps Pags had gone to fetch help? Yet Elinor did not have much time – and nor did Perry. Blood was pooling onto the floor, and his face now looked sickly.

Suddenly, incongruous in the tense atmosphere, a bell tinkled loudly.

Elinor jumped a foot in the air. She was glad to see that Lord Olliot also leapt like a startled deer. Though she didn't like the way the knife quivered.

The bell jangled again. Elinor realised the sound came from a small silver bell hanging on the wall. It was tied to a black and white ribbon that led out the window.

As she watched, the ribbon tightened, and the bell rang once more.

Olliot glared at it. "What the hell is that racket?"

Elinor cleared her throat. "I believe it might be a client for Lady Denier. She is a modiste, you know."

"She would not receive clients at night," snapped Lord Olliot.

"She is a vampiri," said Elinor. "When else would she receive clients?"

"Ignore it," said his lordship, and he gestured with the knife. "Back to the pearls. She won't be receiving clients anymore once I burn this place to the ground."

A voice came floating up through the window. "Tailor? I need a tailor!"

It was Pags, his distinctive voice carrying on the still night air.

"A tailor!" he called again. "I have a clothing dilemma!"

Elinor raised her brows at Lord Olliot, whose hand gripped the knife rather tightly.

"Vampiri often have clothing emergencies," she observed. "Perhaps you should tell him that Lady Denier is not ... in."

The bell tinkled again. Pags's voice floated up again. "This is a most serious matter, and I would be much obliged if you could assist me. I want to make it to the opera tonight, and I cannot appear like this!"

Elinor was fairly certain that the bat in the far corner of the ceiling rolled her eyes.

"Damn the opera," said Olliot. "Who is that fool out there? Not a London vampiri, surely?"

"Perhaps a French one," agreed Elinor.

Perry lifted his head. "I have some vampiri clothes." He raised his voice and shouted back to Pags. "Do you need some unmentionables, my good sir?"

"Quiet!" Olliot jabbed the blade towards Perry. Perry ignored him and fumbled in his waistcoat with his free hand, even though Olliot stepped forward menacingly. Triumphant, Perry pulled out a pair of miniature breeches and a coat. "Here you go," he said. "Pass this down. That should send the fellow off."

Olliot eyed the offering suspiciously. The bell tinkled again, even more peremptorily.

"I'm coming up!" shouted Pags. "My attire is in desperate need!"

The bell jangled. The rope tightened with the weight of a large, presumably naked, vampiri.

Lord Olliot cursed and grabbed the clothes from Perry. He stalked over to the window and thrust it open.

"Here," he hissed, tossing them out. "Now, go away!"

Elinor stepped in front of Perry. Next to her, the door burst open, and Jaq charged in.

Olliot turned, but this time he was outnumbered. Aldreda dropped from the ceiling and landed on his head, flapping her wings over his eyes. Jaq, with determined ferocity, grabbed Olliot's knife hand and swung it down.

The blade plunged into Olliot's leg, and he let out a screech.

Jaq wrestled him to the ground and yanked the knife out. He flung it aside, and Elinor leapt forward to pick it up. Pags, flying through the window, added to the melee.

Elinor, watching, felt helpless even though she now

grasped a deadly knife. Her mind was oddly blank, as if no coherent thought were possible. Should she charge in? But she was just as likely to hit Jaq as Olliot, and Perry would never forgive her if she did that.

Could she somehow pin a coat-tail? Just as she took a tentative step forward, Olliot broke free of Jaq. He staggered back, yanking Aldreda off his face, and reaching into a pocket.

Perry shouted, but Elinor didn't need to hear his words to know instinctively that Olliot was reaching for a gun.

Almost without thought, she stepped forward and thrust the knife-point into Olliot's right arm. It cut through cloth and flesh.

Olliot spun with a howl, his hands empty, his face livid, and blood spurting from his arm.

Elinor glared at him with fire in her eyes and the knife at the ready. But Jaq leapt forward, grabbing Olliot from behind, and Aldreda landed on his head again. This time, with Olliot wounded, the tussle quickly moved to Jaq's favour. Elinor watched, her breath heaving, the knife slippery in her hand.

Once Jaq had him on the ground, Aldreda lifted into the air again, dusting her wings off with a satisfied air. She circled once, then hooked a swathe of fabric in her claws, and flew it over to Perry.

"Good thinking, my dear," said Elinor. Shaking, she threw the awful knife aside and bent to staunch Perry's bleeding. Aldreda fetched more cloth. Perry's eyes were open, riveted with fear on Jaq, who was still holding a grunting, furious Olliot to the ground.

Jaq shouted over his shoulder. "Is Perry alive?"

"He's alive." Elinor gulped at the sight of so much

blood sticky on the floor. "But we need a doctor. Or a Healor."

"Don't die, Perry," said Jaq. "I haven't finished kissing you."

Perry grinned weakly, though he didn't seem able to lift his head anymore. "I'll live."

Jaq smiled back, though he still wrestled with a heaving Lord Olliot. "Help me tie this bastard up," he said, and the bats circling the ceiling went to fetch more reams of fabric.

Shortly afterwards, Beresford and the Duke of Planx arrived. Elinor gladly renounced her place at her brother's side, and the duke set about doing what he could for Perry. Beresford, pale and grim, swept Elinor into his arms and kissed her most thoroughly.

"Why is there blood on your dress?" he demanded.

"Only Perry's."

"Good." Beresford kissed her again. "What in damnation happened here?"

Elinor explained, rather disjointedly. Beresford became confused when the tale diverted to Pags's demands for a coat, but he was suitably grateful, nonetheless, to all of them.

"It sounds like it was a concerted attack," he said, eyeing Lord Olliot's trussed-up form. "Well done, all of you. Good work, Jaq."

Aldreda and Pags nodded, standing on one of the shelves. They were now in human form. Aldreda was hastily dressed in a half-finished blue silk gown that had yet to acquire a hem or sleeves. Pags simply had a piece of fabric wrapped around his waist. His chest was bare, his hair unruly, and Elinor rather thought he was enjoying himself immensely.

"Your Grace!," said Aldreda. "Put on some clothes at once."

Pags ran his eyes over Aldreda. "Your own gown barely meets that description, my dear."

Aldreda blushed. "What of Perry's set of clothes that was thrown out the window? Perry won't want them to go to waste, and it was his dying wish that you wear them."

"Not dying," snapped Jaq, who now sat with Perry's head in his lap.

"Not dying," confirmed Perry, his voice weak. "Still, put some clothes on, Pags, for love of God."

Pags grinned. "Very well." He cast off the fabric from his waist, and Aldreda gasped in outrage. After posing for a moment longer than necessary, he turned into a bat and flew out the window.

Elinor laughed. "We are near the stables, Aldreda – his gracel is on his home ground."

Aldreda shook her head. "Pags has drunk from two Musors tonight. His behaviour should be improving."

Mrs Avely entered the hayloft, flushed and anxious. She threw herself by Perry's side. "I knew this would all end badly!" she exclaimed. "You are both forbidden from Musing from now on!"

"Not much chance of that," said Perry. "I've only just begun."

IN WHICH SEVERAL CAVEATS
ARE MADE KNOWN

Elinor

Two days later, Elinor was finally able to see the Planx library for herself. The duke had insisted Perry stay at the ducal residence while he recovered. So Elinor had to call there to see her brother, and she had done so the previous day with Beresford and her mother. However, tonight a special meeting was arranged.

As the meeting would include vampiri, it was to be held after dusk in the famous library. The butler showed Elinor in, and she looked around curiously.

The duke's library was large, as Elinor had expected, but only two walls were covered in books. A third held a fireplace and paintings, and the fourth was covered in long tapestries, similar to the ones Elinor had seen in the Sapphire Library.

One of these tapestries was drawn back. Behind it

were deep shelves, carpeted and set with furniture in miniature size.

"That must be for you," said Elinor. She helped Aldreda out of her reticule onto the shelf. Aldreda glanced around with approval and sat on one of the tiny straight-backed chairs.

"Indeed," said Aldreda. "I am glad the Vampiri Edicts have been lifted for tonight."

Elinor sniffed. "I hope it is a sign of things to come."

She turned to greet Perry, who had already been tenderly placed in an armchair by a footman. Perry still looked rather pale, but he smiled cheerfully.

"I say," he said, "I wonder what this is all about. All very mysterious, the duke calling us together like this." He lowered his voice. "Do you think the king has guessed that I can Travel now?"

"I hope not." The Avelys had decided to keep Perry's Gift a secret from the royal court for a little longer. Their mother had insisted, and after recent events, Elinor hardly wished to argue against a path of caution.

Elinor went to examine a bookshelf. "I don't think the meeting is all about you, dear brother. I suppose we need to discuss what happened."

"Do you know what is being done about Lord Olliot?"

Elinor nodded. "He is a prisoner at the London Tower, awaiting the next vessel to the Antipodes. Apparently, the king cannot bring himself to execute him, so he is sending Olliot to the opposite side of the world instead."

"Hm," said Perry. "I hope that is far enough away. I have taken an aversion to him myself." He shifted his arm as if it pained him. "I suppose he has to recover from his injuries too. That was a good right thrust, Ellie."

Elinor wrinkled her nose: she could not bring herself to feel guilty for the wound she had dealt Olliot, however unladylike it might been, when her own brother had been stabbed first.

At that moment, Jaq came through the door. He was dressed in his usual elegant fashion, and he gave Elinor and Aldreda a deep, princely bow. Then he strode over to stand beside Perry, dropping a hand to clasp his good shoulder.

"How are you feeling?" Jaq asked.

Perry's hand came up to grasp Jaq's, and they exchanged smiles. To an outsider, it would appear brotherly, but Elinor knew better. She recognised the flash of adoration in Perry's eyes as he looked into Jaq's face, and she suspected that was how she herself looked at Beresford.

Jaq, she could not read as well, but his returning smile was tender. He began speaking in a low voice to Perry.

Elinor glanced across at Aldreda, who shrugged and smiled. Apparently, co-ordinating a rescue with Jaq had softened Aldreda a little towards him. This was the third time Jaq had assisted in rescuing various Avelys, and three times seemed to be the charm. Aldreda had finally (privately) admitted to Elinor that perhaps Jaq wasn't so bad. For a selkie.

The next to arrive was Mrs Avely, wearing a large paisley shawl. After she kissed Perry on the cheek and ascertained he was improving, Mrs Avely held out one end of her shawl at arm's length. A new pocket had been sewn into one side of it.

Out of it popped Pags's head.

"Good evening," said Pags, in his best lordly fashion. "How are we all on this fine night?"

Perry grimaced in surprise. "Good Gad. What are you doing in my mother's shawl?"

Pags twitched an eyebrow. "All these poor Musors without vampiri. I'm merely doing the gentlemanly thing and providing some companionship."

Elinor laughed. "You could be Perry's companion," she teased.

Pags raised a supercilious eyebrow. "I'd rather be a companion to a matron than a puppy." He cast a disparaging eye at Jaq. "Especially if the puppy is spending time with a seal."

"Who are you calling a puppy?" demanded Jaq, and he took a threatening step towards Pags.

"Don't be so rude," said Mrs Avely, though it was unclear whether she was speaking to Pags or Jaq. Then she added, "All of you show some manners to my new companion."

Pags smiled smugly and then caught sight of Aldreda.

"Ah, Miss Zooth. You see me a reformed man," he announced from his paisley pocket, his imperious nose aloft. "Is this not what you wanted?"

Mrs Avely turned to see Aldreda sitting in her shelf. "Good evening, Miss Zooth. May I deposit Pagrilliard next to you?"

Elinor observed that Aldreda no longer seemed so averse to Pags's company. Pags leapt upon the shelf and kissed Aldreda's hand. Then he pulled up a chair rather close and sat next to her. They, too, began conversing in low tones.

Elinor heaved a sigh and looked around. When was Beresford arriving? She wanted someone with whom to exchange intimate looks and converse in low tones. She shifted impatiently, frowning dourly.

Mrs Avely spoke from Elinor's elbow. "I am so relieved you are not any worse for wear, Elinor."

Elinor turned, smiling at her mother. "Only thanks to you. You brought help when we needed it."

Afterwards, Mrs Avely had told Elinor of her sense of foreboding and her determination to follow Elinor to the duke's house. Elinor suspected her mother, Discernment attuned, had heard her own inner plea for help.

Her mother sighed. "Yet, I have been meaning to apologise."

"Why?"

"I kept the truth from you for so long." Mrs Avely's eyes moved to Perry. "I only wished to protect you, but I fear that instead I placed both of you in more danger. If you had known how to discern lies earlier, you might have avoided such a terrible situation. Or," she added, "if I had exposed Perry to the arts earlier, he wouldn't have caused such a scene at the opera."

Elinor laughed. She had heard the tale of Perry's maiden voyage: it had ended on Jaq's lap, with wine spilled everywhere, and Lord Worthing flabbergasted. Jaq, on the other hand, had apparently greeted the event with aplomb, not to mention initiative, and had conducted an inventory to ascertain that indeed all of Perry had arrived. So Perry had been right about opera boxes after all.

Elinor had heard all this from Perry himself. She smiled at her mother. "You need not apologise, Mother. I am merely grateful you Discerned I was in trouble. I doubt I will ever be as proficient at the art as you."

"You can learn," replied Mrs Avely. "I have been thinking, and I have come to the conclusion that you should accept the royal position."

Elinor's eyes widened. "Truly?"

"Your father would have wanted it." Sadness crossed Mrs Avely's face. "Just as he served the Crown."

Elinor reached out to hold her mother's hand. "You must tell me all about him one day."

"I will soon," said Mrs Avely. "You and Perry deserve to know."

Beresford and the Duke of Planx arrived at this interesting juncture, and Lady Denier emerged from the duke's waistcoat pocket. She, too, joined Pags and Aldreda on the shelf, and they exchanged civilities. Elinor watched the three small figures, imagining it must feel like old times to Aldreda if it recalled her vampiri circles in France.

Beresford came over to Elinor. He kissed her hand and wrapped a ringlet of her hair around his finger, and tugged it. "After this, can we go home and be married?" he murmured in her ear.

"Please." She smiled up at him.

"At least here I won't have any Beresford jam to try me," he said and turned to take a whiskey from the duke.

Drinks were handed out to everyone, and then the Duke of Planx cleared his throat. A hush fell over the assembled company.

"Thank you all for coming tonight." The duke nodded to all of them. "My first task is to communicate the royal gratitude for your services to the Crown in apprehending the traitor Lord Olliot. Without you, his perfidy would not have been discovered, and the king would have continued to suffer. His Majesty and the queen also appreciate that the discovery came at great personal risk to yourselves."

Elinor repressed a shudder, remembering the gleam of that long, wicked knife. Jaq gripped Perry's shoulder again, and a sigh rippled around the room. Then everyone drank to the king's health, which was in much better order now Lord Olliot had been dispatched.

The duke continued. "My second task is to reiterate His Majesty's invitation to Miss Elinor Avely to become a Royal Discernor – with a few caveats."

Elinor tilted her head, curious. What kind of caveats could the king place on the position? If His Majesty was going to rescind his offer of making her a viscountess, she would have none of it.

The duke coughed. "The first caveat is that the position is to be shared equally with Mrs Avely, with the title bestowed first upon her, and to pass to Miss Avely in due course. It has come to the king's attention that Mrs Avely is as Gifted in Discerning as her daughter. His Majesty wishes to avail himself of the services of both ladies. Accordingly, and in gratitude for services already rendered, the title bestowed will now be that of Marquess of Lanyon."

Elinor's eyes widened. She glanced over at her mother to see an identical expression of surprise.

A marquess! Elinor grinned. She quite liked the sound of Lady Avely, Marquess of Lanyon. "Mother is far more Gifted than I," she announced. "The king is wise. I will be happy to share the role and the title with you, Mother."

Even as she spoke, Elinor glanced over at Perry to see how he felt being excluded from this bounty. Would he now want to announce his own Gift? However, Perry merely smiled at Elinor and winked.

Mrs Avely flushed. "I will think on it carefully, Your Grace."

Perry scoffed. "Think on it carefully, Mother? You shall be a marquess; you won't be able to resist. And now you even have a vampiri to assist you in your duties."

Pags looked a little shifty where he sat. Elinor

wondered if he had been the one to whisper into the king's ear of Mrs Avely's surpassing talents and bargain for the title of marquess.

The duke spoke. "To avoid giving rise to questions or revealing your Gifts, the title will be bestowed retroactively on the late Mr Avely, for services rendered to the Crown leading to his death." There was a sombre pause as everyone digested this, and Elinor vowed to find out soon the story behind that statement. She glanced over at her mother to see Mrs Avely a little pale and blinking her eyes rapidly. The duke continued. "Hence Mrs Avely will hold the courtesy title. As a gesture of promise, the king sent these two Talisman Stones to present to you today."

He turned to open a box behind him and held out two chains of gold. From each hung a large blue stone set in gold filigree. One was a perfectly round shape, which the duke passed to Mrs Avely. The other was an oval, which Elinor received. It was heavy in her hand; the deep blue shot through with flickers of gold. Catching her breath, she slipped the chain over her head and placed the lapis on her bosom. Immediately, it felt as if it belonged there.

"Very nice," said Beresford, in appreciation, though Elinor rather suspected he was also referring to her bosom. She smiled at him, very pleased. Finally, a Talisman Stone! Nothing could stop her now. She would be able to find any number of liars, murderers, jewels, or missing jars of jam …

The duke cleared his throat. "There is … more."

Everyone turned to stare.

"More?" asked Elinor, clutching at her lapis.

"The title of Marquess of Lanyon comes with lands in Cornwall, near enough to the Beresford property. On this land is an old castle. It is rundown and in need of new management. His Majesty has designated it as the new home for the Sapphire Library to ensure its safety. And the castle will also be the place of the new School of Musing."

A gasp murmured around the room, and Elinor caught her own breath. "A School of Musing?"

The duke nodded. "The king has decreed the arts must be nurtured and taught, and Cornwall is far enough away to keep the matter secret. He hopes that you and your mother will be the heads of the school. As you are both able to easily Discern the spells within the sapphires and pearls, you are the ideal candidates for passing the knowledge on – not to mention your practical experience of the arts."

Silence settled as everyone contemplated this vision. Elinor knew Cornwall was near to Devon, but it would be at least a good day's ride from Beresford Manor. She turned to look at Beresford.

Beresford smiled back. "Of course, you must accept a castle, my love."

"A whole castle?"

Beresford nodded. "If it is the one I'm thinking of, it is supported by a very good dairy. Think of all the cream we can have at the wedding."

Elinor licked her lips eagerly, then caught herself. "But ... teaching? I am not fitted to teach anyone," she objected. "I barely know anything about Musing myself."

Perry spoke up. "You shall have Mother and the pearls."

The duke nodded. "And I will send you other Musors to assist you. In fact, I will also visit soon, once I am certain the king can spare my presence."

"I thank you, Your Grace," said Elinor. "Yet, I still doubt I will be sufficient for the task."

Aldreda put in an observation. "Teaching others is the best way to learn for oneself."

"You will come too, Aldreda?" asked Elinor.

"Of course," replied Aldreda.

"And I too," said Pags. "Cornwall is pleasantly wild. Though I suppose I don't need horses anymore."

"I will come too, of course," announced Perry.

"And I," said Jaq. "My queen's waters border on Cornwall. I'll be able to visit easily if you will allow me."

Elinor rather suspected she wouldn't be able to keep Jaq away. She felt warmth well in her heart that she was so thoroughly supported. "Well, then I suppose the answer must be yes if Mother agrees." She paused and turned to the duke. "Yet what of the Vampiri Edicts?"

"The Castle of Lanyon will be exempt from the Edicts," said the duke, and a rustle of surprise ran around the room.

Elinor smiled with approval and turned back to Mrs Avely. "Well, Mother, what do you say?"

"Cornwall is perhaps safer than London," said Mrs Avely. "Yet, the first thing we should study is Impacting, so we can better defend ourselves."

The duke spoke up. "The first thing you will do is catalogue the Sapphire Library. We will not send you any students or teachers for a year. However, in the meanwhile, we do have one more task for you all."

"What is that?" asked Elinor. She was beginning to see that King George didn't give out titles, land, and cream without exacting a certain amount in return.

"Find the lost vampiri of France."

Everyone sat up a little straighter.

Aldreda was the first to speak this time. "The lost vampiri?"

The duke nodded. "The king recently received information that, in fact, a large population of vampiri escaped France ten years ago. They were last seen flying off the coast near the Guernsey Islands, which is where we suspect they took to hibernation." He paused. "It will be your task to find them and offer them refuge in England."

2 8

IN WHICH PAGS MAKES A PROMISE

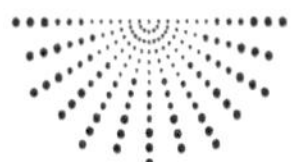

Aldreda

After the duke had finished with his manifold announcements, the conversation broke into excited parts. Aldreda turned to Pags accusingly.

"It was *you* who told the king about the missing French vampiri, wasn't it?"

Pags did not deny it. "I was possibly the last one to see the roost flying out of France. I think they went into hibernation, but it is time the queen is awakened once more."

"Why?" demanded Aldreda.

"Her Majesty and her roost will remember how the Musor arts were applied in practice – something not contained in the sapphires. And your school will need vampiri."

Aldreda sniffed. "It is not *my* school."

Pags grinned. "You will be Vampiri Headmistress, I am certain of it. You are perfect for the role."

291

Aldreda narrowed her eyes. "What is that supposed to imply?"

"Merely a reference to your superior intelligence and high moral standing."

"You mean the fact that I don't drink from horses or attempt mating flights upon strangers?" retorted Aldreda.

"Ah, you remember that, do you?"

Aldreda did not reply that she could hardly forget it.

Pags leaned a little closer. "I am happy to reprise it soon, my dear."

Aldreda felt a shiver run through her and rather suspected it was of pure anticipation. And she could not even blame it on plum jam or tears this time. She cleared her throat. "I am not inclined to marry, my lordel."

"Ah, yes," said Pags. "You remind me that I have lost my title of dukel in bonding with Mrs Avely."

Aldreda met his eyes. "I appreciate it is a step down for you, and I thank you for your humility."

"Ah, well," said Pags, with a smug smile. "Mrs Avely will be a marquess soon, which gives me the title of marquisel. Not so low after all."

"Hm," said Aldreda. "I wonder if you had anything to do with that?"

Pags widened his eyes innocently. "Not at all. Nor with the acquisition of a large castle with plenty of attics and cellars."

Aldreda smiled. "And cream. Elinor will be happy."

Pags raised a brow. "Yes, you picked a winning horse there, didn't you? Miss Avely will be a countess soon enough, which means you will have the courtesy title too."

"Do not *ever* refer to Miss Avely as a horse again."

Pags laughed, and Aldreda smiled despite herself. She realised she was glad Pags would come to Cornwall too.

It *was* nice to have vampiri companionship, as well as human. And Pags's habits had improved since their first encounter on the moors. Indeed, his cravat was almost neatly tied this evening.

Aldreda examined the folds of the material critically, then raised her eyes to see Pags looking at her with an unsettling glint in his golden eyes.

"Miss Zooth, I hope we don't have to leave London immediately. I still have not had the pleasure of dancing the cotillion with you. I will settle for that, in lieu of any other kind of … dance."

To her vexation, Aldreda realised she was blushing. "I make no promises, my lordel." Then she relented. "However, I suppose you deserve a dance after battling the Aubadesol."

Elinor had come up in time to hear this last remark. "Indeed, Pagrilliard, I am very grateful to you."

Pags thrust out his chest and preened. "It was nothing."

Aldreda rolled her eyes.

"Truly," insisted Pags. "I would do it again in a heartbeat to save you, Miss Zooth. Anything at all; my life is at your service." He bowed grandly.

Aldreda pursed her lips at this outrageous gallantry, and she shook her head at him reprovingly.

But Elinor's head was tilted, and her eyes were wide, making her look rather like an inquisitive owl. She held her lapis stone in her hand. "Well," she said. "You'll be pleased to know he is telling the truth, Aldreda."

THE END

AUTHOR'S NOTE

An uncanny fact came to my attention after I completed *The Sapphire Library*. I did an online vocabulary quiz (I'm a word nerd, ok), and 'peregrinate' came up. Unfortunately, I lost that point, as I had never seen that word before. And it turns out 'peregrinate' means 'to traverse', or 'to travel or wander'.

Peregrine's name turns out to mean Travel. And I had no idea. Such are the mysterious workings of the muse.

Thanks for reading the third book in the Lady Diviner series. If you are keen for more, *The Golden Flute* (Book 4) is out now.

And now it is past time for some acknowledgements! On this HUGE journey of writing three books in a series (and then publishing them in quick succession), I was supported by many generous souls.

Firstly, thank you to my alpha readers, **Trine, Anne,** and **Eli,** who gave me such invaluable feedback and cheered me on. You inspired me to press forward.

All my beta readers, you know who you are! Each one of you helped to make these books better.

My cover designer, **Lena Yang**, who designed such beautiful book covers, and who has talent and patience in spades.

My editors, **Cameo Marlatt** and **Tamlin Day**, who between them taught me about bats and commas.

My proof-reader, **Carmen Rutter Hedley**, who pro-bono proof-read every word of this series so far, often on a tight deadline.

And special mentions must go to my lovely author mentors:

H. Y. Hanna, best-selling author of the Oxford Tea Room mysteries (among others), who took me under her wing *years* ago and has been a veritable font of author advice.

Charlotte E. English, author of the House of Werth series (Regency fantasy!), who has been very kind in dispensing her knowledge and wisdom.

Olivia Atwater, author of the Regency Faerie Tales series, who has generously given her time and expertise, helping me at every step of the way in this overwhelming publishing journey.

Jacquelyn Benson, author of the Charismatics series (Edwardian fantasy!) who has been so knowledgeable, supportive, and good at spotting plot holes.

Finally, thanks to my Dad for proof-reading and being a fan, and my Mum for introducing me to Georgette Heyer when I was ten years old.

And my husband, for being like a Heyer hero (the tall, strong, gentle ones) and backing me on this crazy endeavour with so much patience, good humour, and staunch belief.

I couldn't have done it without you all.

And of course, thank you to my readers - there would be no point at all without you.

Yours in gratitude,
Rosalie

The Golden Flute

Lady Diviner 4

Which will cause Elinor the most trouble — dangerous island cliffs, a lurking murderer, or her pretence at matrimony?

Pretending to be already married to Lord Beresford is certainly improper, but only if someone discovers it — or so Elinor argues. The honeymoon masquerade will hide their true purpose in travelling to the beautiful island of Sark: to find the missing vampiri roost, and, of course, sample some of the famous French soufflé.

Yet Beresford is being a stickler about their wedding night, the islanders shoot on sight, and Elinor must also find a tiny golden flute to waken the hibernating vampiri. Unfortunately, she cannot divine gold, especially a magical flute the size of a needle.

When Aldreda discovers a dead body in the attic, the hunt for the missing roost takes on sinister overtones, especially as mysterious mishaps suggest another victim is intended. If only Elinor's charade can hold long enough for her to find the flute, the roost, *and* the murderer — before the killer strikes again or the 'Beresfords' are thrown off the island in disgrace.

What secrets lie hidden on the isle of Sark? How was the murder done in the attic? And just why *do* the soufflés keep falling flat?

Buy *The Golden Flute* for another rousing tale of magic, manners, and mystery set in the Regency era.

OR... A SPIN-OFF

Dear Reader, you have a choice at this point in the Lady Diviner series!

You could charge on with Elinor's adventure to Sark, in *The Golden Flute*.

Or you could follow her mother, Mrs Judith Avely, as she embarks on her own secret journey while her children are thus occupied, in the Matronly Misadventures series.

Mrs Avely - now in possession of a new title - must travel to the Duke of Sargen's estate, where she will find troublesome spectres, a vulgar murder, and an impertinent old flame, in *Lady Avely's Guide to Truth and Magic*. It was refreshing for me to write a heroine closer to my own age, and to give Judith her own adventure.

Either way, I hope you do not find the conduct of either mother or daughter too scandalising…

Happy reading,

Rosalie

HAVE YOU JOINED ROSALIE'S NEWSLETTER YET?

If you've read this far in the Lady Diviner series, you probably have already picked up your free copy of *A Pendant for Trouble* by signing up to my newsletter.

If not, you can sign up at rosalieoaks.com/newsletter. As the price to pay, you will also receive monthly musings from me, including book gossip, book recs, and random pictures of scones.

ROSALIE'S PRIVATE TEA PARLOUR

If you'd like to be part of the lovely community that supports my authorly endeavours, please pay a visit to my Private Tea Parlour (otherwise known as Patreon), where you may read my books before anyone else, as well as peruse deleted scenes, short stories, join in the Castle Lanyon Book Club, and much more.

My wonderful Patrons also gain a secret key to the Lamplighters' Guild Discord community, filled with delightful bookish folk and conversations.

I'd be thrilled to have your support. Pop along to patreon.com/rosalieoaks to have a peep.

Happy tea drinking!

Rosalie

ABOUT THE AUTHOR

Rosalie Oaks writes novels set in a magical Regency England full of manners, mystery, and soothing beverages. As a child, she loved conducting home-made theatre productions with her three younger brothers. Now she directs her characters instead, but like her brothers, they don't always do what she says.

While writing, Rosalie consumes vast quantities of tea and chocolate, and steadfastly ignores the housework.

Further intimate details, such as her favourite books and recipes, can be found in her Private Tea Parlour on Patreon.

Lady Diviner

A Pendant for Trouble (prequel novella)

The Lady Jewel Diviner

The Moria Pearls

The Sapphire Library

The Golden Flute

The Selkie Scandal (an internovella)

Matronly Misadventures

Lady Avely's Guide to Truth and Magic

Lady Avely's Guide to Lies and Charms

Lady Avely's Guide to Guile and Peril

(releasing 2025)

rosalieoaks.com